MOUNTAIN CROSSING

A Jack Kendall Mystery

One man's search for the truth
and his life-or-death choices

JAY B. GREENE

Contents

Prologue: The Mountain I   5

1. Charlie Tolbert   10
2. A Tragic Ending   28
3. Jack's First-Person Story   43
4. Becky Leaves   55
5. Jack at Home   69
6. Driving Fast   75
7. Key West   81
8. Back at Work   84
9. Hot Tip   92
10. Jack's Scoop   101
11. High Seas   107
12. Damage Control   115
13. Jack and Bobbie Talk   120
14. Mountain Dream No. 2   126
15. Next Stop Jamaica   129
16. Mackey's Unfinished Business   144
17. Drinks at Foley's   149
18. Siesta Key   156
19. Drugged and Out   160
20. Jack Who?   164
21. The Hospital   167

22. Talk with Sarah   173
23. Childhood Memories Return   185
24. Jack Remembers Everything   192
25. Long-Awaited News   199
26. Becky's Letters   211
27. Arriving in Jamaica   221
28. A GoldenEye Evening   233
29. Breakfast at GoldenEye   244
30. Jamaican Police   251
31. Shocking News   257
32. The Silver Spoon   267
33. Raleigh Lakes   277
34. Mountain Dream No. 4   283
35. Sarah's Obsession   285
36. Jack Confronts Michael   289
37. Michelle Decides   296
38. Sarah and Robert   302
39. Robert's Final Plans   309
40. Planning the Rescue   314
41. The Mountain II   318
42. Recovering   330
    Epilogue: Going Home   338

    Other Jack Kendall Mysteries 344
    About the Author   350

For Tynan, Casey and Jordan

Boketon Press

ISBN (Paperback): 979-8-9902256-0-2
ISBN (eBook): 979-8-9902256-1-9

Book Design by Adam Hay Studio, UK
E-Pub Formatting by Steve Mead Graphic Design

Printed in the United States of America
This book is a work of fiction. Names, characters, businesses, events, and incidents are products of the author's imagination or used fictitiously. Any resemblance to actual persons, living or dead, is purely coincidental.

Prologue
The Mountain I

Early Monday morning, July 7, 1980

Nine soldiers marched through an old city, past black stone houses, under a dark, starless sky.

A soft, warm wind was blowing, rustling the thin branches of barren trees that dotted the dry landscape. The men marched as if they were in a trance, a spell. Their faces, expressionless; their movements, mechanical.

Dressed in full battle gear—black knit undergarments, black leather vests, and tight-fitting black legwear tucked underneath heavy, dull black boots—the soldiers marched. Some wore swords strapped around their waists, and some carried long-handled axes and sharp-pointed spears. As they marched, the monotonous sound of their leather boots pounded on the stone-covered street and echoed through the desolate town. They marched through the deadened city, past shuttered houses, heading toward a large shadow in the distance that rose above the quiet earth...

Jack Kendall suddenly woke up from his dream to a rustling noise in the bedroom. He squinted and half-opened his light green eyes. He saw his wife, Becky, brushing past their queen-sized bed on her way to the bathroom.

"Baby, are you all right?" he said in a sleepy whisper. She had disturbed his strange dream about marching soldiers.

Becky's sleek figure was barely discernible in the soft light that filtered through the Venetian blinds.

"Yes, go back to sleep," she said quietly.

Even though half asleep, Jack was overly sensitized; the night before, they'd had a repeat of the same old argument. He tried to put it out of his mind, as he always did when they disagreed.

Water began to drain through the bathroom pipes. The sound made him sleepy again, so he lowered his head to the pillow and closed his eyes.

Suddenly, images from the dream—marching soldiers—flashed before him. He opened his eyes and stared at the ceiling. The dream continued. In the milky morning, he could almost see those nine soldiers marching through an ancient city toward a large object. The vision seemed quite clear. Then, in an instant, the men vanished. He shivered.

Flooded with eerie feelings, he closed his eyes and pulled the sheet to his chin. What was that? he wondered. It had seemed so natural, so clear, and so vivid. And frightening, because the men were so serious and intent on what they were doing.

Maybe it was something other than a dream He had no clue. But he had a strange feeling he knew something about the soldiers. He wanted to know more. Why were they marching? Where were they going? What were they doing?

He closed his eyes, calmed himself, and thought deeply about the dream. Was there more about it in his memory? No. That was all he could remember. The men had gone. The dream was over.

Jack then heard a creaking sound in the bathroom as Becky turned on the faucet. He opened his eyes a little. Splashing sounds came forth as she washed her hands. Should he tell her about the dream?

As she was finishing up, his mind wandered back to what he'd seen. Then, the vision became clearer. He was one of those marching soldiers. He was with them. He wasn't sure why or where they were going, but he felt there was a purpose, a reason. But he was getting drowsy.

Maybe the dream was pulling him back. He exhaled softly and fell into a deep sleep. He never noticed Becky sliding back into their bed. His sleep lasted until morning.

*   *   *

Jack awoke to soft music from his alarm clock. He turned and glanced toward Becky. She was sleeping on her left side, facing the door. Looking at her, he thought of the marching men in his dream. He stood up, and his legs felt sore and tired. It was as if he had played basketball for three hours. His back also felt a little strained. Some dream!

Slowly and with a slight limp, he made his way toward the bathroom, taking care not to wake his wife. He bent over to turn on the water in the shower and felt a sharp pain run down his side. Jesus, he thought. What is going on?

In that instant, Jack knew he had experienced an extraordinary dream. He stepped into the shower and began some light stretching exercises under the warm water to relax his tense muscles. He rubbed soap into his hands and spread the suds around his shoulders.

Could this be more than a dream? He wondered as he finished his shower.

Jack stepped out of the bathtub, grabbed a towel, and dried himself as he walked back into the bedroom. He dressed as quietly as he could.

Becky lay on the bed as peacefully as always in the early morning. He gazed upon her and saw that her clear blue eyes were closed. Her thick, gorgeous, wavy red hair was spread across her back, slightly covering her finely cut face. Her long, shapely body was covered underneath the sheets. He always loved to watch her sleep.

Sometimes, when he was watching, she would wake up and become startled when she realized he had been staring at her. She didn't like it when he did that and would always protest and tell him to stop. He always laughed at her pretend modesty.

As he watched her, he wanted to wake his wife, kiss her, and tell her about the dream. But he didn't. She usually thought Jack's dreams were funny. She chalked them up to his exuberant imagination and all the dramatic stories people told him during the day. Most times, he would agree. This time, it was different, so he decided to keep it to himself. He sighed lightly as he turned and left their bedroom.

He strolled into the kitchen to continue his morning routine. He poured a glass of fresh orange juice, set it on the table, and walked outside to pick up the *Herald-Tribune*, which he scanned as he walked back inside. He put the paper down on the breakfast table without taking his eyes off the lead article—a story about another big cocaine bust—took another sip of orange juice, and returned to the bedroom.

Becky had turned over, and her back was to the door now. Jack leaned over, kissed her cheek, whispered "I love you" in her ear, and then walked back to the kitchen table.

He poured a little more juice, opened a bottle of vitamins, and popped one into his mouth. Deciding to take a couple of aspirin for his aching muscles, he swallowed two, took another sip of juice, and then finished it. He placed the glass into the sink and walked toward the front door.

As he opened the door, he heard Becky stirring in their bedroom. He listened for a second to see if she was getting up, but she was only turning over. He closed the door and left for work.

Chapter 1
Charlie Tolbert

Monday, July 7, 1980

Jack peered over the top of the blue and white police cruiser. He squinted in the bright, sweltering early afternoon Florida summer sun.

He held his hand over his brow, a salute to what lay before him: an aging, wood-frame house with an unkempt yard in a poor and forgotten neighborhood of North Sarasota.

Sweat that had gathered on his shoulders and arms dripped down his wrist and onto his hand. It was 1 p.m., and the air couldn't be described as hot. It was a suffocating heat, the kind that smothered people and robbed them of rational thought.

It was the type of summer's day that made him want to be someplace else, preferably with air-conditioning and where drinks were served with crushed ice and giant, juicy pieces of fruit.

Jack hated those thoughts because they were so tempting, and he had work to do.

Even with his sunglasses on, the glare from the white house was intense. He took off his blue tie and slowly stuffed it into his back pocket. He opened the top two buttons of his light-blue, short-sleeved cotton shirt.

He wondered briefly why he wore a tie during the summer. *A parochial school habit*, he remembered with a pained smile.

According to police, an unemployed industrial worker had kidnapped two teenagers and was holding them hostage inside his house. Trusting his well-honed reporter's instincts, Jack came out to find out why. On this side of town, things just happened.

Right after the police arrived, the man had fired a few shots through a window, hitting the windows of squad cars and nearby houses. When Jack heard the APB go out over the police scanner, he didn't waste any time picking up his notebook and tape recorder.

Jack knew this neighborhood. He had been out here many times. Summer was the worst time of the season for the Augustine Quarters, a mix of industrial and construction workers, migrants, people on welfare, and those unemployed or looking for jobs.

Last summer, a man had killed a woman and their two kids in a bloody domestic triple murder. Jack had also went out on that call and would never forget that scene. The blood and bodies were strewn all around the house. Every time he drove past the neighborhood, he thought about it.

When he wrote the story, he learned from police and neighbors that these things had happened many times over the past 20 to 30 years. Only the names and faces changed.

Over the past 30 minutes, the police had been busy securing the neighborhood. They had put up wooden barricades around the house about 50 yards away in all directions. Everything was quiet inside the home.

About 50 onlookers gathered behind police lines. Officers escorted neighbors out of their homes for their protection. Some were complaining, saying it was unnecessary. But police were cautious because the man inside the house had fired gunshots in what seemed to be a haphazard manner.

Other residents quietly followed orders, not wanting to appear uncooperative or scared. Some laughed, thinking it was a joke and a good time to enjoy.

One young man brought out a portable TV to watch the hostage-taking. A local news station sent a reporter and camera crew to cover the situation in live reports.

Patrol cars and officers were everywhere. It looked like they were following proper police procedure in a hostage situation.

After years of covering cops and government, Jack had mixed feelings about public servants. He had respect for the things they did well and contempt for their holier-than-thou attitude when they screwed up. He tried to report both, but his editors only wanted stories about screwups. Jack constantly fought that battle.

He liked working the police beat when he could. Two years of working weekends as a general assignment and features reporter had hooked him on the human interest connected with crime-related stories. Now, as an investigative reporter and columnist with the *Sarasota Herald-Tribune*, his passion for understanding and reporting on crime continued to draw him to police work. He also liked the action involved in a serious crime investigation, the mystery associated with it, and the process of solving the crime.

While detectives and officers were often hostile toward the

press, Jack had cultivated a few good law enforcement sources who helped him gain insight into their work. He went on patrols when officers allowed reporters to accompany them, and he witnessed firsthand the danger cops faced daily.

One night, an APB came out on shots fired inside a house in North Sarasota. He was sitting in the cruiser's backseat with a veteran sergeant training a new patrol officer.

They rushed to the nearby scene and were the first to arrive. Suddenly, shots were fired from the house, hitting the patrol car and shattering the front windows. Nobody was hurt, but Jack felt an adrenaline rush when shots were fired at him.

He often wondered whether he had inherited his late father's ability to remain calm in battle or under fire. His father had survived three years of fighting the Japanese as a Marine in the South Pacific during World War II.

In many ways, Jack was his father. He loved the sting of battle, whether it was a sports game like football, baseball, or basketball, a boxing or karate lesson, or playing paintball, a military-type team sport played with compressed air guns that fired soft, round capsules filled with paint.

Suddenly, a woman's scream pierced through Jack's thoughts and the crowd that was growing behind the police cars. Still standing behind a cruiser, Jack jerked his head back toward the sound and saw a large Black woman yelling at a youthful-looking officer.

"I told you I want to see your boss, man, and I wanna right now! Not later!" the woman shouted in a shrill Southern accent. "What do you mean by forcing me outta my house? I've got work to do. This whole business is a fuss about nothin'."

"All right. All right," the police officer said. "Just wait here, and I'll be right back."

"That's better," she said. "Now we'll see who's in charge."

As the woman waited, Jack approached her for an interview. She eyed him with suspicion.

"Excuse me, mam. I'm Jack Kendall from the *Herald-Tribune*. May I have a word with you?"

"I'm not going to tell you anything I wouldn't tell the police," she replied.

The woman, who appeared to be in her mid-thirties, had calmed down somewhat after the prolonged outburst with the young, rather nervous patrolman.

"What's your name?" Jack asked.

"I'm Loretta Smith. I live two houses down," she explained, pointing down the street.

"Do you know what the man inside the house is doing?" Jack asked.

"Lordie, I know more what's a-goin' on inside than I know what's a-goin' on outside with all these policemen," Mrs. Smith said with a hearty laugh.

"Who is he?"

"Poor ole Charlie Tolbert has been drinking too much the past two weeks. Everybody knows about him. He lost his job a while back and can't straighten hisself out. I think he's on drugs, too. Everybody is these days," she said in a knowing voice.

"Oh, that's right! Yes, he is," said an old man from the back of the group. "I've heard yelling and broken glass and seen empty bottles and cans in the yard. I think his wife left him a couple weeks ago. Took the kids and everything. That's when it really started. It was his wife that done it."

"Now, Chester, you don't know `bout that," said Mrs. Smith sternly. "It's true that his wife left him. I jest don't knows why.

Maybe because of all that drinkin' and drugs he wuz doin'. I do know he don't have no job no more."

"Mrs. Smith," said Jack, "another question. The police told me you were the one who reported Tolbert taking the kids?"

"That's right. I wuz in my kitchen and heard a young girl scream. I looked out the window and saw Mr. Tolbert forcing a boy and a girl into the house," Smith said, shaking her head. "But when I saw that gun, I knew I needed to call 911. I've seen my share of violence in this neighborhood, and I knew nothing good was going to happen."

Just then, Jack saw Lt. Stevens, second in command. "Thank you, Mrs. Smith," he said. He walked over to the lieutenant to get an update.

"I'm sorry, Jack. All we can say right now is the area is secured," said Stevens, anticipating Jack's question.

"C'mon, Jim, you can tell me if he's made any threats or demands," Jack said impatiently.

"Okay, he did say something like 'Stay the hell away from the house' and 'I've got bullets for these kids,' but don't quote me on that, Jesus, please, Jack. You can get it from the police report later."

"I just want background quotes now. I won't attribute it to you," Jack replied. "Thanks, Jim."

"Right," said Stevens with an unbelieving tone. "I am sure we'll get this settled soon. The hostage team is coming."

As Jack walked back to his car, he wondered what was going on inside with Tolbert and the kids.

But for now, inside the house, everything was quiet. Jack looked at his watch. It was 1:20 p.m., and the minutes seemed to be passing slowly.

Unexpectedly, Jack felt a cold, eerie sensation rush through him as the dream from the night before about soldiers marching toward a mountain flashed through his mind.

Simultaneously, a sickening feeling about Becky washed through his body. Something wasn't right. He felt something terrible was happening at this precise moment.

He took a few more steps and reached out to his car for balance. What just happened? Soldiers marching? Becky?

As he leaned against his vehicle, Jack took a deep breath and wiped the sweat off the side of his face. He noticed his shirt was becoming damp. He reached into his car for a water bottle and took a sip. It made him feel a little better.

He needed to get out of the sun. He looked around for shade but didn't see any. Whoever had built this subdivision removed most of the trees—stupid bastards, clumsy developers with their mindless bulldozing mentality.

It seemed hotter just now because the light breeze had stopped. It could be worse, Jack thought. It could be nighttime, out in the country, with mosquitoes hacking away, sucking blood. He hated mosquitoes. But he didn't like these boring hostage situations, especially on hot summer days.

He looked at the house and made mental notes of its condition. What a dump. The white paint on the siding was dry and chipped. The shingles on the roof were severely worn. This house is suffering, he thought. The small front lawn was no different. Months had passed since anybody had mowed the yard. Weeds grew in bunches among the litter.

Parts of the near-north side of Sarasota looked like refugee camps, with junk cars on the streets and kids walking around in tattered clothing. The country was in a recession, and jobs were scarce, especially for the uneducated.

Most of this neighborhood's houses were owned by out-oftowners or semi-affluent south-side slum lords. They didn't care. All they wanted was the rent and the tax breaks.

This area starkly contrasted with most of Sarasota, nationally known as a tourist and retirement haven for the rich, famous, and trendy.

Jack knew the history of Sarasota by heart. Growing up in the city, he had heard dozens of stories from his parents and the old-timers.

Sarasota's north side was the town's garden spot forty years ago. In 1926, the Ringling Bros. Circus family built their mansion along Sarasota Bay. In those post-World War I years—immortalized by F. Scott Fitzgerald in The Great Gatsby—it appeared that Sarasota would take off as a major tourist destination.

But then came the real estate land bust, then the Great Depression, then World War II. It wasn't until the late 1960s that the world began to rediscover Sarasota and its sandy beaches as a quiet getaway.

With runaway growth in the late 1970s, the once-small airport suddenly faced a noise problem from large jets carrying international passengers, prompting developers to abandon the north side. They began building in central and southern Sarasota County instead.

Over the past ten years, Sarasota's near-north and northwest sides, given their proximity to the airport and industrial area, had slowly died of neglect.

There was some hope. With the new interstate opening east of town to connect Tampa with Naples, the northeast side could get a development boost. The *Herald-Tribune* had reported all the changes.

That highway could help stimulate the whole north side,

but only when companies start hiring people again. Jack laughed at himself. What am I thinking? This heat is making me daydream.

Still, nothing was happening. The police, the onlookers, and probably even Tolbert were waiting. For what? Jack continued to stare at the old house like everyone else.

He began to think again of his hometown and what Becky had said about it. Maybe he should take her advice and get out. He told her about his dream of taking a sabbatical, going to Jamaica for a year, chilling out, and writing something other than hard news or feature stories. He wanted to write a mystery novel, but he had no time.

She wanted to move to Seattle, Phoenix, or Chicago. But he wasn't sure. Except for five years in college and another year spent traveling in Europe and South America, he had spent nearly his entire life here.

He wasn't opposed to moving away. Sarasota was changing, and he didn't like it. He felt slightly angry when he thought about the growth and the people overlooked by the political-developmental establishment.

The house before him epitomized how city officials ignored community problems and embraced newcomers and their money. Local politicians hoped the new money would stimulate the economy and increase jobs, part of an old, failed "trickle-down" economic theory that led to the Great Depression of the 1920s. It gained new supporters today because of the stagflation of the 1970s.

Community problems were one reason Jack liked to cover the underprivileged. Their stories needed to be told. If papers didn't recognize the poor as human beings who demanded respect or at least understanding and compassion, the public wouldn't know. He knew nothing would be done to correct class inequity without public knowledge.

Jack again wiped his brow with his sleeve. He looked around. The police were consulting with each other more now. They had set up a listening device to pick up conversations inside the house. Everything was still quiet. He wondered how long it would stay that way.

In the corner of his eye, standing by the police cruiser, was a man in a white suit with extra-dark sunglasses. Jack wouldn't have noticed the man if it weren't for that white suit. It stood out.

The mysterious man in the white suit just stood there, watching. He seemed out of place compared with most people in the crowd, who appeared to be neighbors. Who is this guy, and what is he doing here? Jack wondered.

Maybe he had been driving around, had a police scanner in his car, and stopped to see the fuss. But why stand out in the hot sun without a good reason?

Jack noticed something else about this man: something was wrong with his expression and body language. He had a scowl on his face, and he was angry. Maybe he knew Tolbert?

Jack decided he would go over and strike up a conversation. He'd started walking when he heard a booming voice.

"All right, Mr. Tolbert. We know you're upset, and we all sympathize with you," said Police Chief Tom Bagley through a bullhorn. "Losing a job is a hard situation. But this isn't going to solve things. The teenagers' mothers are outside, and they're very worried. Why don't you let the two youngsters out, and we'll talk?"

Bagley paused momentarily, then said, "Rest assured, you will not be harmed. Just let the children go."

A veteran beat cop who had risen through the ranks over the years, Bagley stood behind the horn, his cheeks puffed out and his broad chest heaving as he spoke.

Jack observed Bagley fidgeting with his bullhorn, aware that the seasoned officer hoped to resolve the standoff peacefully before violence erupted, as the officers were eager for action.

Over the past few months, the police department had been wracked with dissent. It wasn't Bagley's fault. The mayor had nearly busted the police union, and some officers were bitter about the way they were treated. Some quit, and some were forced to resign under intense pressure. Morale was low, and the city's people knew it. The police's actions had been documented primarily through Jack's columns.

This was the cops' first chance to make the public forget about how divided the station was during the union battle with city hall.

The cops, especially Bagley, were on the spot just as much as the man holding the kids inside. Jack knew Bagley was thinking about it. Bagley wanted a clean bust. Nothing fancy. No one hurt. No heroes. Just good, clean policework. Something positive the papers, and especially Jack Kendall, could write about.

As Bagley waited for a response from Tolbert, Jack looked around and saw that the police department's new hostage team had arrived. They were gearing up. Was Bagley going to use them? So far, he'd seemed to be taking charge of the situation rather than turning it over to the lead negotiator, Lt. Nicholas.

Maybe Bagley also sensed something was going to happen. Police were on the telephone with Tolbert to talk him down, so it was unusual for Bagley to use the bullhorn. Maybe he wanted to get it on the public record that he was in charge and doing everything he could before acting.

Jack also noticed sharpshooters had positioned themselves on roofs around the house. Gas masks had been passed around, and two cops were attaching tear gas canisters to their rifles.

"Chief, everyone is in position," Jack overheard Lt. Stevens say. "We're ready if you want to go in. He's in the living room with the kids."

But Bagley seemed hesitant, saying, "Let's wait until his wife arrives. We'll give him more time, but I don't feel good about this one."

Oh, great, the chief, Jack thought. His deadline to finish his column for the afternoon edition was in about two hours. Time was running out.

One of Jack's strengths was also one of his weaknesses. He was sometimes impatient and impulsive. He always wanted things to happen sooner rather than later.

But he knew anything could happen at any second. In his job, Jack had met plenty of lunatics. Not all of them were criminals. Some were law-abiding citizens. Some even ran for political office. You just never knew until they snapped, just like the guy inside.

That's what fascinated and disgusted Jack about covering crime. Every person has their breaking point, the point that snaps people from being fools into bloodthirsty murderers. Sometimes, turning a person around takes only one moment of anger.

Charlie Tolbert remained silent in the house. He still had not responded to Bagley, which was not a good sign.

Jack wondered what Bagley was waiting for. Was he going to give the order to tear-gas the house? He suspected the chief was right to wait and be patient, especially with one of the mothers of the hostage outside and TV crews filming.

He had been involved in hostage situations before. They could last for five minutes or for five hours. You could never tell with a confused, trapped, potentially dangerous person like Tolbert. One problem was that nobody seemed to know much about the guy.

But what if the guy is crazy? Maybe by waiting, he is getting more desperate? He'd threatened to blow away the kids earlier, so Lt. Stevens had said. Perhaps he will if he doesn't get his way. The police must be thinking the same.

At that thought, Jack realized nobody else from the newspaper had arrived. "Where is my goddamn photographer?" he said to himself. He returned to his car, reached for the phone, and called the paper.

"This is Kendall. Rick, are you there?"

A voice crackled back over the line. "Sure am. What can I do for you, Jack?"

"Where the hell is Alex? I have a feeling something might happen very soon. The cops aren't going to wait on a photographer before they toss in tear gas, raid the house, and shoot this guy dead."

"He's coming. He should be there by now. Anything to report?"

"Can you check out a guy named Charlie Tolbert? He worked at Tropicana in Bradenton until about a month ago.

He might have been fired for some reason. His wife left him two weeks ago and is probably staying elsewhere."

"Okay, I'll get Bobbie on it. Anything else?"

"How about sending over some cold lemonade? Over and out," said Jack, not waiting for Rick's reply.

Out of the corner of his eye, Jack noticed a middle-aged woman talking with Chief Bagley, Lt. Stevens, and Lt. Nicholas. She was tall and dark-haired, probably in her early 40s. Jack inched closer to the chief to hear what the woman was saying.

"I'd like to speak to whoever is in charge here," she said in a shaky, nervous voice. "I'm Liz Baker, and I have been waiting, and nobody is telling me anything. My 15-year-old son, Jamie, is in there, and I want to know what's being done to have him released?"

"Let me introduce myself, ma'am," said the Chief. "I'm Thomas Bagley, chief of police. First, I want to assure you that we have everything under control."

"Control?" shouted Mrs. Baker. "Control? Is that what you call it? It looks like the only thing you have in control is your men, and I wonder how long you can control them. All these guns. Why are they necessary? Can you control them? You're probably making the man inside more desperate. Why don't you tell him to release my boy and his girlfriend? He has no right to hold him."

Chief Bagley had met women in situations like this before. She is probably a perfect mother, but she clearly doesn't understand the complexities of it. You can ask for the hostages to be released, but you can't just order him to do it.

Should he explain police procedures to the mother? First, you must set up lines of communication with the kidnapper. Try to reason with him and find out what he wants. Then, you must try to defuse the situation and lower the temperature. That takes time.

But all Bagley said was, "Ma'am, we are doing the best we can."

The chief's calm words seemed to settle her down. "I know.

I'm sorry. I know you're doing everything humanly possible to get my son out," Mrs. Baker said, having let off steam and seeming to relax. "Is there anything I can do? Can I talk to my boy? My husband is coming from work. He can help, I'm sure."

"We appreciate that, ma'am. We really do. Why don't you stay by the cruiser in case we do need you?" Bagley asked, turning to Lt. Stevens and whispering, "If Tolbert's wife doesn't get here pretty soon, let's see if we can get a relative here, or a neighbor, to talk with him."

Lt. Stevens nodded and ordered several police officers to canvass the neighborhood.

Bagley motioned for Lt. Nicholas to come closer. "Jon, when Mrs. Tolbert arrives, I want you to take over. He's getting pretty negative. I'm not sure how long I can keep this up."

"Yes, sir, Chief," Lt. Nicholas said. "You're doing as well as can be expected. I talked with him on the phone for a while, but he hung up and isn't answering our calls."

Jack went up to Lt. Stevens again. "I overheard what the chief said. Are you guys going to make a move?" he asked.

"Don't worry. You'll be the first to know," said Lt. Stevens sarcastically as he walked away, then spun around. "Oh, Jack. Maybe you want to talk with one of the mothers, Mrs. Baker. She's over there," he added, pointing at the woman.

"I will, thanks," Jack said.

Jack edged closer for an interview with a troubled and nervous Mrs. Baker.

"Hi, Mrs. Baker. I'm Jack Kendall with the *Herald-Tribune*. I know this is a tough time. Could you tell me about your son and the girl inside?"

"Well, Mr. Kendall, I'm not sure what I can tell you. My son, Jamie, is an honor roll student at Sarasota High. He and his girlfriend, Leslie Pulaski, were going out to the beach with some friends this morning," she said in a breathless voice.

"I was told by one of their friends that there wasn't enough room for everyone in the car, so they decided to take the bus. They must have decided to hitchhike," she said, pausing for a second and putting her hand over her mouth.

"Yes, so the man inside picked them up. Go on, please," said Jack.

"We're pretty sure the man who picked them up brought them here; at least, that's what the police told us.

"We know they never got to the beach, and their friends became worried. One called me at home to find out if Jamie had gone home. I called the police," said Mrs. Baker, who added that she also had two other children, ages 10 and 12.

"Thanks, Mrs. Baker," said Jack. "Take it easy. I will check with you later."

Jack heard Lt. Nicholas talking on his police radio. "Chief, we found the Tolbert woman. She seemed reluctant but said she would try to leave work."

The chief nodded, picked up the bullhorn, switched it on, and put his mouth to the built-in microphone.

"Charlie. We have contacted your wife. She is on her way to talk with you. Just relax. Everything will be all right. We want you to feel comfortable. No one wants to hurt you," Bagley said.

Jack had to smile. Despite the heat and situation, the chief was at the top of his game today. Old Bagley should have run for sheriff years ago, he thought. He was a natural-born politician.

But the chief liked working for the city. He'd started as a beat cop some 35 years ago. Now, the chief was the chief, and he would retire as the chief; that's how this husky man with four children and seven grandchildren wanted it.

Jack's thoughts about the chief were interrupted when someone in the crowd yelled that the door was opening. A boy's head popped out, his mouth taped.

Mrs. Baker screamed, "Let my baby go!"

A man's voice rang out behind the boy. "I know what's going on out there. I've been seeing you cops with your guns and… that tear gas. I don't want any of that in here. Do you hear me? If any come in, I'll kill these kids right away and then start killing you cops, one by one!" the man shouted angrily.

While Jack couldn't see the man's face, he could now see his forearm and hand as he waved what looked like a .38-caliber pistol. He didn't think the sharpshooters would try a shot at the angles they had. Too risky with the boy in the way.

With those words, Mrs. Baker started screaming and crying and had to be held back from the police line by officers. The second mother, Mrs. Pulaski, tried to comfort her while holding back her tears.

"And I don't want to see my wife. If I see her, I'll shoot these kids and throw them out one by one. Do ya hear me?" said Tolbert, closing the door.

As soon as he heard Tolbert, Jack switched on his micro-cassette tape recorder—which Becky had given him for his birthday—and began writing down every crazy, deranged word in his notebook. The guy was disturbed. But at least something was happening.

Bagley also became very concerned about the outburst.

"All right, Charlie, all right. We don't want to use tear gas. We don't want to use anything. We want you and the kids to be safe. All you have to do is let the kids out and walk outside without the gun and your arms raised," the chief said. "Everything will be all right. You will not be harmed."

Then, from inside the house, came the booming voice one more time. This time, asking a question. "Is Jack Kendall out there?"

Hearing his name, Jack looked up from his notebook, turned his head to the side, lowered his eyebrows, and then raised his head with a half-smile. He thought he had heard right, but you never could tell, especially on a hot day like this.

Chapter 2
A Tragic Ending

Monday, 2 p.m., July 7, 1980

Through an open window, Charlie Tolbert yelled again, this time in a scratchy voice, "I want Kendall! If he isn't here, call him. I'm not going to talk anymore until Kendall gets here. You got 15 minutes!"

Jack Kendall walked over to Chief Bagley, who had a look of complete bewilderment on his face.

"Do you know this guy?" the chief asked accusingly.

Jack had been reporting on crime and domestic matters for the past eight years. Had he met Charlie Tolbert? He didn't recall the name, but he had talked to hundreds of people in this town, some on the phone and some in person. Tolbert's name didn't ring any bells.

"No. Not that I can remember," Jack said.

"Good," the chief said.

"But I—"

"Now, Jack, before you say anything else, there is no way

I will let you go. I already have two hostages to rescue," the chief said.

All Jack could do was smile. He had already made his decision. It was a good story, but a direct interview before the arrest would be even better. It would clarify the man's state of mind. For a second, he thought about what Becky would say. She would think he was crazy, and he would have to agree. But he had done crazier things before in the name of a story.

And he wanted this story.

"Chief, I'm ready to go."

"Forget it, Kendall."

"Tom, come on. You know what you've got. Think about it. There's a seriously confused, troubled, scared man in that house, holding a gun on two children," said Jack in his most persuasive voice. "The way I see it, you have three choices: wait for hours in this heat and hope he gives up or passes out with a drug overdose; rush the house like John Wayne with your SWAT team, guns blazing; or three, let me go in to find out what he wants. Regardless of what he yelled out the door a minute ago, you can see he doesn't want to hurt those kids if he wants me in there with him. He's got something else in mind. He wants to tell a story."

Jack paused. "He apparently is familiar with my work."

"Kendall, shut up," Bagley said.

"Do you want to wait him out?" Jack asked. "If you do that, he will get even madder because he isn't getting his way. He had already shot up the neighborhood a couple of times. You saw how panicky he became when he saw the tear gas."

"Lieutenant, get Kendall out of here," Bagley said. "He thinks he's a goddamn psychiatrist."

"Yes, sir. Jack, beat it," Lt. Stevens said.

"Okay. So, you're going to rush the house like John Wayne. You don't have more than a 50-50 chance of getting the kids out alive. You've seen this movie before. Go ahead. I'll go interview the parents as you shoot your way in," Jack said as he turned around and waved goodbye.

"Now, hold it, Kendall. I suppose the brighter idea would be to let you go in?" said Bagley, taking Jack's bait. "And what if you get shot? Your replacement and editorial writers will crucify me for putting you in danger."

Jack turned around with a big smile. "Don't worry about that. I volunteer. You have witnesses. He asked for me. With me in there, you've got someone who can talk and listen to the man. You don't even know what he wants. I'm betting all he wants is to tell a story. He wants some attention. Let me give it to him. Anyway, what have you got to lose: a reporter who's been on your heels for the past eight years?"

Lt. Stevens acknowledged Jack's point with a nod and a quick smile. But the chief didn't say anything. He knew Tolbert didn't want to see his wife. She hadn't arrived yet and may not have been coming anyway.

Jack saw Bagley's indecision. "You let me in, and I'll be out in half an hour. The kids will be reunited with their parents, and you will look like a great genius for having such insight, patience, and understanding. I'll have a fantastic story. Everybody will come out looking good. And the poor, dumb bastard in there will be relieved that he isn't dead or sitting on death row waiting for our dear old governor to send him to the electric chair."

Jack paused, then said, "What do you say, Tom?"

The chief removed his cap and ran a hand through his damp white hair, and Jack could see the strain etched across his face. He hated moments like this—especially when the press, and Kendall in particular, had been right. Worse still was knowing he had no real choice. Hostage situations were chaotic by nature; all the firepower surrounding the house meant nothing if the man inside had already decided to die. The chief knew it, and Jack knew he knew it. In the end, persuasion—not force—was the only weapon that mattered.

"Jack," said the chief. "If I let you in, you promise not to try anything foolish. Just listen to the man. Don't try to analyze him or counsel him. And for God's sake, don't promise him anything. You are not a negotiator."

Jack nodded. "Give me a couple of minutes," he said as he turned to phone in the news to his editor.

Damn, Jack, you are going to get an excellent story, he thought as a ripple of adrenaline surged through his body. He walked to his car and saw that his photographer, Alex Mahoney, had finally arrived.

"Tell Guy Caballero that Johnny LaRue went in for a first-person scoop. Send reinforcements," Jack said to Alex, who shook his head, not entirely understanding the oblique reference to the old television comedy, Second City. It was Jack Kendall's inside joke with Rick, the city editor.

Alex snapped a couple of pictures of Jack with his Nikon F-3. "Right, Kendall, I'll send these photos to your next of kin," Alex said as he turned to walk to the newspaper car to radio the photo department to let them know what Jack was doing.

Jack didn't hear Alex. His large, light green eyes were shining. He forgot about the hot day and the long wait. He was already thinking about the story's lead. Something like, "How many Charlie Tolberts are out there? No job, no friends, no hope, no future. Nothing except a needle and a bottle of booze. A rebel with a curse." Nah, too dramatic. Delete. Jack was riding high, very excited. What fantastic luck, he thought with a little laugh. A first-person interview with a kidnapper. And on a Monday!

As he waited for Bagley to give the go-ahead, Jack wondered whether he should have asked Alex to call Becky at home. His smile faded, and his bravado waned.

For a moment, he allowed himself to think of last Saturday. After a long night on the town with friends, they had argued again about Becky's increasing cocaine use and how to pay for their next vacation.

Jack insisted she keep her savings intact. It was an old, never-changing argument. He did regret bringing up her cocaine use, a very sore subject.

A few months earlier, they had compromised. Becky promised to cut back, and Jack agreed to use some of the savings from that change to fund their annual fall vacation.

But she couldn't cut down, and Jack knew it. He'd accused her of spending too much money on cocaine and insisted that they needed to save more if they expected to take the vacations they loved to Jamaica, Chicago, Seattle, and elsewhere.

She cried when he told her in anger that she was turning into a coke junkie.

But today, as the long afternoon wore on, Jack began to change his mind. Maybe he had been wrong to come down so hard on her. She needed professional help, not angry condemnations from her husband.

She needed to stop using so much. But they should live for today, like she always said, and not worry about tomorrow. If she wanted to spend her savings, why not let her? He was worried about her health and where the money would come from in an emergency. That was his dilemma.

He was trying to be practical. But what was more important? Being practical or making Becky happy? It was ironic. But at times like this, when he risked his life, he wished he weren't so pragmatic. He suddenly wanted her there. But he had work to do. He shook his head and decided to think about it later.

The seconds passed slowly. Jack checked his tape recorder. It was working. He looked around and saw Mrs. Baker clinging to her husband, who was soothing her. Mrs. Pulaski was standing beside them. They were staring at him with terror in their eyes.

He nodded to them and gave a reassuring smile. Then he turned toward the house and thought, I hope old Charlie Tolbert isn't actually crazy. If he is, the kids and I are dead.

The chief walked over to find out if Jack had changed his mind. He had not.

"Okay, Kendall, don't mess this up," Bagley said worriedly.

"Don't worry, Chief. I plan on writing this story in exactly 90 minutes for the afternoon paper," Jack said with a smile.

The chief stared impassively at him as he picked up the bullhorn for a third time. "Charlie, this is Chief Bagley. Jack Kendall is here. He has agreed to talk to you, but only for 15 minutes, tops, and then you will let him out. We want you to promise that he will not be held hostage. Do you understand?"

The door opened a crack. "Let Kendall come in. I'm not making any deals with all those guns and cops out there. Kendall has to take his chances like me and these kids."

The chief started to respond, but Jack grabbed his arm. "Let me go. It's okay."

"Go on, get the hell out of here," the chief said, waving Jack off in frustration.

Jack took a deep breath and was off before the chief had

finished his sentence. As Jack walked toward the house, Bagley was on the bullhorn.

"Jack Kendall is on his way. Alone," the chief said.

The front door was slightly ajar. Jack knocked three times. It opened a little more, and a voice on the other side said, "Don't try to be a stupid hero, Kendall. Just be a fucking reporter. Remember, I've got a gun here, and it can go off mighty easy. So don't tempt me."

Jack hesitated a second, took another deep breath, then walked through the front door and into the living room. He saw the two kids, their mouths taped closed with duct tape and their hands tied behind their backs. No wonder they weren't making any noises. He glanced at Tolbert but didn't recognize him. Must be a reader, he thought.

The house was a mess. It looked like it had been weeks since anyone had cleaned it. Empty TV dinner tins lay around the ragged couch in front of an old television set. Beer cans and liquor bottles were scattered around the floor. The house smelled of stale alcohol and garbage.

Charlie Tolbert, dressed in wrinkled, dirty clothes and looking like he hadn't slept in days, watched Jack as the reporter made mental notes of the house. Nothing was said in the first few seconds.

Finally, Jack sat on a brown recliner, took out his tape recorder, opened his slim notebook, and began jotting down some notes, hoping Charlie would start the conversation. There was silence, so Jack looked up.

"Well, you have me here, Charlie."

The man sat there, saying nothing.

"Do you want an interview?" Jack began to get nervous at the man's strange silence.

Charlie just sat there staring at Jack. His bloodshot eyes had a wild look. This guy wasn't acting like he knew what he was doing. Jack wondered if he had made the right decision by coming in with only the tools of his trade.

Jack had half-expected the man to welcome him in because he was a member of the press, not the cops, and to start talking away. But Tolbert looked like a lost soul who had gotten on the wrong subway train and didn't know how to get home.

"Just wait," said Charlie as he got up to look nervously out a window to see if the cops were using Jack to sneak up on him.

"I take it you want to get your side of the story in the paper," Jack said. "I want to understand everything. Maybe I ought to ask you some questions."

"No," Charlie said abruptly, stepping away from the window. "I want to do the talking. Just turn on that machine. Don't take any notes. I want this word-for-word."

Jack closed the cover of his reporter's notebook and put it in his back pocket. He put his pen in his top shirt pocket, turned on the recorder, and laid it on his lap.

"Why am I here, Charlie?"

"Shut up, I'll do the talking," Charlie replied loudly. He then continued in a softer voice. "Please. I don't know how much time I have.

"First of all, these two kids here, I don't want to hurt them. I never intended to hurt them. This wasn't my plan. I just picked them up hitchhiking. They seemed so happy, and it got me mad. This whole thing has gotten out of hand. It's driving me crazy," said Charlie, suddenly crying.

Jack realized he was right all along. This poor, pathetic bastard is hurting terribly and is absolutely confused. But he sensed something else was at work here—something far worse than losing a job and having his wife walk out.

"Why is this happening, Charlie?" Jack asked in his most understanding voice, one well-rehearsed for situations like these. He leaned forward in his chair.

"I told you to shut up; I'll do the talking." Charlie's face suddenly changed from pathetic to passionless ice, as if he had just figured something out. "Have you ever worried about something so much that you couldn't get it out of your mind? Whatever you did, whoever you were with, it was there?"

Jack sat there and nodded like he knew exactly what the man was talking about. He didn't. Everything in life had always come easily for him.

"First of all, it all started about six months ago. My wife just came out and told me she wanted a divorce. Right out of the blue, she says one night: 'Things aren't working out. I'm not happy. We need to separate.' She's saying this, and we have two little kids in the next room.

"I couldn't believe it at first. I kind of took it lightly for about four months. Sure, I was worried. But Betty didn't leave, and she didn't say anything more about it. I was afraid to talk about it, and I suppose she had nothing more to say.

"I tried to change a little, make things more exciting for us, but I had a full-time job to worry about," Tolbert said, his voice shaking. "People were getting laid off, transferring, leaving for better jobs.

"She changed a whole lot during that time. Never wanted to do anything with me, always demanding the world and criticizing me," he said louder. "You know, like picking little fights over nothing. It got to the point where I couldn't do anything right.

"Two months ago, on our fifth wedding anniversary, she didn't want to go out," he said, shaking his head in disbelief.

"She said, 'Let's not make a big deal.' I didn't say anything. We stayed home," he said in a deflated tone.

Jack sat there, wondering where Tolbert was going with this line of thought. At this point, he knew the kidnapping was not just about his wife leaving.

"Finally, just four weeks ago, we got back home from hitting a few bars with friends. I knew something was up. She was quiet on the way home. I pulled into the driveway, and before I could turn off the car, she said she was leaving," Tolbert said in a softer voice. He was now fidgeting more with his handgun.

"I said, 'Leaving? Where are you going?' She said she didn't know. She needed time away. She said she would come back later to pick up her stuff. It was 2:30 in the morning, and she was talking about splitting up a marriage, a home, kids, and our life together."

Jack was getting increasingly worried. Where was this going? He saw Tolbert change from angry and nervous to sad and angry.

"I pleaded with her to come inside and talk it over. I told her she had to look at the kids and say she still wanted to leave. She refused, and I sat in my car, watching her go.

"Next, I saw her mother, who was babysitting, come out, almost on cue. Betty said something to her mother, and they both went inside and brought out the kids, who were still sleeping. I got out of the car and watched them as they walked out, got in, and drove off. I was stunned.

"I went inside and drank a half bottle of Johnny Red and passed out. When I woke up the next morning with a terrible hangover, she was there with a friend, and they were packing her stuff. I begged, pleaded, and promised everything I could to get her to change her mind. But when Betty makes up her mind, it's unchangeable. That's one of the reasons I married her. She's so strong-willed."

During what seemed to be a lengthy confession, Jack had hardly taken his eyes off Charlie, except for a glance at the two kids, who were squirming and mumbling frightened, unintelligible words through their gags.

"All this happened 30 days ago. I can't sleep at night. I lost my job because I missed too many days."

Jack nodded and wondered when Charlie would tell him something more about this hostage-taking.

"At work, I met a guy who told me of a way to make extra money. I got involved in other things that I shouldn't have. It seemed easy, and I thought it would help with Betty and our situation. Maybe take some pressure off her. But nothing I did mattered. Everything I did made things worse because I can't escape from the things I've done."

What, thought Jack, were the things he had done? Jack was confused at Charlie's change of topic. Making money? He was now discussing something other than his love and sadness over Betty leaving.

But before Jack could interrupt and ask about it, Charlie spoke again.

"Listen, I just want to make a short statement, and this whole thing will be all over," said Tolbert, his voice rising.

"I know I've lost Betty. I've lost my kids. I don't want to go to jail for this and other crimes I've committed. It doesn't matter anymore without Betty. I worry about my kids. But I don't have any choice."

The tone of his voice suddenly changed from bitterness to

soft melancholy. Jack became extremely worried about what was happening in the room.

"Charlie. It's all right. I will write this story, and people will understand you didn't mean to take these kids. Put the gun down, and you and I walk out together," said Jack, trying to calm Charlie and give him a way out. He'd expected crazy, not such hopelessness.

Charlie just sat there with a queer smile on his face as he fidgeted with the gun.

Jack looked over at the two kids on the sofa. Their eyes were wide open in astonishment. He quickly turned around to face Charlie, who had raised the gun to his own head.

Without wasting a moment, Charlie desperately yelled, "I love you, Betty! Forgive me! You aren't to blame!"

The gunshot was loud and crisp. The blood splattered against the ceiling, over the floor, and on the front of Charlie's dirty white shirt.

Jack jumped up from his chair and yelled, "Oh my God! Damn! Oh my God!"

The kids ran out of the house. Jack stood there, looking at the man he had been interviewing just two seconds earlier.

His eyes watered, and he clutched his tape recorder and said in a stunned, shaky voice, "Oh my God. Jesus. God Almighty. Oh my God. What have you done, Charlie? What have you done?"

He felt cold all over. He kept repeating, "Oh my God, oh my God."

Skin tingling, Jack felt sick. The last words Charlie said—*I love you, Betty. Forgive me. You aren't to blame.*—echoed in his head, with the sound of the gun drowning everything else out.

Jack had heard his share of sick stories. He had seen many

crime scenes. But he had never witnessed anything as ghastly as this. His knees became weak, and he reached out for the sofa to keep from falling over, staring at Charlie in horror.

In seconds, Jack went from being a reporter to feeling like a victim. He was a pawn in a tragic sequence of events that he had no control over. He was completely numb. He began to shake and sweat, but he couldn't make himself look away from the corpse.

A second later, Charlie's lifeless body slumped off the sofa and onto the floor. The heavy, dull thud startled Jack.

"Oh my God," he said again. What the hell am I doing here? I've got to get out. Get out now. Move your feet and leave. Walk outside. That's it, Jack, move.

He forced himself to step away. He turned slightly away from Charlie, still watching him, as he slowly made his way step by agonizing step toward the front door.

Outside, everyone heard the gunshot, and Jack felt the moment tighten around his chest. He saw it register on Bagley's face—Bagley thought the shot had been meant for him. That fear hardened into certainty when the front door flew open, and the two kids burst out alone, sprinting into the night with no sign of Jack behind them.

At the sound of the shot, Bagley and police officers rushed to the house from about 30 yards away. They were nearly at the house when they saw Jack backing out the front door.

Several officers pushed past Jack to enter the house. Bagley approached the reporter, who turned to look blankly at the chief. His face was ghostly white.

"You are safe now, Jack. Go talk with Lt. Stevens," said Bagley, placing his hand on Jack's shoulder.

Jack nodded, but the chief's voice seemed a mile away. He

stumbled out of the house, stunned, speechless, in shock.

People ran up to him, asking questions. A slew of other cops followed Bagley into the house.

Lt. Stevens came up to Jack as he was walking away. "I need to talk with you about what happened."

Jack gazed at Lt. Stevens blankly and continued toward his car.

"Jack! Can you hear me?" Lt. Stevens said. "We need a statement. Where are you going?"

Jack wasn't listening.

"Well, okay, we can talk later. Go sit down in your car and wait for us."

As Jack walked out in a daze, the mysterious man in the white suit leaned into his black BMW. He picked up his car phone and began speaking to someone.

"He's dead," the man in the white suit said.

A voice replied, "That dumb son-of-a-bitch."

Jack wasn't aware of what was happening around him. He was numb. He was in a vacuum, swallowed up by what had just happened.

An ambulance's siren went off. A dog barked. The crowd rumbled. Questions were directed at Jack as he walked past. What happened? What did you see? Are you all right?

Jack didn't hear a sound except for the ringing in his ears from the gunshot. Seeing Tolbert's death had put him in a state of shock. He was oblivious to what was happening around him.

What should he do? He had simple thoughts. Get away. Leave. Becky. Go home to Becky. She was a safe zone for him.

But what just happened? He was a witness to a suicide. A recorder of death. He had his story, but he was now part of the story.

Then, he saw a vision of Charlie sitting before him, talking. Again, he heard him say, "I love you, Betty. Forgive me. It's not your fault."

Then, the gunshot. Surprising. Bang. Charlie slumped over. Blood ran down the side of his head. Blood on the floor. Blood all over.

The grisly recollection snapped him entirely into the present. He looked at his hands.

Jack glanced over to the kids and their mothers. They were all hugging each other and crying. He heard the pop of the gunshot again.

Then he heard his mental voice asking: Did you help Charlie kill himself? Would Charlie still be alive if you hadn't gone inside looking for a story? Why didn't you listen to the chief?

It didn't matter. Charlie was dead. And Jack was a reporter. He knew what he had to do: write a story for the afternoon paper.

He walked over to his car, opened the door, started the engine, and drove away.

Chapter 3
Jack's First-Person Story

Monday, 3 p.m., July 7, 1980

Jack walked slowly through the front entrance of the newspaper's blue-carpeted lobby. The atrium behind the reception area on the first floor glowed with light from the skylights six floors above. It was a warm feeling in the winter, a grim reminder of the heat in the summer.

Making his way past Curtis Nettles, the middle-aged security guard who stood by the door, scrutinizing each person as they entered, Jack's eyes remained fixed ahead.

The slightly overweight receptionist, Kathy Hopkins, who was punching buttons on the wide switchboard with the expertise of an airline pilot in heavy weather, cheerfully greeted Jack, as was her custom. Hearing his name called out cut through the numbness that lingered from Charlie's suicide; Jack glanced at her with a quick, weak half-smile.

Sometimes, he would chat with these familiar staff members for a quick minute. Today, he hardly noticed they were there.

As he walked past, they stared at him. They had already heard the news about the suicide at the police stakeout and were expecting to see him in the newsroom.

But Jack was still experiencing shock from the strange sequence of events that had ended only 30 minutes before, when Charlie Tolbert had suddenly ended his life.

As a writer, he could always detach himself from whatever he was writing or whomever he was writing about. It felt strange to be more a part of the story than he had ever been. Maybe, if he could sit down and write about what had happened, the ugliness and horror and pain and confusion he felt would leave.

The newsroom was between the advertising and production levels on the fifth floor. He got on the elevator and pushed the button for the third floor, where the snack bar and library were located. He wished he had a stiff drink—like his favorite, Jack Daniel's Old No. 7 Black Label—but he was going for coffee at the newspaper by habit. He got off the elevator and stepped into the snack bar, then walked toward the coffee table.

"Jack!" said Tom Justice, his close friend at the paper. As usual, Tom was loafing around, talking to several good-looking young ad reps. "Jack!"

Jack ignored his friend. He reached into his pants pocket for change to drop into the coffee donation can.

"I heard you had a close one out there...Jack? Are you here?" Tom said, knocking on the top of the coffee table. "They have a space saved for you on A-1. 'Man kills self as brave reporter takes notes,' the headline reads in boldface. Nice package. I guess you really knock 'em dead with your interviewing skills, old boy."

Jack turned around quickly as if he were waking up from a trance. His drawn, tired face stared off Tom.

"Screw yourself, Tom," Jack finally said in a whisper.

"That's an idea," said Tom, winking at the two young women.

Jack looked at Tom once more, expressionless, while Tom kept on grinning broadly.

In a stern voice, Jack said, "Why don't you cover cops for a while, bright boy? Maybe you're the type who'd be able to laugh when somebody blows their own head off."

Tom's smile faded as he studied Jack, and Jack could see the question forming behind his eyes. This wasn't the Jack Tom knew, and they both understood it. Tom glanced at the girls and gave a slight shake of his head, and Jack watched as they quickly made their excuses and slipped away.

Jack picked up the coffee pot and slowly poured the black liquid into a Styrofoam cup. He wondered how tremendously desperate or sick Charlie must have been to kill himself.

He shuddered at the thought of Charlie slumped over, the life rushing out of him. He remembered how helpless it had felt to sit there and watch. There had been no time for him to act. If he'd only had time to lunge over and knock the gun away...

Even if there had been time, would he have taken the chance? The man did have a gun. If they had struggled, and if the weapon had fired, who knows who might have been shot? Damn it. Why didn't I anticipate something crazy like that? Charlie's attitude and body language signaled disaster during the interview.

Suddenly, Jack realized he had to try to contact Charlie's

wife. What was her name? Betty, that's right. She never showed up for him when she was called. Very odd. Jack didn't want to get into their domestic affairs too much, although he knew he would have to ask many embarrassing questions. All he wanted was her reaction and whether he had given any warning signs.

But there was something else going on in Charlie's life. He had implied other crimes than the kidnapping. What, Jack had no idea.

He paused for a second. This is good, he thought. You are starting to feel like a reporter again, rather than a victim or an enabler. You have a story to write.

Tom, who had left Jack to his thoughts, waited patiently by the door as Jack walked back to the elevator. He stared at Jack with a serious look on his face.

"Going up?" Tom said.

Jack looked at Tom, paused, and raised his eyebrows. "Unless you got tickets to the ball game."

"Listen," Tom said. "I didn't mean to make light of your situation. You know me better than that, Jack. I suppose covering politics has warped my sensibilities."

Jack shrugged. "All I want to do is finish this damn thing and go home."

"Sure, of course. I understand. No problem. Accept my humble apology, and forget I'm a jerk sometimes, especially around pretty young ladies. Listen, I know you've got to file the story, but let me ask you something."

"All right," Jack said as he exhaled.

"What's up with Becky?"

"Becky?"

"Yes, Susan asked me about her the other night. She hasn't been able to get a hold of her for two weeks, and we haven't seen you together in a while."

Jack tapped the elevator wall with his three middle fingers. "Great timing, Tom. Becky has been working a lot, so we haven't had much time together. We talked about that the other night—how we need to find more time. Maybe we can get together with you and Susan sometime soon."

"Sure, we'd like that—just like old times. Go to dinner, do a little dancing, go to the bottle club, stay out all night, watch the sunrise, get breakfast, collapse, that sort of thing," Tom said. "Let me know when. I'll talk with Susan. You need a break."

Jack nodded. "I'll talk with Becky tonight, maybe just about dinner. We're getting a little old for all-night partying. It would be good to get out, though."

The elevator lurched to a stop at the fifth floor, and the doors slid open. Jack barely noticed. He was staring past his reflection in the metal wall, lost somewhere else, until a sudden wash of noise hit him—the clatter, the voices, the familiar din of the brightly lit newsroom spilling into the car. He could feel Tom watching him, waiting for a cue, but Jack had none to give. He had never walked into the newsroom feeling this heavy.

"I tell you what. We'll cook at our place. You guys come over, and you won't have to do a thing," he said, pausing for a second. "Okay? See you later, Jack."

Tom walked out first, before reverting to his old sarcastic self. "I'll be looking for a heart-wrenching story from you. Let me know if you need any pills or narcotics."

Jack nodded and walked over to the circle of desks that comprised the city desk.

"Kendall, I've got Bobbie phoning Charlie's boss at

Tropicana," said Rick Wiseman, Jack's editor, a guy with more energy than the power and light company. "We're giving this front page, and we want a lot of color in the story. Don't worry about the details. Just write what you've got. Bobbie will fill in his background and any hollow spots."

"Rick, I need to talk to his wife. That's an unknown part of the story," Jack said. "I don't know anything about her."

"Of course, talk to her. Write the news story first with the parents and all the colors of what happened out there, and fold in the wife. And then, I want you to write a sidebar in first person about the suicide," Rick said. "I've never heard of something like this happening in front of a reporter."

Jack nodded, walked over to his desk, pulled out his reporter's notebook and tape recorder, and looked at the blank terminal screen.

But before he did anything else, he tried to call Becky at home to tell her what had happened. First, the line was busy. Five minutes later, there was no answer.

It was now 3:30 in the afternoon. Thinking of Becky, the same terrible feeling Jack had at the crime scene returned. He couldn't identify it.

Was Becky all right? He felt something was wrong. Maybe she went shopping. He wanted to talk with her, but Wiseman wanted the news story immediately. That needed to be dealt with first. Luckily, the story had already taken shape in his mind.

Jack thought of several questions to ask Charlie's wife. He felt he needed answers because Tolbert had talked about her so much.

He looked up Charlie's phone number and dialed, unsure she'd be available because the police would be there collecting evidence. He needed to ask about the breakup and his state of mind leading up to today. His heart began to pound as adrenaline surged through his body. It was always that way when calling a survivor of a tragedy.

Betty Tolbert picked up the phone on the fifth ring. "Hello," she said in a monotone voice. Jack was somewhat surprised. So, she did come back to the house, although a little late to be of help.

"Is this Mrs. Tolbert? Mrs. Betty Tolbert?" Jack asked.

"Yes. Who is this?" Betty said casually.

"Jack Kendall. I'm a reporter with the *Herald-Tribune*. I'm sorry to bother you, but I want to talk with you about Charlie. I was with him this afternoon."

"Oh, it was you," Betty said flatly. "I...I really can't talk right now. I don't have anything to say, really."

"Mrs. Tolbert. I want to say how sorry I am about Charlie. How do you feel?" Jack asked awkwardly.

"He's dead, and there is nothing left to say. I've got two little girls here who need me. The police are here, searching the house for some reason. They let me in for just a few minutes to gather some things. I...I can't talk."

"I'm sorry, but just one minute," Jack said. "Were you and he going through a breakup? Did you know he was this troubled? Was he doing drugs? Had he given you any signs that something like this might happen?"

She paused and took a deep breath. "That's a lot of questions. Yes, I had left him. He was upset about it. He was working very hard at Tropicana before he was laid off. He started doing a second job. I didn't know too much about it. I can't get into anything more right now."

"But can you tell me why he would take his life?" Jack

asked quickly, urgency clear in his voice.

"Well, I did leave him about four weeks ago. Our marriage was over. You must know that, if you talked with him," Betty said. "He acted very different after that. I didn't believe he would go so far—kill himself. Now I've got to go."

"One more question, please," Jack said, "What about this second job? He said he was going to make a lot of money. He suggested it was illegal and that he didn't want to go to jail for committing other crimes. What else was he doing?"

"I didn't ask. But Charlie acted like he was going to get a big inheritance or something. He begged me to wait, and soon he'd be able to buy me things," she said.

"Mrs. Tolbert, he told me to tell you he was sorry, that it wasn't your fault. But he also specifically said he was committing crimes. What crimes?" Jack asked.

"Sorry, I just can't talk anymore," said Mrs. Tolbert as she abruptly hung up.

Jack was surprised at the tone of her voice. Unemotional. Cold. She could be in shock. No. He sensed there was something else.

He knew he should have interviewed her in person. If not to get more answers, at least to see her body language. But he was on deadline and didn't have time. She did confirm a few things and shared her reaction. At least he had enough information for the breaking news story.

He wondered if Betty knew something more about the money and didn't want to say it. Was she hiding facts? Maybe it was nothing.

Jack leaned back in his chair, looked at the ceiling, then focused on the keyboard and began to punch words into the terminal.

He typed Betty's section into the story and then read it back to himself silently. He wasn't satisfied; he knew there was more to the suicide than just Betty. There was money, and Charlie had mentioned other crimes. He had to leave the money part out of the story because there was no explanation for it.

Jack hadn't even given the police a statement yet about what he saw and heard before the suicide. But Betty had mentioned that the police searched the house while she was there. Jack picked up the phone.

"Bobbie, could you talk with Lt. Stevens about why they're searching Tolbert's house and what they're looking for?"

"I talked with him already. He said they're investigating the circumstances of Charlie's death and have no further comment because it's part of an investigation," Bobbie explained. "He was oddly irritated with you."

"I promised him I would give him a statement. I'll call him later," Jack said. "Can you send over some quotes for Rick to add to the story? Thanks, Bobbie."

Jack's instincts told him the search was related to the money. But he had a deadline to meet. Maybe something would come up eventually.

A half-hour later, Rick came over as Jack was finishing the story.

"I meant to tell you earlier. Becky called you around two o'clock. She didn't leave a message, but she told me to tell you she called and would contact you later. It was a little strange at the end. She mumbled something like, 'Tell him I'm sorry.' What do you think that meant? I didn't understand it. Then she said goodbye."

Sorry? Odd, Jack thought. Two o'clock. That was when

he'd walked toward his car, having that first awful thought about her and his mountain dream.

"Did she sound all right?"

"I don't know, Jack. She tried to act normal, but she sounded nervous. Probably nothing. I didn't tell her anything about what you were working on, but she might have heard something on the radio and guessed you might be there. I don't know," Rick said.

"Thanks for the message. I'm just about done with the news story," Jack said. "I'm going to write the first-person story now; then I have to call Lt. Stevens, then I'm going straight home. I'll let you know when I'm done, and then you can call me at home if you have any questions."

"Sure, Jack. I'm sure it'll be fine. Good job. Finish up, then go home and get some rest."

Jack nodded. As he punched the key to send the story to the city desk for editing, he thought about how it had seemed to write itself. It was like somebody had helped him, putting words into his fingers. He visualized each sentence, and the words flowed from his memory to the computer. He changed very little from the first draft.

On the other hand, the first-person account of Jack's interview with Charlie Tolbert before he killed himself was a little more challenging to get started. He was calmer now than in the first hour after the incident, but he was still a little upset.

He listened to the tape again and relived the experience. It seemed incredible, almost surreal, that it had happened to him.

A real person had died in front of him. He thought about the dozen or more people he'd "killed" in his paintball games.

But they were just shot with a soft capsule filled with red paint, not killed with a .38 caliber bullet.

He took a deep breath and began to write the first two sentences of his first-person account for the afternoon paper.

"Charlie Tolbert took his life today in front of a reporter and two teenagers he had kidnapped earlier. I was the reporter."

Like the news story, he wrote it as clearly as possible to bring the reader into the room with Charlie, the two kids, and Jack. Because he couldn't understand this second job and Mrs. Tolbert hadn't said much about it, he left that part out, as he had in the news story.

He needed more information, maybe from the police or coworkers at Tropicana. He wasn't sure what the next day's story would be or if there would be a follow-up.

Once he started writing, the words came fast. He finished the story and sent it to Wiseman.

Now, he just had to contact Lt. Stevens. He hoped a phone call would do.

"Jack, you have to come into the station and get it on the record," Lt. Stevens said. "You're lucky I didn't send a squad car over to pick you up."

"I'm coming right over," Jack said.

He drove to the police station, spoke with Lt. Stevens for over an hour, and felt drained when he left.

During the 15-minute drive to his apartment, Jack felt a little more energized at the thought of coming home to Becky.

She was special. She was so optimistic about whatever she did. He admired that in her. Sure, they were having some growing pains, but didn't every relationship at one time or another? But he was sure they could work things out, if only they could get through their present difficulties. He promised to work harder to understand her and change many things in their relationship.

Jack felt eerie and empty as he reached for the front doorknob. It was similar to his feelings at the stakeout and the newspaper.

A cold rush flashed through him. Something was wrong. He turned around and stared at the driveway. Becky wasn't home. Her car should've been out front, but it wasn't. She wasn't supposed to be working tonight; she should've been here.

Rick's words suddenly came to mind: "Tell him I am sorry."

Jack opened the door and automatically looked at the kitchen table, where they usually left notes. He saw a piece of paper and recognized Becky's handwriting.

Chapter 4
Becky Leaves

Monday morning, July 7, 1980

With Jack at work, Becky could finally pack.

She had put it off as long as she could, hoping something might change—hoping Jack would back off, or at least stop looking at her the way he had lately, as if she were someone he no longer recognized. But the questions kept coming. How much cocaine was she buying? Where was the money going? Didn't she think they were starting to have a problem?

Jack believed they were crossing a line. More than that, he was scared. The police were cracking down on dealers, the newspapers were full of drug busts, and Jack worried that being anywhere near it could cost him his job—or worse. He talked about saving money, cutting back, focusing on their careers, and planning vacations instead of late nights fueled by lines of white powder. He wanted them to stop. Completely.

Becky didn't see it the same way.

She knew she was using more than Jack realized—after

work, with friends, on nights when she didn't feel like going home to another lecture. But she told herself she had it under control. She always had. What bothered her most wasn't Jack's concern; it was the way he framed it, as if he were issuing rules instead of talking to his wife. She didn't like being told what to do, especially by someone who seemed to think he knew what was best for her.

She had tried to explain herself, to tell him why she felt boxed in and why quitting now felt like surrender. But the conversations always ended the same way—Jack insisting, Becky pulling away. Staying meant lying to him. Leaving meant hurting him. Either way, something was breaking.

Then there was another issue: Jack wanted children. Not someday in the abstract, but soon. He spoke about it carefully, hopefully, as if patience alone might change her mind. Becky deflected, joked, and changed the subject. It wasn't just difficult for her—it was impossible. Quitting cocaine felt negotiable by comparison. This was something she couldn't fix, compromise on, or explain without opening a door she'd spent her whole life keeping locked.

She shook her head—as if that gesture could erase those memories—zipped the last bag, and lifted it from the bed. As she turned toward the door, her eyes drifted to the small table by the wall.

Their wedding picture sat there, angled slightly, the two of them frozen in a moment when everything still felt possible. She looked at it for a second longer than she meant to, then reached out and straightened the frame, as if that small act might set something right. It didn't. She picked up the bag and carried it to the front door, afraid to look back.

Outside, the morning was already warm and bright. The

ocean breeze drifted inland, stirring the palm fronds along the street. Becky stepped out, closed the door behind her, and turned the knob twice, just to be sure. The apartment felt different now—like a place she no longer belonged.

It was just after eleven. Traffic moved steadily along the road, the sound of it constant and indifferent. Becky paused, her heart thudding, and glanced around to see if anyone was watching. No one was. She walked toward her car—a dark green Buick Century—then stopped.

She turned back and looked at the apartment again.

For a moment, she wasn't sure whether she wanted to cry or feel relieved. She told herself this was temporary, that she needed space, that Jack needed time to stop trying to save her from herself. Still, the weight of what she was leaving pressed down on her.

"Goodbye, Jack," she said quietly, her voice unsteady. Then, almost as an afterthought, "Till we meet again."

The passing traffic swallowed the words.

Becky opened the car door, started the engine, and pulled away from the curb. She checked the rearview mirror once— just once—then forced herself to look ahead.

She had made a plan.

And she intended to follow it.

* * *

It was only a 15-minute drive to Michelle's house, where a friend who had moved from Chicago a year earlier lived. Jack didn't know her. He also didn't know many of the things Becky had been doing lately, which was good, considering what she had planned.

Becky pulled into Michelle's driveway.

"I didn't think packing a few bags would take so long," Michelle said as Becky got out of the car.

"It took longer than I thought," Becky said.

"Did you forget anything?"

"Oh, yeah…"

"We can go back and get it."

"That's not what I meant," Becky whispered.

"What do you mean?"

"Do you mind, Michelle?" Becky said, growing increasingly impatient with Michelle's questions.

"I'm sorry, Becky," said Michelle, biting her lip. She always said things at inappropriate times.

Becky knew she meant well. She took a deep breath, looked at Michelle for a moment, then said, "Can you help me bring my bags in?"

"Why, sure, kid. I was just worried you'd change your mind and stay with Jack. I know how much you've been agonizing over this."

Becky nodded. "It's been a rough morning," she said.

She had packed three suitcases and four boxes of her belongings, leaving only a few things. She wondered if she'd done that as an excuse to go back, but she wasn't sure right now.

Jack would wonder why she'd left her seashell collection. They had collected it on Sanibel Island one late summer evening, when the tide was low and the sun peeked above the shoreline. She'd also left behind other things: a four-piece glass set with a matching carafe, a Christmas gift from Jack's mother, and a picture collage of their vacations in Key West and Jamaica. Jack had made the collage for Becky last year as a birthday present.

It wasn't much, but Becky was sure Jack would care for them.

"Are you thinking about him?" Michelle asked.

"Of course I am," Becky said.

"Well, you can stay here until you decide what to do, but I've got to warn you: I'm expecting company tonight."

"Oh, Michelle," Becky said. "I didn't know. I'll watch TV."

"I know it's early, but Michael is bringing a friend over. Someone you know . . ."

Becky cut Michelle short before the friend could be named. "I don't feel like seeing anyone tonight," she said as she picked up one of the bags and walked into the house. "I'll just stay out of the way."

Michelle followed her, carrying one of Becky's cardboard boxes.

The house was large in front, stretching across the lot. It had a two-car driveway with an enclosed garage on one side. It wasn't an old house, but it was aging. Some white stucco on one side was crumbling and needed to be replaced.

Becky walked up to the small patio near the front entrance, put down her bags, and opened the heavy, solid oak door.

Michelle walked up behind her and put the box on the living room's rose-spotted sofa. "I'll give you the room on the other side of the house. The people who built the house used it as the maid's room. There's also an attached bathroom."

"I want to thank you for putting me up."

"Hey, no problem. What are friends for, if you can't use them occasionally?" Michelle said with a small laugh. "I've got to make a phone call. Why don't you put your stuff away, and when you're ready, come out, and we'll talk."

"Okay," Becky said. She picked up two suitcases and carried them to her new room.

*   *   *

Michelle went into the kitchen and dialed her boyfriend, Michael LeCare, who lived in a house on Siesta Key. He was the manager of The High Seas, an upscale seafood restaurant on the island, and Becky's boss.

Michelle and Michael were a perfectly matched couple physically. Michelle had long, thin brunette hair and a sleek body with broad, full breasts that curved upward. She usually wore baggy clothes to conceal her outstanding slim figure. Standing at 5 feet 11 in her bare feet, she was taller than most men.

At 6 feet 4, Michael was muscularly built and had sandy, sun-bleached hair. He lifted weights and knew martial arts, which he'd learned while in the U.S. Army's Special Forces in the late 1960s.

Shortly after Michelle introduced Becky to Michael, he'd hired her as assistant night manager for The High Seas. Within two months, business dramatically increased.

Becky started in the restaurant business as a table server at a posh dinner club when she moved to town six years ago after college in Illinois. She met Jack there.

She moved up quickly and became a maître d at the restaurant thanks to her excellent, natural marketing skills. Learning quickly how to be a good manager, she found she instinctively knew how to handle employees and customers. She made many friends at work, most of them people Jack didn't know.

Michael was very pleased with Becky and would tell people, only partly in jest, that she had made his restaurant a success and had made him a lot of money.

Michael answered the call on the second ring.

"Yes," he said in a deep, resonant voice.

"Michael, Becky came over 10 minutes ago. She's unpacking her bags right now. I'm going to talk with her."

"Have you told her about Robert tonight?" Michael asked.

"Not yet. I think it will be all right. She always liked Robert. Just don't expect too much from her tonight. She's been through a terrible thing today."

"I know. I've told Robert. He knows about it. You know how Robert feels about her. He's excited about seeing her again," Michael said.

"Michael. Don't let Robert push it."

"Believe me, Michelle, Robert will make her forget all about her ex-husband. I guarantee you," Michael said.

Michelle paused, then said, "Jack's not an ex yet. Just be careful. Dinner will be ready at eight sharp. I've gotta go."

* * *

Becky's new room was large, with a queen-sized waterbed in the middle and two windows facing the side and backyards. There was also a large walk-in closet by the bathroom door.

She looked around the room again and then put one of the suitcases on the bed. After opening it, she took out her overnight case and carried it into the bathroom. She wouldn't unpack everything, just what she needed for tonight.

After she brought the rest of her suitcases and boxes into her room and put them in one corner, she sat on the bed.

Well, you've done it, she thought. Jack should've been at work. He wouldn't get home for several more hours.

Becky was having second thoughts about what she had done. It was rather cruel and cold. But she was tired of explaining why she was coming home late from work after partying with friends and coworkers. She also didn't want anyone, especially Jack, to question how much cocaine she had bought and used.

She also thought back to happier times with Jack. Sometimes, he'd come home early in the afternoon as a surprise and always make up some excuse. They'd make love for an hour, he'd go back to work, she'd get dressed, do several lines of cocaine, and leave for her shift at the restaurant, which usually started around 6 p.m. That was nice, she thought, suddenly missing him.

At the thought, Becky impulsively picked up the phone by the bed and decided to call Jack to explain why she'd left when she did. She started to dial, but then realized Michelle was still on the phone. She quickly laid the receiver back down.

She had second thoughts about calling him. Maybe the note was enough. She was torn.

Becky also had an odd feeling that something had happened to Jack at work. It was a nagging worry she'd had all day. She decided to call to find out.

After waiting another two minutes, Becky picked up the phone. The line was clear. She dialed the number slowly, and with each turn, she decided whether to continue. It started to ring, and someone answered.

"City desk," answered Rick Wiseman, Jack's plain-talking editor.

"Is Jack Kendall there?" Becky said weakly, hoping Rick

wouldn't recognize her voice.

"He's out. Can I take a message?"

"N-n-no, I don't think so," Becky stammered, not knowing what to say next.

"Is this Becky?"

She paused, almost hanging up, then said in a tearful voice, her throat choking. "Yes, just tell Jack I've got to go." She moved the phone away from her mouth, whispering, "Tell him I'm sorry."

She quickly put the phone down, falling onto the bed as tears streamed down her face, her body trembling with frustration and sorrow.

A knock came on the door. It was Michelle.

"Are you all right, dear?"

"Not really," Becky sobbed as she lay on the bed with a pillow over her face.

Michelle entered the room and lay beside Becky, who had turned onto her left side. She touched Becky's shoulder gently.

'There, now,' Michelle soothed gently, her tone reassuring. 'It's good to get it all out,' which might help the audience feel a sense of relief and understanding for Becky's emotional process.

"I hated to leave him the way I did," Becky said.

"What choice did you have?"

"None. I repeatedly tried to tell Jack to stop telling me what to do and what was best for me. He wouldn't listen. I told him. I told him. I told him."

"He wasn't listening," Michelle agreed.

"He didn't want to listen because I disagreed with him. That's his problem. He's used to getting his way so often when making plans that it doesn't occur to him that other people might have other plans, other ideas," Becky said, her voice stronger now.

Michelle listened, then said, "Let's go into the living room. I'll make some coffee, and we'll talk it out." She got up off the bed.

"I'll be out in a minute, Michelle," Becky said.

"All right," Michelle said as she left the room.

Becky lifted herself out of bed, straightened her shirt, and went into the bathroom. She looked into the mirror and saw bloodshot eyes, then turned on the faucet and washed her face with clear water. After drying her face, she walked into the living room.

Michelle had two cups of coffee ready. She handed one to Becky.

"What time is it?" Becky asked.

"It's about thirty minutes after two," Michelle said.

"Something has happened to Jack today. I can feel it," Becky said.

"What do you mean?"

"It's just a feeling I get sometimes. I'm usually right," Becky said. "I suppose living with Jack for five years has given me an even closer connection to him."

"Whatever it is, he'll be all right," said Michelle, pausing. "I think leaving him will be good for Jack. From what you've told me about it, he's always gotten what he wanted. Maybe this will wake him up, and he'll learn something from this experience. Men always seem to think they can get what they want all the time, especially when it comes to women."

Becky took a sip of coffee and let out a deep breath. "He's got to learn to get along without me now. When I think about the last three months, I wonder how I stayed that long. I guess it was… the sex."

Michelle laughed. "It was good?"

"Yes, it was, but it wasn't enough to keep going. I was fooling myself into thinking I could follow his crazy plan."

"What plan was that?"

"As I told you before, Jack had this plan to go to Jamaica for a year or two and write a book. He told me about his story and the plot and described all the characters in great detail. He was excited about it. It was fascinating.

"I'd tell him to write it all down, and he'd say he would when he had the time, which he never seemed to find. One night, after we'd snorted a lot of coke with some friends and were pretty wired, Jack told me he wanted us to stop using cocaine, save money, and move to Jamaica in a year," Becky said.

"Stop using coke? You?" Michelle asked.

"Like I wanted to stop. He even wanted me to go into drug rehabilitation. Can you believe that? That was a non-starter, and I pretty much ignored what he said about it," Becky said. "I focused on talking about Jamaica. I love that country."

"I've been there with Michael," Michelle said. "It's beautiful."

"Jack knew somebody, an artist, who owned a house in the mountains above Kingston. He said we could rent a house near him and live, as he said it, as expatriates for a year or two, depending on how long it took to write his book."

"What did you say?"

"I laughed. I told him we could go immediately, even though I wanted to go to Seattle. We didn't need to wait. I had $20,000 in the bank from when my mom died. Jack has never wanted to touch that money," Becky said.

"Why?" Michelle asked.

"I don't know. Just foolish pride, I suppose. He said he wanted to save it for an emergency. Anyway, I didn't give his plan much thought after he told me about it. We were doing a lot of coke, and I thought he'd forget it the next day.

"I told him if he wanted to move to Jamaica, Seattle, Key West, or anywhere, I'd support him for as long as he wanted to write. He didn't want my money. He wanted to do it his way."

"Yeah, they usually do," Michelle commented sarcastically.

"But the next day, Jack told me he was serious about it. I couldn't believe him. We argued. I didn't want to give up coke, my lifestyle, to sacrifice like that when I had the money. I told him I was going to use my own money to buy coke whenever I wanted. We finally agreed to cut down to once a week," Becky said.

"How much were you doing?" Michelle asked.

"A lot. Some weeks, four or five days. We were spending all we had on coke, vacations, and parties. It was a lot of fun, and it wasn't hurting anyone," Becky said.

"Now I think I understand why you didn't want to introduce me to Jack," Michelle said. "You didn't want him to know you were still partying."

"That's right. I couldn't do it in front of him," Becky said. "If he knew I was spending my money on coke, he would have had a fit because it wasn't part of 'The Plan.'"

"How much money do you have left?" Michelle asked.

"I don't know, maybe $5,000," Becky said. "It's not the money. I couldn't care less about it. When I spend it all, I'll ask Michael to give me a raise or make me a partner." She laughed. "He doesn't pay me enough as it is."

"You should tell him that. He brags about you so much. Make him put his money where his mouth is," Michelle said.

"Michael knows what you're worth. I know he'd hate to lose you."

"I might. Don't tell him this, but I don't know how long I want to work there now that I've left Jack. He knows Michael and often came into the restaurant when I worked."

"Does Jack know where I live?" Michelle asked.

"No. Thank God. He'd be over here in five minutes if he knew. I'm not going to tell him either."

"Good," Michelle said. "By the way, Robert's coming over tonight. With Michael."

When she heard Robert's name, Becky's mouth dropped open. She just stared at Michelle.

"You remember Robert, don't you?" Michelle teased. "He's the Australian guy who lives in that big mansion in the mountains of Jamaica with all those servants and all that money."

Becky frowned. "I know who Robert is. I don't want to see him tonight."

"We'll just eat dinner and have a quiet evening at home," Michelle insisted.

Looking up at Michelle, Becky said sternly, "I wish you hadn't done this, Michelle. I'm a total mess today."

"I told Michael to let Robert know what happened."

"I'm not sure that will help," said Becky, taking a deep breath and looking into the coffee cup as if it held an answer. Then she took a deep breath and shook her head.

"I suppose if I am really leaving Jack, I must start my new life sometime," she said. "I hope he understands I need space tonight."

"You'll know what to do," Michelle said.

"Just don't push me into anything with Robert. He has a

crush on me."

"Crush? Is that what you call it?" Michelle exclaimed in an incredulous voice. "He's just crazy about you, and you know it!"

"Yeah, that's right. He is. I couldn't do anything about it before, even if I'd wanted to, because of Jack," Becky said, feeling a little guilty about her feelings.

Thinking back to the last time they'd met, Robert had come on to her, and she had to cool him off by telling him she didn't like foreign accents.

Despite her mixed emotions of the day, she smiled at the thought.

Becky got up, walked to the window, and looked out into the sunny yard. Her life was already changing.

Chapter 5
Jack at Home

Monday, 5:30 p.m., July 7, 1980

Jack stood by the kitchen table, staring at Becky's note without reading it, just staring at it.

He knew what it was. This letter was the terrible thing he had felt all day, starting with his dream the night before. He'd ignored his feelings, as he had many times before, to get on with the day or moment, not wanting to be negative.

His hand shook as he picked up the handwritten letter. The note began with a simple "Jack," not "Dear Jack" or "Darling Jack," just "Jack." He quickly scanned the letter. The words were blurry. Overcome with emotion, he dropped it on the table and ran into their bedroom.

Maybe she had left for just a few days to cool off, like the time before. The bed was made, as usual, but the portable beach stereo he had given her for Christmas was missing from her nightstand.

Jack ran to the closet, threw open the door, and looked

in. Her clothes were gone.

He walked back into the bedroom and sat on the bed. His heart was beating madly. He couldn't seem to catch his breath. The room was quiet, except for the traffic outside. He took a deep breath and stared at the emptiness that was once their small yet comfortable apartment.

The whole day had been a nightmare. He closed his eyes for a few seconds and relaxed his mind. Take it easy. Don't overreact. Stay calm.

He opened his eyes. Everything was the same. He shook his head, slowly stood from the bed, and walked to the bathroom. Everything of Becky's was gone.

He clenched his teeth and stared at himself in the mirror. For an instant, he saw Charlie's bloody face glaring back at him. No, not happening, he thought.

Yes, it is. She left. He walked into the kitchen and sized up the situation. This was planned. But for how long?

He thought about the past weekend. It was the one weekend Becky had off each month. Saturday evening started the same way. They went to a movie, then to dinner. They drank a lot, as usual, and did cocaine, as usual. But it wasn't fun; it was more mechanical, both trying to act as if they weren't going through problems.

Later, at home, he made the mistake of bringing up their drug use, and they argued. She went to bed without a word.

On Sunday, she hardly smiled, except when they were watching a movie with horses.

She noticed tears in Jack's eyes after a scene in which an older horse had died to save a younger horse. She saw the tears and asked if he was sad. No, he replied; he just loved horses. She smiled for a brief moment.

But he knew Becky was unhappy. He didn't know what to do. He made it clear he wanted them to stop—or at least slow down—the drinking and cocaine use. It was becoming too much for him. He told her he worried it was interfering with his job. How could he report on the dangers of drug use, the way dealers were taking over streets and hooking young kids on dope, when he was buying and using? But she didn't think it was her problem. She thought it was his problem.

He could quit using cocaine in a day and not think twice about it. She couldn't. He knew it. And, despite her denial, she knew it.

What happened to them? How did it come to this? He thought about their last five years. It seemed like he had proposed only yesterday; she had said yes, and they were married and living together.

Until now, he hadn't realized how much he had taken her for granted. For the first three years, they had been almost inseparable.

Then, she took that two-week vacation to Chicago, then started that job at the High Seas out by the bay. Things were never the same after that. She became secretive, and he was certain she had friends he didn't know about. Her cocaine habit increased month after month. He tried to reason with her about her growing dependency, telling her it was getting worse, but she wouldn't listen.

Now, at home after a terrible day at work, he realized he hadn't been prepared for Becky to leave. Despite his reporter's intuition, he thought they were moving toward a resolution, a peace, a good place.

"Becky, do you know what happened today?" He paused and answered, "No, you don't." She hadn't been interested in his work for the past year. How could he have been so wrong?

He drifted back to what Rick had told him about Becky's phone call to the newspaper that afternoon. Was she calling to say goodbye? Or had she left this note instead?

There was nothing left to do but read the letter. He slowly sat down in the wooden chair at the kitchen table.

It was handwritten and filled both sides of the paper. She was sorry. Things weren't working out, and she was unhappy. She'd probably stayed six months too long. She ended it by saying she would call when she was settled.

He shook his head in disbelief. Why didn't he come home this morning when he had that funny feeling? Why did he have to go to that police hostage stakeout? For a story?

He again saw a vision of Charlie's body slumping lifelessly in front of him. He began to understand how Charlie must have felt in those last moments: devastated by terrible pain.

It was hauntingly familiar. He remembered the thing, the old pain, that he had promised himself that he would never think about.

Johnny. A drunk driver had killed his childhood friend as he rode his bike over to Jack's 6th birthday party. They were best friends at school and lived less than a mile apart in the same neighborhood.

After that day, Jack vowed he would never cry over anyone again because of the pain he had felt. But it was not an easy promise to keep, because Johnny's ghost often returned in emotional times like this.

Johnny had been so young and was so unfairly killed. He'd had so much life in front of him. At the thought, Jack cursed and pounded his fists on the table.

Where was Becky? He knew she was in trouble. He felt it.

He had to find her.

On impulse, he decided to call his mother. Once, after a long argument, Becky had stayed the night there. Maybe she would be there again.

The phone rang five times at Laura Kendall's apartment.

"Mom, is Becky there?" Jack asked in as calm a voice as he could manage.

"No, Jack. Why?" Mrs. Kendall said.

"She's not here. I thought she might be over with you. She's gone, and she took everything with her this time."

Listening, Mrs. Kendall finally said, "She left? Oh, no, Jack. I was worried something like this might happen."

"I've got to find her," he said. "She may be in trouble."

"Why don't you come over here?" she suggested. "You can stay with me until she contacts you."

"I am not sure she will," he said.

"She will. You need to take it easy, especially now," Mrs. Kendall said. "I heard what happened on the radio. That poor man you were with today. You must still be in terrible shock from that."

"That doesn't matter now. I've got to find Becky."

"Don't do anything rash."

"I think I'll go over to Tom's house. Maybe Susan has an idea where she went. I've got to talk to her. I'll call you later. Don't worry."

"That's a good idea. Just drive carefully," Mrs. Kendall said.

Jack hung up and walked around the room. He grabbed a beer from the refrigerator and chugged it as he stared at the 32-ounce Diet Coke bottle Becky had left. She knew Jack hated Diet Coke. Did she leave it on purpose? No, she wouldn't do that.

The shock had worn off, and Jack was losing his temper. He did his best to remain calm, but it wasn't easy. He needed to do something; he couldn't just wait around for her to call. Grabbing another beer, he angrily stalked out of the house.

Chapter 6
Driving Fast

Monday, 6 p.m., July 7, 1980

Jack's gold Cutlass Supreme blazed through the city streets on his way to Tom Justice's home.

Trees, mailboxes, houses, speed limit signs, and people flashed past his bloodshot eyes. He had his window down, and the wind was gushing through the car and swirling around his head like the sound inside a conch shell.

He accelerated faster, passing slower cars, running red lights, and taking side streets to avoid traffic. Speed seemed to soothe him temporarily, helping suppress the anger, pain, and confusion roiling deep in his chest.

Racing down a straight, open street, he wished he could drive fast enough to lift off the ground and fly away.

But then he visualized Charlie's head jerking back and blood spraying across his sofa and floor. At the same time, he saw Becky sitting at the table, writing her letter, and Charlie's body slumping on the couch. He saw it all merge into a single, sizable spherical mass.

Then it hit him: he knew why Becky and Charlie were connected. Becky had left him for her freedom, and Charlie had killed himself for his. It was that simple. They wanted to be free.

He could only think of Becky and Charlie as he approached 50 mph on a street through a residential area. "You're both free," he said.

Into dusk, Jack drove like a maniac, turning corners too fast, screeching his tires, not noticing people along the streets waving at him to slow down.

Then he heard a mysterious voice in his head, sounding an alarm. Slow down!

He quickly took his foot off the accelerator. Suddenly, out from a side street, just ahead, a kid on a tiny bicycle was rolling down from a driveway.

"Oh, my God, Johnny!" Jack yelled out instinctively as he reacted immediately, swerving to the left and braking hard. As the tires screeched, the car came to a halt, and Jack's forehead violently smashed into the steering wheel.

Dazed, he sat in the driver's seat, shaking. What was he doing? Nothing made sense. He felt someone tugging at his arm and looked up sluggishly.

"Hey, are you all right?" someone said. "Are you hurt? Your head is bleeding."

His eyes out of focus, Jack shook his head.

"You could have killed that boy at the speed you were driving!"

Jack got out of the car. His legs felt weak. Blood dripped down his brow from a nasty gash on his head. He wobbled over to where the bystanders gathered around the boy who had fallen off his bike.

The boy's mother came out of the house. She ran over to her son, looking at the torn pants and bloody bruise on his leg. The boy wasn't crying, though, just in shock from seeing Jack's car come straight at him and hearing the screeching tires.

Stunned and uncomfortable, Jack mumbled in a low voice, "He just shot out of the driveway."

The mother stood up with tears in her eyes. "Maybe he did, but what right do you have to drive through this residential area at that speed with kids playing in their yards?"

Jack stared at the woman. Her barrage of words was all jumbled. All he could sense was her mouth moving. His head was throbbing. People seemed to be floating around him, angry and threatening.

"Can't you even look me in the eye? I should report you to the police. You have no right to speed around in our neighborhood!"

Jack looked around at the crowd of neighbors who had heard the commotion and come out of their houses and yards. He felt disoriented. He knew he was in the wrong.

The scene reminded him of a minor accident Becky once had. She had run into the back of an older woman's car, which was going only about five mph. There wasn't even a scratch. But the old lady got out and started yelling at her, making the bump seem like a big deal.

Becky grimaced at him and said, "Jack, do something." Jack told the woman firmly that no one was hurt and that if she wanted to discuss it further, she should follow him. He pointed to a nearby parking lot. The woman left without another word.

Now, Jack felt utterly helpless. As he looked at the child he had nearly run over, he thought of what had happened to

Johnny 25 years before.

He felt so many emotions. Johnny, the boy, Becky. He wanted them to stop. This mess started over the weekend, when he and Becky argued. It had gotten worse today, when Charlie died, and he discovered Becky had left. And now this. Jack felt embarrassed by what he'd done. He knew he was in the wrong.

Suddenly, people stopped talking, and the mother stopped yelling. It was quiet. Jack looked up and noticed everyone was staring at him. He became dizzy and sat down on the curb.

Just then, Tom Justice pulled up in his car to see a crowd around Jack and his gold Cutlass.

"Hey, Jack. Are you all right?" Tom said.

"Yeah, but my head hurts."

"Your forehead is bleeding and swollen," Tom said. "Let me get you home."

"How is it you're here?" Jack asked.

"Your mother called and told me you were coming over. I waited, but decided to drive over when you didn't arrive. I spotted the crowd on the sidewalk and saw your car," Tom said.

The neighbors, who had gathered on the sidewalk to chatter about the incident, watched Tom arrive and talk with Jack. They decided the drama was over and went back to their houses. The mother took her son inside their home.

As Jack stood up, he whispered to Tom, "I'm worried about Becky. She left the house today. Something may have happened to her."

"I heard. It's a little strange. But everything will work itself out. We'll get things sorted. Would you like to go to my place for a while?" Tom asked.

"I just want to go home. Can you ask Susan if she knows

where Becky is?"

"Sure. Are you all right? Can you drive home by yourself? If you can, I'll get Susan and meet you there. You almost made it to my house. This is my neighborhood you were speeding through, dude."

"I know. I'm sorry. I don't know what came over me," Jack said apologetically. "I'm better now. I can make it home."

"Drive slowly," Tom ordered. "See you in a few minutes."

At home, Jack went into the bedroom and lay down. He felt dazed. It was like the time after he had a concussion playing baseball in high school. He had spent the night in the intensive care ward, where he kept telling people he needed to leave because he was late for a Jeff Beck concert. Everyone had humored him.

A few minutes later, Tom arrived with Susan, who applied a large band-aid to Jack's forehead. She found a bag of frozen peas in the freezer for the small knot on his skull.

"What am I going to do now?" Jack asked Susan. "Where is she?"

"I don't know where Becky went. She didn't tell me anything," said Susan, standing over him with a worried look. "I hate to say it, but Jack, she has been very secretive the past few weeks. I thought she was acting very unusually. I was worried."

The phone rang. It was Mrs. Kendall. Tom answered.

"Oh, Tom, I'm so glad you're there. How is he?"

"Good. He had a small accident and bumped his head, but he's okay. Very tired. I hope he'll go to bed soon. Do you want to talk with him?"

Jack waved his hand, indicating he didn't want to talk with his mother.

"Jack's starting to nod off. I think he wants to go to sleep," Tom said. "We're going to leave shortly."

"Let him sleep. I'll call him in the morning," Mrs. Kendall replied.

It was 10 p.m., and Becky had not returned home or called.

Exhausted, Jack closed his eyes and fell asleep.

Chapter 7
Key West

Early Tuesday morning, July 8, 1980

He was dozing off one moment, and the next, he was with Becky.

They were together again, almost as if nothing had happened in the past 24 hours. They were in Key West, where they loved to go for long weekends, walking arm in arm through a light rainstorm on their way home from dancing at Rocky's, their favorite bar. She was wearing her light blue jumpsuit, which she had bought with Jack at the start of the summer. He'd wanted Becky to buy the green one because it made her long, thick red hair stand out. Becky had laughed and purchased both.

There was the sound of thunder and the flash of lightning in the distance, across the key and off in the Atlantic. They watched the flashes of light illuminate the southeastern horizon, turning night into day for brief moments—milliseconds that filled them with a sense of oneness.

They laughed as it started to sprinkle. She held his waist

tight. They talked about the months they had been apart and how lucky they were to be back together again. They promised they would never part again.

"Oh, Jack. All I needed was some time. I know it was tough letting me go. But it all has worked out for the best," she said. Her red hair glistened as the rain kept up its steady drizzle.

Jack nodded and kissed the side of her face.

The lightning crackled again. This time, it was much closer. The storm was starting to come ashore from the south. They didn't care.

"Are we really together, Becky?" Jack asked. "Or is this just a dream?"

Becky laughed. That throaty laugh. The laugh Jack had always found so reassuring.

"Is it a dream, Jack?" she teased. "What do you want it to be? Does it seem too good to be true? Can't you accept how things are?"

"But what if you aren't with me in the morning?" he said. "If this is a dream, I don't want to wake up. I'll stay here with you."

"We can't stay here, Jack," Becky said, laughing. "We've got to get back to the hotel. Remember, I promised you sex in the pool before we go to bed."

Becky reassured him that it was real and that he could believe and trust her. He was relieved and smiled sincerely into the blue eyes he loved so much. Everything felt so right, so true, so easy, so comfortable. They were happy, as happy as they always were in Key West. They had all the time in the world.

Suddenly, Jack saw Charlie sitting in the chair where he had killed himself, with a hole in the side of his head and dried bloodstains down his neck and chest.

Pale as a ghost, Charlie smiled. "You know, Jack, it's not so bad. I didn't even feel it."

Jack lurched forward in bed. He began to shake at the thought of Charlie's words. Then he thought of Becky. Was she here beside him?

The dim glow from the streetlight outside his window cut through the slightly open Venetian blinds, zigzagging across his head in light and dark stripes. He exhaled, feeling all the air leave his body.

Key West was only a dream.

Chapter 8
Back at Work

Tuesday, 8 a.m., July 8, 1980

When Jack walked into the newspaper office, the echoes began. Flashes of her, things she had said, and the plans they had made popped into his head as he saw people he knew, people Becky knew, and people who knew them as a couple.

It was an odd feeling, to be sure. The past 24 hours had been so stressful. He took a deep breath.

"Hey, Jack. Jack!"

Jack heard Bobbie's voice but didn't want to talk to anyone. Instead of saying something nasty, he decided to be rude in a different way by saying nothing.

But he liked Bobbie and always got along with her. He took another deep breath and stopped in the hall. He dropped his head and let Bobbie catch up.

Bobbie Jackson, the cop-beat reporter, was a little younger than Jack, in her mid-20s. With blonde hair and blue eyes, she always had a cheerful face and kind words. It was her charming smile that made her most attractive. She hardly ever had dates—her choice, as she was asked out quite frequently—because she was dedicated to and immersed in her work and the people surrounding it.

"Bobbie," Jack said in a low, monotonous voice. He glanced at her briefly and then looked away, barely making eye contact. He didn't feel like himself and didn't want her to see him that way.

Jack and Bobbie liked to have lunch together when they happened to be at the paper and weren't in the middle of a story that required them to be at their desks, waiting for a phone call, wading through government or police documents, or chasing down people on the streets.

Bobbie had a crush on Jack from the first day she met him, a year before Becky entered the picture. They liked each other and often talked at work, at office parties, while playing in the company bowling league, and at the many bars the staff frequented after work. But Jack had never asked her out. She was disappointed to hear that Jack was dating Becky.

Bobbie had met Becky several times, attended the wedding, and even liked her, though she always told Jack that Becky would have been a better choice for him. But Bobbie knew that Jack was committed to Becky and made the best of it by being his most faithful friend and best confidant.

She knew him well enough to recognize immediately when something was amiss.

"Jack, what's up? You haven't said anything about my dress. You usually notice when I've bought something new," said Bobbie, trying to start small talk. She didn't have a new dress.

Jack wasn't going to look, but it wasn't Bobbie's fault that Becky had left or that Charlie had killed himself. One little bit of conversation couldn't hurt.

"It's nice," he said, not even looking at the dress. "I'm sorry. I've got to... I..." He abruptly stopped, turned, and said, "I can't talk now. Maybe later."

Jack walked toward the stairs to avoid getting into the elevator with her. He didn't feel like talking about Becky.

But Bobbie was persistent. She followed him up the stairs and walked with him, not saying a word.

At the top of the stairs, she tugged on his arm. "Jack, I heard you had a little accident last night. What happened?"

Jack stopped, turned to Bobbie, and said, "I'm okay, but Becky's gone. I don't know where. Bobbie, I can't talk about it now. Maybe later."

Bobbie nodded. "Tom called me last night. He said you were struggling and asked if I could talk with you today. I could tell he was very worried," she said. "I assumed it had to do with the story you wrote yesterday, but it was odd that he wouldn't tell me what happened."

"Yesterday was bad all around. All I know is that she left me a note saying she had gone somewhere and would be in touch," Jack explained. "It is mind-boggling that two of the worst things I've ever experienced happened on the same day."

"Oh, I'm so sorry!"

"Thanks, Bobbie."

"Becky doesn't know what she's doing."

"She's in trouble; I can feel it," Jack said as he turned to walk down the corridor. Bobbie held his arm tightly, and they walked to the newsroom. Her eyes were a little moist.

"I know it's about the cocaine she's been using. She left because she got tired of hearing me tell her to stop," Jack said. "But I was worried about her turning into a junkie. Bobbie, you should have seen her sometimes. Line after line, vodka after vodka."

"You did the right thing to warn her. Maybe she'll think about it on her own," Bobbie said.

Jack shrugged. "I don't know."

When they reached the newsroom door, she said, "Let's talk some more when you're ready. I'll be here."

Without an expression, Jack nodded and walked toward his desk to start another day. It was a day unlike anything he had ever faced before. He had never felt as helpless as he did now.

As he sat down, he thought he should have stopped by his brother Ed's detective agency on the way to work to talk with him about looking for Becky. He also wondered why he hadn't stopped at one of the dozen liquor stores along his route to pick up a bottle of Jack Daniel's. He'd need it later.

But he hadn't done that either. He'd driven mechanically straight to the newspaper, thinking about Becky's whereabouts. He decided to call Ed later in the morning.

Everything on his desk was exactly where he had left it the night before. There was the notebook he used to record his impressions from the police stakeout, the tape recorder, and the cassette tape of Charlie's last words. He must have picked it up automatically as he left the house. Amazing.

Jack plugged in an earphone, switched on the recorder, and listened to the end of the tape. It was like a bad movie. He heard Charlie's voice shift from desperation to an eerie elation.

The single gunshot rang out, and he heard himself scream in disbelief. It was all on tape; he'd left the recorder running. He could hear his own footsteps as he walked out of the house. Voices asked him questions and expressed surprise and confusion.

"Are you all right, Jack?" the chief asked.

"What happened in there?" asked someone else.

Most voices were drowned out by the shouts of paramedics as they rushed inside to try to save Charlie. There was little hope; a point-blank shot to the head had killed him instantly. He was dead before he hit the sofa.

Jack turned down the volume on the recorder and picked up the phone to make a call.

Rick Wiseman strolled over, sat on Jack's desk, reached over to the phone, and disconnected it. "Sorry, Jack. Why don't you take the day off?"

Jack shook his head. "I want to work on a follow-up to the Tolbert suicide," he said.

"I don't think that's a good idea," Rick said. "You wrote two great stories on it yesterday. Why don't you let Bobbie do the follow-up if there is one? Cops are her beat anyway. She will make the rounds soon. I think you could use a change of assignment."

"Bobbie might find out some news. But I've got certain angles I want to follow up on, Rick," said Jack abruptly. "We've got to know more."

"All right. I still think you ought to drop it. It's too close," Rick replied, pausing, trusting Jack's instincts. "Don't press, but let me know if you come up with something."

"Sure. Thanks, Rick."

He picked up the phone again and dialed Bobbie's extension. She was still in the office, reading notes on her computer screen.

"Hi, Bobbie. I forgot that Mrs. Tolbert told me the police had searched her house. Can you find out why? And can you get an update on the Tolbert suicide investigation?"

"Sure. You think they found something?" Bobbie asked.

"I have a feeling the search has to do with something Charlie told me about something illegal he was doing to make a lot of money."

"Sounds like drugs," Bobbie suggested. "I've been seeing more cocaine busts than usual lately."

"I'm going to check with the parents of the two kids, just to see how they're doing and if they know or saw anything. Then, I want to try talking with Charlie's wife again. She's hiding something," Jack said. "Let me know what you find out."

"I'll be back sometime after lunch," Bobbie replied. "How do you feel?"

"A little better, but I am just trying to work. See you later," Jack said as he clicked off the line and dialed Betty Tolbert's number.

"Hi, Betty. This is Jack Kendall with the *Herald-Tribune*. I'm sorry to bother you again, but could I come over and talk a little more about Charlie?"

The phone line was silent.

Jack said, "I was the one who called you yesterday at the house."

"Yes, I know. I talked with you. You wrote the story this morning. It sounded more about you than Charlie," said Mrs. Tolbert in a shaky voice. "What do you want now?"

"I'd just like to sit with you and talk."

"I don't have anything more to say."

"I understand. But have the police talked with you yet?

I had to go in and give a statement, and they implied they would talk with you," Jack said.

"I'm sorry. I can't tell you anything that I told the police.

Besides, I'm busy. Goodbye."

Click. The phone went dead.

Jack slowly set the receiver down and wondered whether she had told the police anything about the money. He'd told Lt. Stevens about his suspicions. He was convinced she knew something, but he needed more details about the search at Tobert's house before he tried to talk with her again.

Jack decided to call his younger brother, Ed.

Ed Kendall had started working as an investigator in their late father's law office. After Ken Kendall died suddenly two years ago at age 61 from a heart attack, Ed started his agency, serving mostly businesses and higher-income clients.

Maybe Ed could shed some light on Becky's disappearance.

"Hey, Ed, how are you?" Jack said.

"Jack, I'm glad you called. I've been thinking about you."

"Did you hear what happened? About Becky?" Jack asked.

"Yes, Mom called me last night," Ed said. "I don't understand Becky at all. You need me to do something?"

"Yes, could you make some inquiries about her? See what you can find out without raising any suspicions. I don't want the bosses at the High Seas to know we're looking."

"Sure, Jack. I'll check the usual places—trains, planes, and automobiles," Ed said.

"Don't forget the hospitals," Jack said. "She might have overdosed."

"You think? I was going to check the hospitals first. I didn't want to worry you by saying that, but you're always a step ahead. We'll treat her as a missing person," Ed said. "I'm sure we'll hear from her soon. Don't worry."

Next, Jack called Mrs. Liz Baker, the mother of one of the two high schoolers Charlie had kidnapped, to find out how they were doing.

She picked it up on the first ring.

"Hi, Mrs. Baker. This is Jack Kendall with the *Herald-Tribune*. Just wanted to see how you and Jamie are doing?"

"It was quite a scare yesterday, but I'm fine. I wanted Jamie to stay home, but he wanted to go out with his friends. It's summer vacation, and he doesn't like missing anything. They all went to the mall," Mrs. Baker said. "How are you? You saw the whole thing."

"I understand him. Jamie wants to get back to normal as soon as he can. I'm working. Keeps my mind busy," Jack said. "Do you know how Leslie is doing? I don't have Mrs. Pulaski's phone number."

"She's with Jamie. They learned a hard lesson. Maybe they will listen to us about how dangerous hitchhiking is. There are people out there with many troubles," Mrs. Baker said.

"Glad to hear it. One more thing. Could you tell me if Jamie talked with the police about what happened?" Jack asked.

"They asked him many questions about what the man talked about when he picked them up. They wanted to know if the man said anything about selling or having cocaine," Mrs. Baker said. "It was an odd set of questions."

"Do you think the police were looking for cocaine?" Jack asked.

"I don't know, but Jamie said when they got back to the house, the man, Mr. Tolbert, took out a big plastic bag of white powder and was sniffing it and drinking shots of whiskey."

"Thanks, Mrs. Baker. Hope you and the kids have a good summer."

Jack put the phone down. He was sure now that the money Tolbert was making came from selling cocaine.

Chapter 9
Hot Tip

Tuesday, 4 p.m., July 8, 1980

The telephone rang when Jack was sitting at his desk, pondering what to do next.

"*Herald-Tribune*. Jack Kendall."

"Bagley here."

Jack paused, somewhat surprised by the unexpected call. "Chief?"

"I just wanted to let you know that we found a pretty good cache of drugs in Charlie Tolbert's house. Thought you could use the tip if you're interested," said the chief in a muffled whisper. "Call Lt. Stevens for quotes. He's handling it."

Jack pounded his desk and exclaimed excitedly, "I knew it! Son of a bitch. He was dealing. What?"

"Cocaine," Chief Bagley said.

"Just as I thought," said Jack, his mind racing. "He said he needed money. But he was too disorganized, too messed up to deal coke."

"You were there."

"He was whacked out. Emotionally disturbed and strung out. How much did you find in the house?"

"About two pounds. Street value is a little more than $300,000."

Even though Jack wasn't surprised by the cocaine, he was stunned at the size of the stash. Everything made sense now. Charlie wanted to make Betty happy and keep her from leaving. He thought selling coke could give him the money to buy the things he thought she wanted.

"Did you talk with his wife?" Jack asked.

"Not yet, but we will," the chief said.

"This is my speculation based on my interviews with her. She knows something about the cocaine and that he was going to get a lot of money dealing it."

"Possible. We're looking into that."

"Did you do an autopsy on Tolbert?"

"Of course."

"What did you find?"

"Preliminary results show heavy cocaine and alcohol use," the chief explained. "The cocaine put him in bad shape. He was healthy otherwise."

"Just what I thought," said Jack. "You know Tolbert couldn't afford to buy two pounds of cocaine. Somebody fronted him."

"We also are looking into that," the chief confirmed.

"Any other clues?"

"Nothing we can say right now," said the chief, pausing for a second. "There's one more thing, Jack. It's the main reason I called."

"What's that?"

"This is off the record. Totally."

"Chief, what if I attribute it to a background source?"

"No, totally off the record," Bagley insisted. "You'll understand once I tell you."

"Okay. Agreed. What is it?"

"We found a phone number in his wallet. We called the number."

"Yes."

"It was the High Seas restaurant."

"The High Seas?" said Jack, perplexed. "Why would he have that?"

"You tell me," Bagley said.

"Well, Becky works at the High Seas," said Jack, growing nervous as he slowly pieced together what Bagley was telling him.

"Yes, I know that. That's also where Tolbert's wife works."

Jack nearly dropped the phone. "Betty, Charlie Tolbert's wife, works at the High Seas with Becky?" he asked, hardly believing it.

"Yes," the chief said.

Jack took a deep breath and exhaled. "What does that mean?"

The chief didn't reply.

"Wait a minute. Are you telling me you believe the cocaine you found at Tolbert's house came from the High Seas and that Becky and Betty are involved?" Jack asked.

Bagley paused and said, "Jack, I wish I could tell you more. We're investigating."

"Are you investigating Michael LeCare? He's Becky's boss and the owner of the High Seas. Is he trafficking cocaine?" asked Jack.

The chief said nothing.

Now, Jack was worried. That Bagley wasn't saying anything more likely meant the cocaine came from the High Seas. And if Becky worked at the High Seas and bought cocaine there, did Bagley know that?

"Do you think Becky's involved?" Jack asked.

"Just be careful," the chief said.

"What about Betty Tolbert? Did she get Charlie involved in this?"

"I can't say."

"You have other leads, don't you? About where the cocaine came from and who is involved?" Jack asked, in a state of disbelief at how the conversation had turned.

"I've told you enough," Bagley said. "This is an ongoing investigation. I'm trusting you on this, Jack."

"Have you thought about the possibility that Tolbert had the High Seas' phone number in his wallet because his wife works there?" said Jack, trying to be as logical and calm as possible.

"Jack, we have other indications about the High Seas besides the phone number and the cocaine at Tolbert's house. But I can't tell you any more. Again, this is way off the record," Bagley said.

"I understand. I won't print anything about the High Seas," said Jack.

"Now, Jack, I've got to ask you an important question. I heard you two might have split up. Have you spoken with Becky today?"

Jack was surprised that Bagley knew. He didn't say anything for a moment. He wondered what Bagley would say if he found out that Becky had left him.

"Chief, you have good sources. No, I haven't seen her since

Monday morning, before Tolbert's suicide," Jack said. "This is why I'm worried, not that she is involved with cocaine. For personal reasons."

"I see. Now I've got to warn you not to get involved in this investigation," Bagley said. "I know how you are once you start snooping around. We can't have you tip her off on what we are doing. I don't want you to get into any trouble."

"What do you mean by trouble? Is Becky in trouble?" Jack asked.

Bagley ignored the question. "Listen to me. If you talk with Becky, tell her to call us or come to the station. Tell her to ask for Lt. Stevens."

Jack suddenly felt cold. He knew what Bagley was saying about Becky. She could be involved in cocaine trafficking, or she could be in danger.

"What do you want me to do?" Jack asked.

"Just have her call us. Nothing more," Bagley said.

"I'm sure she will cooperate. I don't see how she could be involved with cocaine trafficking without me knowing, and I swear I don't know anything."

"I believe you, Jack."

"I expect to hear from her soon. She said she'd contact me once she got settled. I will make sure she calls you."

"I'm sorry to hear all this, Jack. I've really got to go. You should talk with Lt. Stevens," Bagley said.

"Wait, what are the chances she's involved? 50-50? Less?" said Jack, pushing Bagley.

"Jack, you know better than to ask me such a question," the chief replied. "I suppose I could tell you this. We think she could be a material witness to what she saw. That's why we want to talk with her. But the longer it takes us to find her, the more it looks like something else."

Jack had been trying to remain calm throughout his conversation with Bagley, but it was turning into a nightmare. He couldn't tell Bagley that he was most concerned about Becky's cocaine use or that she might be part of a drug-trafficking ring without implicating himself.

For months, Jack had worried about Becky. Her cocaine habit was worsening, and it sometimes made her act differently. He had nearly quit, using with her only once a week.

"I know it might look bad, but I want you to know that she may appear to be hiding because she wants space. She knows I would look for her. We have been dealing with some problems at home," Jack said. "I want to give her time to contact me before I start looking for her."

"It may be we can't find her because it's about you two. But listen, Jack, your wife works at the High Seas. If the restaurant is where the cocaine is coming from, she could be involved, even if she knows about it and says nothing. You understand?" the chief asked.

"Yes, I know," said Jack in a soft, sad voice.

"You're a good reporter, and I like you. I feel bad for you having to go through this. I don't want you getting involved in this investigation over a woman, even if it is your wife. It's dangerous," Bagley said.

"Chief, I appreciate you telling me all this. It helps," Jack said. "Do you have a few more minutes? Just so I fully comprehend."

"Just a few."

"You said you have some suspicions about the High Seas. I think you said 'indications,'" Jack said. "Have you any evidence, even before this, that the High Seas is trafficking dope?"

"Again, off the record. We've heard some things about that place for a while. Just rumors from informants and users we have in jail who are talking," Bagley explained. "I can't get into specifics."

"I told Lt. Stevens last night in my statement that Tolbert probably had some drug connection at Tropicana, where he worked. He told me he got involved with someone there who might have involved him in some crimes. I thought it might be cocaine."

"We are looking into Tolbert's employee friends at Tropicana, but of course, that is off the record, just like everything else we're talking about. You can ask Lt. Stevens for any on-the-record comments," Bagley said.

The chief continued. "By the way, Bobbie is working on a story about crack cocaine and the extra resources we're putting into drug investigations. We think people working at Tropicana and the High Seas could be involved, along with several other places."

"I've noticed there's been more drug arrests," Jack said.

"Bobbie talked with one of our detectives about the crack problem. It's getting worse and seems to be driving car thefts and burglaries, but also drug overdoses and deaths."

"Does Bobbie know anything about what you are telling me?" Jack asked.

"No, nothing about Tolbert, the High Seas, and Tropicana. Jack, I can't give you definitive answers. This is an ongoing investigation," Bagley said. "I'm taking a big risk in telling you all this."

"I know. What's the next step?" Jack asked.

"Now that we have this possible connection between the High Seas, Tolbert's suicide, workers at Tropicana, and the cocaine stash, we're hoping that it will be enough probable cause for a judge to issue a search warrant on the High Seas," said the chief. "We have a couple of suspects at Tropicana, but not the company itself."

"Will you let me know if you get a search warrant?" Jack asked.

"I can't tell you about that beforehand. Bobbie will be told once it is completed," Bagley said. "It's too sensitive to ask Bobbie along this time."

"Chief, I'm sorry, but I have to know more about Becky. It sounds like you think she could be involved," Jack asked as calmly as he could.

"I can't say yes or no. I do know she didn't go to work on Monday night. They said she was off," said Bagley. "Michael LeCare also is not around. We want to talk with both of them right now."

"I don't like LeCare. Never did. I hope you arrest him," Jack said.

"We know he bought the restaurant with cash a few years ago," Bagley replied. "He had no restaurant experience. He had been in Vietnam and the Army before that. He hired several award-winning restaurant professionals at top dollar."

"Like Becky, I know. She loved working there," Jack said in a defeated voice. All this new information had worn him out.

"Listen, you've got a good story about the cocaine stash at the house. I've authorized Lt. Stevens to tell you and Bobbie that we've investigated Tolbert and his possible connections to the drug trade. That's about all we can say for now. We've got other things we need to keep under wraps."

"Yes, I know. Thanks for calling, chief," Jack said.

"Don't mention it. Seriously. Call Stevens," said Bagley,

hanging up.

Jack slowly put down the receiver and tried to absorb the news he had just heard.

As a journalist, Jack knew he needed to write a news story on this latest development immediately. He'd never expected his follow-up story about the suicide to focus on a cocaine stash.

But all he wanted to think about was Becky. Where was she?

Chapter 10
Jack's Scoop

Tuesday, 4:30 p.m., July 8, 1980

Jack sat at his desk, stunned by the news Chief Bagley had shared. But turning off his thoughts of Becky, where she was, and what she was doing was hard. While it had been only two days since she had left, it felt like many more.

But Jack was a reporter. And he had a scoop. And he had to put aside personal thoughts.

He usually relished scoops, especially those that came out of the blue—whether a phone call, a confidential meeting, or just hard work pouring through documents. It was these moments that Jack, as a journalist, lived for. They were magical.

But this scoop was different. He was numb to what the chief had told him about the High Seas, the pending search warrant, Becky's possible involvement, and the police wanting to talk with her. He also realized what Bagley's information about Tolbert's cocaine, the High Seas, and Becky meant: he would have to turn the story over to Bobbie once he finished writing the article about the cocaine found at Tolbert's house.

Jack hated to give up the story. It had kept him going as he dealt with the implications of Becky's abrupt departure.

However, the investigation involving Becky created a severe conflict of interest, which meant he could not continue covering the story. He knew that if he didn't remove himself, Wiseman would surely pull it from him.

He looked at the clock. He had several things to do before he began writing.

But before he could start, he thought about the one thing he feared most: had Becky heard about Charlie Tolbert's suicide, and had she gone missing to evade the law?

Even if she was innocent, her disappearance looked terrible. Whatever the reason she couldn't be found, Jack knew it spelled trouble for Becky, especially given her cocaine addiction.

She was hooked, and without him telling her to slow down, she was free to do as much as she wanted.

Although he was mad that she hadn't listened to him, he didn't blame her. He was sure it was the cocaine that had twisted her thoughts and driven them apart.

The other thing was this: even if she was on a cocaine binge and wasn't involved in the High Seas drug ring, it was only a matter of time before the police closed the restaurant, started arresting people, and began seizing assets.

Becky would be out of a job, stuck with her addiction, and have no money to pay for it. But at least he'd have her back. Then he could convince her to go into drug rehab—something she'd always laughed at whenever he brought it up.

Enough thinking about all that, he said to himself. He had to get back to his reporting on the cocaine found in Tolbert's house. He needed to tell Wiseman about the scoop, make a few calls to confirm the facts with Lt. Stevens and other sources, talk with Bobbie, and write the story.

Jack took a moment to think about how to structure the article. He sat back in his chair, closed his eyes, and visualized the piece. Like magic, as always, he knew exactly how to write it.

He turned his head around to see if he could spot his editor. Wiseman was talking with Bobbie, who must have arrived when he was on the phone with Ed. He wanted to speak with them, but decided to be polite and wait until they were finished.

Jack looked around the newsroom. It was late afternoon. There was a buzz of reporters writing stories and checking their facts with last-minute phone calls. Meanwhile, editors yelled questions to reporters as they reviewed stories.

Most of the time, he loved this part of the day, especially when he'd been a beat reporter. As a young reporter, it took him a little while to block out the noise. Even though Becky was missing, he still loved it—maybe like a baker loved the smell of freshly baked bread or just-made doughnuts. It felt normal.

His fellow reporters had already done the hard part of their jobs: gathering the information. Now came the fun part: the organizing and writing.

Jack remembered the fun part. He didn't feel that today.

While waiting for Bobbie, he created a new story file on his computer: "Cocaine Found at Hostage-Taker's Home." He was sure the copy desk would tweak that headline, but he was in a hurry.

He began furiously typing the article about the cocaine discovered at Tolbert's house.

Bobbie came over from behind him and looked over his

shoulder at the lead paragraph on the screen.

"What do you have there? Police find a cocaine stash at Charlie Tolbert's house? It sounds like you have a good story—and on my beat again," said Bobbie, teasing Jack about his ability to find a crime angle in any story.

"Hey, Bobbie. Cops still know who to give the good scoops to," Jack teased back as he continued to type.

"How are you doing? You sound better than this morning," Bobbie said.

Jack stopped typing. "I'm feeling better. I'm working. I've got a good story to write. I'm still worried like crazy, and I haven't been sleeping well."

Bobbie looked at him reassuringly.

"I can't get my mind off what's happening with Becky," he sighed.

Bobbie nodded. "I completely understand. I'll do what I can to help."

"Thanks. Did you ask Lt. Stevens why the police were at Tolbert's house today? Chief Bagley called a little while ago and told me about the coke."

"Stevens didn't tell me anything about that. How much cocaine did they find?" Bobbie asked.

"Two pounds, probably a kilo. I think he was using more than he was selling," Jack theorized. "He was a very troubled drug dealer."

"So, is the investigation over?" Bobbie asked. "Is that why Bagley called you?"

"I can't tell you everything he said, only that I'd like you to call Lt. Stevens back and see if there's a report. Bagley gave us the green light. Get some quotes and anything else he can give you."

"I'd like to, Jack. It sounds like a great story. But I'm working on a piece about the growing number of crack cocaine overdoses police and hospitals are seeing. I've got an interview with an ER doctor at Nokomis Hospital tomorrow. Rick wants me to write it for Sunday. I'm not sure I can finish it by then."

"Oh, yeah, Bagley mentioned something about that. Let's talk about the crack story later, maybe at dinner? I could help," Jack said. "There could be a tie-in to my story."

"Sure, Jack. After work, if you feel like talking. I've got a few police briefs to write."

"I'd like to do that. Right now, we both have some writing to do. I'd better call Stevens and confirm everything."

"Okay, Jack. I'll talk to you later," she said softly with a gentle smile.

After talking with Bobbie, Jack felt better. He was working on a scoop, and his friends supported him.

Jack spent another five minutes writing several more paragraphs about the cocaine stash found at Tolbert's house. He just wanted to get it done, then think about what to do about Becky.

He typed as much as he could based on what Bagley told him on the record. Then he looked over to see if Wiseman was free to be briefed on the cocaine stash. His editor was talking with another reporter.

He still needed to call Lt. Stevens to confirm everything and get quotes for the story.

As he dialed the lieutenant, he thought of his beloved Becky, the High Seas, and then of cocaine. His trauma from witnessing Charlie's suicide seemed far away from where he was now.

Everything seemed to have fallen into place, except for

why Becky had vanished. But they were all connected to the High Seas in some way.

Chapter 11
High Seas

Tuesday, 7 p.m., July 8, 1980

Now that the story was written, Jack wanted to do more to find Becky. He couldn't wait any longer for her to contact him.

Sometimes, he hated having to follow the rules of journalism. His hands were tied in his reporting because he'd agreed to keep quiet about Bagley's off-the-record information linking Tolbert's cocaine to the High Seas.

He couldn't tell Bobbie that—at least not yet—so she could pursue the story about the High Seas drug connection.

But he could call his brother. He picked up the phone and dialed the number.

"Ed Kendall Detective Agency, may I help you?" Ed answered.

"I thought you would be working late. How is the search for Becky going?" Jack said.

"I'm doing everything I can to find her. She just vanished."

"The police can't find her either," Jack said. "Keep on it. Ed, I need some more help. I talked with Chief Bagley just now, off the record. He gave me disturbing information about Becky and the High Seas."

"Becky and the High Seas?" Ed asked

"Just between you and me, Bagley said the High Seas is a front for a cocaine trafficking network."

"Uh-oh. Is Becky involved with that?"

"I don't think so. The chief doesn't know either. But I'd like you to find out, very quietly, about the High Seas," Jack said. "Look into what they are about."

"Sure," said Ed.

"You will also need to look into Michael LeCare. He's Becky's boss and the owner or manager of the High Seas. I'm sure he's the one the police are focusing on. He has a house on Siesta Key near the High Seas. Bagley said he's a suspect."

"Do you think he is the one who involved Becky?"

"If she is involved, yes. I'm unsure, but we need to find out who he is and if the High Seas is dirty," Jack said. "It sure sounds like the cops think so."

"So, you want us to run quiet background checks on the High Seas and this LeCare?" Ed asked.

"And LeCare's house. Track the funding for the restaurant," Jack instructed. "Be careful, because Bagley gave me this tip off the record, and I don't want it getting back to him."

"All right. And what if we find other people connected with the ownership?" Ed asked.

"Check on everybody you find above LeCare's level," Jack said. "Impress upon your people that we can't let the police know we're running a parallel investigation."

"I know how to handle this. Anything else?"

"Have a man check on Charlie Tobert. He's the dead guy I wrote about. His wife, Betty, worked at the High Seas. Go from the assumption that Charlie was working for LeCare as well."

"Will do. I'll need to assign several men for these jobs. It's going to get expensive."

"Send me a bill," Jack replied in a half-joking tone.

"I hate to say it, but it sure looks like Becky must know something about the drug trafficking ring," Ed said somberly. "She's a manager there and is supposed to know what's going on."

"You may be right. I hope she isn't involved, but maybe," Jack said. "She always knew where to get good coke. She never wanted to explain where she got it. I never pushed her."

Jack listened to his own voice and heard the strain in it. He knew it was there, even if he didn't say anything about it. Part of him wondered why he wasn't doing more himself to find Becky—why he was handing off work he would usually chase down without hesitation. That wasn't like him, and he knew it.

"Becky is a missing VIP, Jack, and we are going to find her. Don't worry," Ed said.

"Just make sure your men know this is a confidential investigation. Don't go near the High Seas or talk with anybody there yet. We don't want to interfere with what the police are doing," Jack replied.

"Right," said Ed. "I have a good police source, an old friend from high school. He will give me the skinny and won't say a thing."

"Just tell him to be careful," Jack warned.

"We got this," Ed insisted.

"Call me as soon as you have something," Jack said as he placed the receiver down.

He looked over to see how Bobbie was doing with her

story. She was typing. He picked up the phone and dialed her extension.

"Hey, Bobbie. How are you coming along?" he asked.

"It might be another hour," she said.

"Still want to go out later?"

"Sure."

"I'm waiting for Rick to edit my story and Ed to call me back about Becky. I'll be here for a while. Will check with you later," he said.

"Okay, bye for now," she said.

It was now past 7:30 p.m. He decided to walk to the break room for a cup of coffee. He had a flask of Jack Daniel's in his desk drawer and wanted to make a quick Irish coffee.

Jack wondered how he could have been fooled into thinking the High Seas was legitimate. He sometimes went to the restaurant with friends while Becky was working. He knew a few people there. It was a fun, upbeat place.

While he didn't particularly like LeCare and sensed something was wrong with him, he'd wanted to believe Becky was safe at work.

Now, he wondered whether there was another reason she had been hired as night manager. Maybe LeCare was using her. There was no doubt that Becky was a talented, charismatic, and beautiful professional, all of which were apparent reasons for LeCare to hire her and put her out front in a position of responsibility.

Jack walked into the deserted break room. Then it came to him. What if LeCare also hired her as the night manager, serving as the restaurant's honest public face? She would be the perfect person to provide cover for LeCare's illegal drug trafficking operation.

As the night manager, Becky could have been fooled about what was happening at the restaurant during the day.

Now, as he walked back to his desk, Jack felt relieved that at least some of the pieces that had baffled him about Charlie's suicide and Becky's departure were falling into place.

Poor Charlie. He'd just needed a little more faith that things would improve. Maybe Jack needed a little more faith in Becky.

He wanted to give her time to contact him, as she'd requested in her letter. But after Bagley told him that the High Seas was likely the hub of a significant cocaine network and considering what he knew about Becky's cocaine addiction, Jack knew he must increase his efforts to find her to protect her.

Jack returned to his desk, reached into his bottom drawer, pulled out his flask, and poured two ounces of Old No. 7 into his coffee.

Just then, the phone rang. Jack picked up the receiver. It was Ed.

"Jack, I made a few calls," Ed said. "She isn't in the hospital. I'm still checking on her car. We don't have any leads."

"Damn it, where the hell is she? I know something is wrong," Jack growled, trying to keep his voice down. "Did you find anything about the High Seas?"

"Yes. My police friend confirmed that the investigation into Tolbert's suicide led directly to the High Seas. They found the phone number you know about. They also have other information on the connection he couldn't tell me about," Ed said.

"Do you know what he meant?" Jack asked.

"Not exactly. I confirmed the police are conducting background checks on all employees, including Becky," Ed replied. "I also thought the High Seas could be connected to a larger investigation."

"What do you mean?"

"My source said they are looking into ownership of the High Seas because of possible money laundering," Ed said. "Sounds federal."

"I hope they find something on LeCare and nail him first. I knew Bagley would investigate Becky," Jack said softly.

"She's not a suspect yet. But the police seem to know quite a bit already. For some reason, they have hesitated in making arrests," Ed said.

"Why would they hesitate?"

"A couple of reasons. The police may have an inside source at the High Seas or somewhere in LeCare's distribution network," Ed explained. "I got that impression from talking with my friend."

"I thought the same. Bagley seemed to know a lot. For example, how did he know Becky wasn't at work Monday night? He also knew Becky and I were having trouble. How did he know that? Were the police watching the High Seas, or did they have an inside informant feeding them information?" Jack said.

"My source implied the High Seas is where Tolbert got the coke," Ed said.

"Bagley said the same thing."

"If that is true, the narcotics unit would have made some effort to develop inside contacts."

"Is that why the police haven't yet asked for the search warrant? They want to use the inside source, maybe with a wire, to get more hard information?"

"Maybe. The cops also check employee criminal records,

FBI records, immigration records—even traffic infractions, domestic abuse problems, everything," Ed said.

"The investigation sounds much more advanced than what Bagley told me," Jack said. "Why do you think they have an informant?"

"My source implied that they are developing information on the High Seas by alternative means," Ed replied. "That is code for someone inside feeding them information."

"Hmm, that's great intel, Ed," Jack said as he sipped his Irish coffee.

"You mentioned a search warrant. The cops also need more information to present to a judge for probable cause to get the search warrant," Ed said.

After a moment, he continued. "There is another possibility for why everything is going slowly. This is just a guess. As I said before, the feds may be involved as well."

"Feds? That means what?" Jack asked.

"Only a guess, but the feds, either the FBI or the DEA, means that the High Seas cocaine network could be a multi-state conspiracy," Ed said.

Jack nearly fell off his chair. The news was getting worse.

"Ed, if the feds are involved, we must be even more careful. Just find out about LeCare, who he is, where he is, if he owns the High Seas, or if it's somebody else, like you said," Jack said.

"My police friend was as worried as I've ever seen him when I asked about this," Ed said.

"I'm worried about Becky. She should have contacted me by now."

"I'll keep looking. But I have a feeling she's left town."

"I hope so, but keep looking," Jack said. "Thanks."

Ed's report was what Jack had expected. The High Seas

was a target of a major drug investigation, and someone was feeding information about it to the police. Becky had vanished and covered her tracks.

Jack was surprised at how fast Ed had learned about the High Seas investigation from his source inside the police department. Bagley would be ticked off if he knew one of his officers was leaking information to a private detective, especially Jack's brother.

Chapter 12
Damage Control

Monday, 5 p.m., July 7, 1980

Michael LeCare listened on the phone, growing angrier.

It was only two hours after Charlie Tolbert kidnapped two teenagers for no apparent reason and killed himself in front of a *Herald-Tribune* reporter with a kilo of cocaine inside his house and half the Sarasota police force surrounding his home.

LeCare had known screwups before, but this one, he thought, was inexcusable. Worse, he didn't know who to blame.

He had decided to expand his operation into the north side of Sarasota and Bradenton. He had handpicked Charlie Tolbert to distribute the merchandise based on a recommendation from one of his best bagmen in Bradenton. Tolbert worked at Tropicana, the biggest factory and employer in Bradenton. He was gregarious, street-smart, and well-connected.

But Michael had no idea Tolbert had deep psychological problems and that his marriage was breaking up. Who could have predicted he would do something as stupid as suicide,

115

especially with a fresh cocaine stash worth $300,000 in his house? Michael had been completely fooled, and that irritated him more than anything.

"You saw all this?" asked Michael. "There were lots of other people outside of Tolbert's house? Jesus. Nobody noticed you?"

"I waited until it was all over. He's dead," said Gordo, LeCare's right-hand man, a blond, native Floridian with a penchant for white suits and violence.

"All right, Gordo. Get back to the restaurant and stay on top of things. We may have to go into damage control. You know what that means." Michael hung up the phone.

"God damn it," Michael said with a scowl as he turned to face a puzzled Robert Mackey.

A smooth-talking Australian with light, prematurely graying hair, Mackey headed up the drug-smuggling operation that stretched from South America to Jamaica to Florida and several of the South's biggest cities, including Atlanta, New Orleans, and Nashville. The dope mainly was cocaine and marijuana, the latter known in Jamaica as "ganja."

While Mackey spent most of his time at his mountain retreat in Jamaica, he supplied dope to many regional dealers who were part of his international network.

But he often visited Michael LeCare, a Vietnam vet he had met in Jamaica in the late 1960s. By 1980, they had built the operation into a $100 million-a-year drug ring.

By fate, coincidence, or bad luck, Robert was in town that summer to discuss complicated political problems brewing in Jamaica.

"What's the matter, mate?" Robert asked, his drawl edged with curiosity.

Michael turned and said slowly, sincerely, "Bad news.

One of my new bagmen killed his stupid, fucked-up self this afternoon. The police found the dope in the house. We don't know much more than that. Gordo will talk with everyone in our network and is taking care of security at the restaurant, just in case we have to shut down fast."

"The cops aren't on to us, are they?" Robert asked patiently.

"I hope to fuck not! But how in the hell am I supposed to know? Tolbert fucked up. I don't know what the pigs know," said Michael.

"Now, take it easy, Mike. No one's pointing the finger at you," Robert said evenly. "Maybe we moved a bit too quickly with the supply—spread it out too wide to the bagmen and runners. Just been too much bloody demand."

Michael nodded. "I can only keep so much stash at the restaurant."

"I don't want no more bloody surprises," Robert said. "From here on out, this shop's shut. Tell Gordo to spread the word—everyone goes underground. No sales, no movement, nothing."

Michael nodded.

"Do we have any other problems?" Robert asked.

"A little one. We have a goddamn shipment that is supposed to go out tonight to Atlanta," Michael replied.

"How much?"

"Twenty-five pounds," said Michael. "This is terrible timing."

Robert shook his head in disbelief. "Has it been cut?"

"No, thank God. Gordo knows what to do," Michael said. "He will pack it up this afternoon and drive it to a rendezvous with our Atlanta dealer."

"Gordo's a solid bloke. I've got full confidence in him," Robert said, pausing. "But I didn't come all the way to Florida to get nicked by the locals. We've gotta tread carefully. I'll need you to come with me to Jamaica—sort out a few headaches with the pollies and cops we thought were playing on our team."

From Robert's serious tone, Michael knew he shouldn't argue or complain. The operation had been run without a hitch for nearly five years since they opened the High Seas. The network was tight—or it had been until now—and the cover was secure—until possibly now.

But he knew that with the risks of expansion, there would come a time like this when they would have to close it down, just like they had in Miami and Tampa when things got too hot. Maybe this was the time.

He had millions of dollars in his bank account in Bogotá. Maybe he should cash out and retire. He knew it wouldn't be easy because Robert had deals worldwide and needed the cash cow that was the American market.

"You and I are supposed to go to Michelle's house for dinner tonight," Michael said. "Should I cancel so we can straighten out this mess?"

"No way, I'm not keen on that. Didn't you say Becky's gonna be there?" Robert asked.

"Yes, but I ought to get down to the restaurant just to make sure Gordo has help if he needs it."

"Gordo'll handle it fine," Robert said evenly. "I don't want you near the restaurant. We'll wait till he clears the gear before we do a thing. No drama so long as Tolbert wasn't one of your lot—the cops can't trace what they can't link. I need you to take me to see Becky. I've been looking forward to that."

"That's right. There was a little something between you two last time you were in town," Michael recalled.

"I've got a thing for redheads—and she's the best I've ever

laid eyes on," Robert said with a grin. "When do we head off?"

"We have to wait until Michelle calls," Michael said. "Have a seat. I'll dig out some of the local stuff."

"Alright," Robert agreed coolly. "Before we go, send someone 'round to check on Gordo at the restaurant. I want to make sure it's all under control."

Chapter 13
Jack and Bobbie Talk

Tuesday evening, July 8, 1980

It was 9 p.m. by the time Jack finished his news story about the cocaine that was found at Tolbert's house. Wiseman put it on the front page, along with Bobbie's story about the troubling increase in crack cocaine deaths and robberies.

According to the off-the-record agreement with Bagley, there was no mention of the incriminating phone number or its possible connection to the High Seas. That would be a future story. Police said they were still investigating the drug cache and Tolbert's suicide.

The news story about a man high on cocaine, desperate after losing his wife and committing suicide after she refused to reconcile, would indeed cause a stir even without the High Seas connection.

Jack grimaced at the possibilities suggested by the headline: "Man dies after realizing money can't buy love."

Before he left the office, Jack stopped by Bobbie's desk to find out when she'd be done. She said she'd leave in a few minutes and meet him for a late drink and dinner at Trader Tom's.

He arrived first and ordered two drinks, appetizers, and small salads. Twenty minutes later, Bobbie arrived.

"Jack, you've been through a lot. I'm glad you wanted to go out," said Bobbie with a smile.

"I promised to talk, and we both have to eat something besides vending machine junk," Jack said. "You still like cranberry breezes?"

"Yes, thanks. And these mini crab cakes look delicious," Bobbie replied. "I'm famished."

"You can order dinner if you want," Jack said. "I already ate one of the crab cakes and had a salad. These are yours. I can't stay long."

"Maybe just what you ordered, then," Bobbie said. "You know I don't eat a lot."

"Bobbie, I've got something to discuss with you."

"About Becky?"

"That too. First, about Chief Bagley. He told me some things off the record that mean I have to pass this story to you about Tolbert and the cocaine," Jack said.

"I thought the chief told you more today," Bobbie guessed. "I don't understand. Clearly, there's more to the investigation into Charlie's suicide and the cocaine than you've told me."

"Yes. Just keep asking Lt. Stevens about the Tolbert investigation. He will eventually tell you the whole story, and then I will feed you information that I learn," Jack said. "I have a conflict of interest at this point, beyond just being a witness to Charlie's death."

"Sure, I understand. I can handle it however you want," Bobbie said. "Can you give me a hint of what's happening?"

"The story you did tonight about the crack cocaine explosion is probably related to the Tolbert story," Jack said.

"Cocaine and suicide? You can't tell me more?" asked Bobbie with a wink.

"No, sorry," Jack replied.

"Okay, let's talk about something other than work stuff," she said.

"You mean Becky?" Jack asked.

"If you want. I don't want to intrude."

"What is bothering me right now is something specific Bagley gave me off the record. I can't tell you about that because I don't want to get you started on a backstory investigation," Jack said, not wanting to tell her the whole truth.

"Jack, I'm a reporter, remember? You're saying Becky is somehow involved in Charlie's death?" Bobbie asked, sensing he was holding back.

"No. I guess it sounds that way because of how I said it," Jack replied. "They're related, but not that way. I shouldn't have said anything. I wish I could talk with you more about this cocaine stash. I can't right now."

"You mean where Tolbert got the cocaine?" Bobbie said. "It was unsaid in the story, but a guy who works at Tropicana whose wife is leaving him—partly because of money issues— wouldn't be able to buy that amount of coke on his own."

"My exact thought," Jack said.

"I am going to guess that Becky bought the coke from Tolbert because his wife, Betty, worked at the High Seas,"

Bobbie said. "Is that what Bagley told you? Maybe she didn't know it came from the High Seas?"

"No, I don't think that's it, but it's probably close," Jack said. "How did you know Betty worked at the High Seas? You are a good reporter. Say, I am not a source. Let's leave this alone."

"I just guessed about Betty. Okay. I won't ask anymore. How do you feel about Becky leaving?" Bobbie asked.

"I'm doing my best to keep it together. At first, I was shocked, and then I got furious. I went on a reckless drive over to Tom's house and nearly ran over a kid," Jack recounted, voice tinged with disbelief.

"That's how you got that bump on the head?"

"Yes. We argued on Saturday night. I said some things I regret. It was the same old argument, you know. I got home Monday after the suicide and found her note," he said with a sigh.

"That was a low blow," Bobbie said.

"Now, I'm trying to do my job while I wait for her to contact me so I can hopefully work things out."

"I know how hard you've tried to get her to stop using so much cocaine," Bobbie said. "I thought something would happen to her, but from a medical standpoint."

"I've told you before that I'm worried Becky will do more coke than she can handle and overdose, right?" Jack said.

"Yes," she said. "I've seen her act bizarrely. Like at that Christmas party last year. She was hilarious but super hyper, talking nonstop. I saw her drink shot after shot, and it didn't seem to faze her."

"She could get pretty wild," Jack said. "Since then, she has kept increasing her use, more and more, and kept spending more and more. She wouldn't stop. Working at night made it worse because she was around all those people at that God-damned drug restaurant."

"I can't imagine what you're going through. I know you've been worried about how much cocaine Becky has been using. So, you think it's somehow tied to her job at the High Seas?" Bobbie asked.

"You are on the right track, but please, Bobbie, keep asking Lt. Stevens about the investigation. I have a feeling there will be a break soon. Maybe in the next couple of days. I can't talk about that," Jack said.

"Do you want me to go to the High Seas to see if she is there and report how she is acting to you?"

"No. Don't do that. She isn't there anyway."

"She quit the High Seas?"

"No, she's just missing," said Jack, gulping down the rest of his Jack Daniel's. "I have Ed looking. Can we talk about something else?"

"I'm sorry. Jack, I'm just concerned. I've seen you exhausted in the morning. I didn't want to say it, but Jack, she was wearing you out."

"You noticed that?"

"I know you. As you said, I'm a reporter too, remember?" said Bobbie with a little laugh.

"I am worn out," said Jack, pausing. "I suppose I should head home. It's been a long day, and I need to get some sleep if I can."

"It's okay. When you want to talk, you know I'll be around."

"Thanks, Bobbie," said Jack. "I wish I could tell you everything. You've always been a good friend."

"You know I could be more," she replied, giving him a slight smile.

Jack looked at her and smiled back. "I know," he said. "I promise we'll talk about everything when the time is right. I've got to go now. Finish your drink. You haven't touched your crab cakes and salad."

"Bye, Jack. Go home and get some sleep," said Bobbie softly. She watched him get up from the table and walk away.

It was hard for her not to tell him more about her feelings. It wasn't the right time. Maybe in a few days, depending on how things worked out with Becky.

*   *   *

Although it had been one of the most challenging days of his life, Jack felt a little better about going home now. He'd had a nice talk with Bobbie. She'd been supportive and understanding, even though he couldn't tell her the whole story about Tolbert and Becky.

He also had written another scoop, which always made him feel good. Still, it was a hollow feeling.

Ten minutes after leaving the restaurant, he arrived home. As he pulled into the driveway, he hoped Becky had changed her mind and returned.

But the apartment was just as he had left it. It was 11 p.m. He took another sleeping pill. After some tossing and turning, he fell deep asleep.

Chapter 14

Mountain Dream No. 2

Early Wednesday morning, July 9, 1980

Sometime during the night, Jack had another dream about the mountain.

As before, he marched through a medieval city. Oddly, he felt conscious while dreaming. It was strange to see himself marching in a military column with eight soldiers, all dressed in black leather. He could see they were going to a place he had been to before.

He marched with the group up a small ridge until they reached the bottom of a steep mountain. Then, one of the soldiers, who appeared to be the leader, climbed onto a rock at the base of the hill and began to speak.

"Men, we are going on a mission. Not all of you are coming back alive."

Jack woke up with a start. Outside, the rain was beating hard on the roof and pouring down the gutters. Lightning crackled in the sky, and a thundercloud clapped.

He sat on his bed and instinctively looked over at the empty spot where Becky had once lain. Then an eerie thought filled him: Not all of you are coming back alive? Coming back? From where?

Feeling confused, he lay back on his bed. What was going on? Becky was missing. The High Seas, where she worked, had become a target in a drug investigation, and Charlie Tolbert was dead.

Jack suddenly realized that the drugs at the High Seas and Becky were connected to the two dreams about the mountain.

He didn't understand it yet. What was the mission? Why wouldn't everyone come back? Why did he think he was a soldier?

He hadn't had many recurring dreams. But in three nights, he'd had two about marching with soldiers toward what clearly was a mountain.

The first dream occurred the night before Becky went missing. It seemed to tell him they were going on a long, mysterious journey.

The second dream foretold danger. Both had been interrupted.

Jack sensed he should listen to whatever the dreams were trying to tell him. The pieces of these dreams wouldn't settle, and that bothered him more than the storm outside. Becky's disappearance, Charlie Tolbert's death, the drug investigation circling the High Seas, and the strange pull of the mountain dreams all pressed in at once, as if his mind were racing to connect truths his heart wasn't ready to accept. He wasn't a soldier, yet in his sleep, he marched toward danger; he wasn't on a mission, yet everything inside him said one had already begun. His thoughts blurred together, leaving him wide awake at 5 a.m., listening to the rain hammer the roof and realizing sleep would no longer protect him from what was coming. Whatever the warning, preparation, or prophecy—they were insisting he pay attention, because the journey had already started, and this time there would be no turning back.

He looked at his bedside clock. It was now 5:15 a.m. The rain continued to beat on the roof with ferocious force. He was wide awake and couldn't go back to sleep. So he showered, dressed, and drove to work. There weren't many cars braving the dark storm.

Chapter 15
Next Stop: Jamaica

Monday night, July 7, 1980

Becky was in her bedroom, getting dressed, when the telephone rang.

"I got it!" exclaimed Michelle, who was preparing lobsters and corn for dinner in the kitchen.

Becky, her hair uncombed and wearing a striking black satin dress, heard the phone and walked into the kitchen. She wondered if Jack had somehow found her. "Who was that?"

Michelle turned from the stove. "You're a little jumpy this evening." Gazing at Becky's dress, she added, "My, you're looking quite the fox tonight."

Becky didn't reply but stood there with a questioning look.

"That was Michael. They're on their way over," Michelle said. With a little wink, she teased, "You wouldn't be looking forward to seeing Robert, would you?"

"I still wish you hadn't invited them over. You know how bad I feel about leaving Jack, but I don't want to let you and Michael down," Becky replied sarcastically.

She wanted a quiet night at home, but Michelle made other plans without asking. So, she'd decided to make the best of it.

"Besides, I've got something to talk with Michael about," Becky said mysteriously. "I'm going to brush my hair. I'll be right back."

Michelle took the rooster-shaped potholders off the wall hangers and opened the stove. Heat and the smell of broiled lobsters poured out. She inspected the four crustaceans, removed them, wrapped them tightly in aluminum foil, and set the plate in the oven.

"Would you like a glass of wine?" she asked Becky as she opened the refrigerator and took out two bottles of very cold California chardonnay.

From the bedroom, Becky yelled, "A big one!"

As Michelle poured the wine, the doorbell rang.

"I'll get it," Michelle said.

She opened the door, and there stood Michael, dressed in black leather slacks with a dark gray satin shirt. Robert wore a loose-fitting peach suit, a low-cut white dress shirt that showed the top of his chest, and a white carnation on his lapel.

"Hi, darling. How did you get here so quickly?" Michelle said as she leaned over to kiss Michael.

"I've got a new car phone. They come in quite handy," Michael said.

Just then, Robert stepped around Michael, smiled, and handed Michelle two sweet-smelling roses. "These are for you and Becky," he said, his voice smooth but edgy.

"Why don't you give them to her yourself?" Michelle asked with a playful wink.

"I think I will," Robert replied with an easy grin. "Where is she?"

"Now, don't be impatient, Robert. She's dressing. We didn't expect you to get here so fast. She'll be out in a moment," Michelle said.

She invited the two men in and closed the front door.

"You're lookin' just as lovely as ever," Robert said, the warmth in his voice not quite hiding the edge beneath.

"When was that—March in Kingston? I've gained two pounds, but I'm still too skinny for Michael," Michelle laughed.

"No, I like you just how you are," Michael said. "I made that one crack about how little you eat, and you've never let me forget it."

"As long as I've still got my figure, I won't let you forget it," she said.

"You'd still look bloody fantastic even if you put on ten pounds," Robert said with an easy grin.

"Don't give me any ideas," Michelle said. "It's hard enough to keep my figure as it is with Michael owning a restaurant." She laughed.

"Speakin' of good figures, where's Becky?" Robert asked, a sly glint in his eye.

"Down, boy. She'll be out when she's ready. I want us to start dinner soon. I finished it and don't want it to dry out. Are you hungry, Robert?"

"Yeah, hungry, I am," he said with a wry grin. "The food on that flight outta Jamaica was rubbish, as usual. Haven't had a bite all day. Michael's been talkin' up your home cookin', though."

"Good things, I hope," Michelle said with a playful leer at Michael.

"Oh, yeah. Only the best, I promise," Robert replied with an easy grin. "From what I've heard, you ought to be the one running the kitchen at the restaurant."

"Never. I would never work there. And that is not a reflection on you, honey," she said mischievously. "Cooking is a hobby for me. Doing it for a living would take away the fun."

Michelle beckoned the two men into the dining room. "Michael, you know where the wine is. Can you get some for yourself and Robert? I'll go see how Becky's doing."

Michelle went into the kitchen and picked up Becky's glass of wine. She walked down the hall and reached Becky's door in five long steps.

"May I come in?"

"It's open."

Becky was sitting in front of a vanity mirror, combing her long, wavy red hair.

"Here, take a sip of this," Michelle said.

"Thank you," Becky replied, taking the wine glass with her free hand.

"The boys are here. Will you be all right?"

"I suppose so," she muttered as she brushed her hair and stared into her face in the mirror with an expressionless, pensive gaze.

She slowly put the brush down and pressed the glass to her lips. Without breaking eye contact with the mirror, she tipped her head back and swallowed half the contents. She put the glass down, leaned over to her purse, and removed a zipper bag containing a mirror, a one-sided razor blade, a glass pipe, and a small, dark brown vial.

"Do we have time for a few lines?" Becky asked.

Michelle laughed and pulled up a chair. "I'll take two."

Becky poured the vial's contents onto the small, four-inch-square mirror. The white powder had only a few chunks, held together by moisture. She cut the chunks into four thick, inch-long lines.

She bent her head toward the mirror, put her nose to the glass pipe, and quickly inhaled. The line of cocaine vanished. She held her other nostril closed with her finger, sniffed again, exhaled, and handed the pipe and mirror to Michelle.

"It's pretty clean," Becky said.

"You always seem to find the good stuff," Michelle said.

"Michael doesn't do too bad either," Becky replied.

"No, he has his connections," Michelle chuckled as she snorted a thick line.

Becky set down her wine glass and stared at her friend with a serious expression.

"You know, Michelle, Jack thinks I left because of the coke, or because I wanted more freedom than he could give me," Becky said quietly. "That's part of it, sure—but it's not the real reason."

"What do you mean?"

"The truth is, he wants children, and I don't. Not ever. I grew up watching my mother ruin everything she touched, and I see too much of her in me. Jack believes love fixes things. I know better. I'd rather walk away now than become the kind of mother a child spends their whole life trying to escape."

Michelle didn't answer right away. She studied Becky's face, usually full of confidence, now like a lost little girl's.

"You never told me this. Listen, not wanting children

doesn't make you broken," she said finally. "It doesn't make you selfish, either. It just means you know your limits. Jack doesn't see that as clearly as you do."

Becky shook her head, a humorless smile crossing her lips.

"That's the problem," she said. "I don't just know my limits—I know my flaws. I like my freedom too much. I like choosing myself. And the day I had a kid, I'd resent them for taking that away. I couldn't live with myself if I turned into my mother... or worse, if I turned into someone who pretended she wasn't."

Michelle lowered her voice. "Jack wants a life that's simple and straightforward—roots, a future, maybe kids. You don't. That doesn't make either of you wrong, Becky. It just means you were heading in different directions. And the longer you stayed, the more it would've hurt him."

Becky's expression hardened, all warmth draining away. "Exactly, Michelle. I knew I could talk with you. He's a good man; I wish you could have met him. He's too good. He deserves someone who wants the same things he does, not someone who'd lie to him and hope he'd change. I don't want kids. I don't want the guilt that would come with pretending I do. And I'm not going to wake up one day and suddenly be different. So I left before I turned into the woman who ruins his life by staying."

Michelle studied her for a long second, then nodded. "All right. I'm glad we talked about this. If you want to discuss it further, I'm here for you."

She glanced toward the door, lowering her voice. "But you should pull yourself together. Michael and Robert are in the kitchen. They're probably wondering what we're doing. Neither of them needs to know anything about Jack or see you vulnerable right now."

Becky's mouth tightened into a thin, knowing smile. "Don't worry," she said coolly. "They won't. I'll put on my game face after a few more lines."

* * *

As they passed the mirror back and forth and chatted, Robert and Michael waited in the living room, talking about Charlie Tolbert.

"We haven't heard from your man about Gordo. Let's call the restaurant to see if he's left with the merchandise," Robert said.

Michael nodded, picked up a phone, and dialed the number.

"Gordo? What's up?" Michael asked.

"It didn't get done, boss," Gordo reported. "Too hot. Too hot. I'm going to try something later tonight."

"Right," said Michael, hanging up.

"What is it?" Robert impatiently asked.

"It sounds like the police are watching the restaurant. Gordo couldn't make the move right now," Michael explained. "He'll try later."

"This is exactly what I was worried about," Robert growled, his tone low and dangerous. "Somehow, the police have made a connection with the dope and the restaurant. It will only be a matter of time before they get a search warrant, find the rock, and then come looking for you."

Michael nodded dejectedly. "It's my fault," he said. "What are we going to do?"

"We've got to get you out of the country, mate—and fast," Robert said firmly. "You're too hot for this town. Don't even think about going home—they could be watching the place."

"Yes. All right. But what about the coke?" Michael asked.

"I'll see to it," Robert replied, his voice low and steady. "If Gordo can't shift it tonight, I'll burn the joint before the cops get there."

"Oh, Jesus, Robert. You know, I was thinking…" Michael said. "It's possible Tolbert's wife, Betty, may have talked with the police about the coke."

"What do you mean?"

"I should have told you before, but she also worked for me. The police must know that. She knows Charlie was working for us."

"Are the cops onto her, then?" Robert asked, his voice low and controlled.

"She's not involved. She was just a server, but she knew about the cocaine trafficking. If they found the coke at Tolbert's house—which is almost certain—they might pressure Betty into telling the whole story," Michael said.

"You reckon she'll sing to the cops, or keep her mouth shut?" Robert asked, his voice flat and dangerous.

"She is smart and a tough cookie. I don't think she'll rat on us, but of course, it's still possible. Tolbert told Kendall something, and he could have told police what he knows about Charlie's work for us," Michael said.

"You might be right—the missus working there shifts the angle a bit. Still, we've got to assume both of them could talk to the cops sooner or later," Robert said, his voice flat and dangerous.

"But if the police had real evidence connecting us to the dope, wouldn't they have raided the restaurant and searched it by now?" Michael asked.

"They mustn't have enough for a warrant," Robert mused, his tone calm but sharp. "That gives us a bit of breathing room."

"For what?" Michael asked.

"Never mind. I have to talk with Gordo before we make our next move."

"Maybe the police are just waiting for us to panic."

"I'm not panicking—just a bit hungry," Robert said, his tone calm but edged with impatience. "Speakin' of food, I'm wonderin' what's keeping the girls so long?"

"Michelle's probably trying out some of the stuff we just got in," Michael said. "She's my harshest critic."

"A real coke connoisseur?" Robert joked.

"If she likes it, everybody will," Michael said sarcastically. "I still want you to leave Sarasota as soon as possible."

Robert kept his voice low and controlled. "I'll make the arrangements. But I need to speak with Becky before we lock anything in."

*　*　*

While the men talked in the other room, Michelle and Becky polished off half a gram. "Are you ready now?" Michelle asked.

"Go ahead. I'll be finished here in a few minutes," Becky said.

"Don't be long. I'm going to put the food on the table."

Michelle returned to the dining room, where Robert and Michael whispered. They stopped as Michelle stepped into the room.

"What are you two just talking about?" Michelle teased.

"Just wondering what you girls were doing," Michael said.

"That's none of your business," Michelle playfully said to Michael as she took his hand. "Becky will be out in a few minutes. Now, I want you to remember what I told you about how difficult it was for her to leave Jack. She is very shaky and emotional."

Michael and Robert exchanged opportunistic glances.

"I know," Robert said, his voice smooth with a hint of danger. "I'm lookin' forward to seein' her—maybe makin' her forget all about her husband."

"That's exactly how I thought you'd react, Robert. I know you've got the hots for her. But be easy with her tonight. Give her time," said Michelle, pausing for a second. "Can you just do that for me, you two? Will you promise? She'll be out any second."

Michael nodded. Robert just smiled. He had other ideas. Tonight was the perfect moment for him, with Becky on the rebound.

Just then, Becky's footsteps tapped on the wooden floor in front of the dining room. The three turned around at the same time as she strode majestically into the room.

"So, what's all this talk about me?" Becky asked with a hearty laugh. "I need another drink, Michelle—a big one."

Robert roared with approval. "That's the feisty girl I know! How are you, darling?" he said in a booming voice.

"Well, Robert, I've been better, but I can't really complain. As long as I've got a job with Michael, at least I'm not at square one again," she said, turning to her employer.

"You'll always have a job with me," Michael said. "Robert, I hate to admit it, but I couldn't have made the restaurant as big a success without her. She's a wonder. I love ya, doll."

Michael leaned over to Becky, kissed her cheek, and

whispered, "Let me know if you need anything." Becky nodded.

"Now, Michael, you're making me jealous," Michelle piped in. "I thought it was me that made you such a success?"

"Both of you, of course," Michael added, amending his previous statement.

They all laughed. Becky smiled, and Michelle noticed how cocaine had transformed her mood from melancholy just a few minutes earlier to the joy she now displayed.

She was hyper, and while the cocaine contributed to her energy, Michelle admired the little performer within her friend. Becky had always seen herself as an actress waiting to be discovered, and tonight, given the circumstances, she was delivering an Academy Award-worthy performance.

"Now, enough of this coddling of the poor girl who has no home and no one to love," Becky declared in mock outrage. "I'm not going to cry on my pillow, so don't feel you have to hurl compliments my way all night."

"That's gonna be a tough one for me," Robert said with a wry grin. "I've been practicin' all these compliments for the past hour."

"Touché, Robert," Becky said.

Robert looked deep into Becky's blue eyes. She was truly an amazingly beautiful woman. Maybe she would concede to his advances now that her husband was out of the picture. But he decided to wait for her to make the first move. He owed her that, especially after the last time they'd met.

Becky also remembered that meeting. It was earlier that year. Michael was hosting an after-work house party. She had come directly from work. Jack was at home, probably sleeping. After the restaurant closed, it was late, and couples were pairing off in bedrooms.

She was in the kitchen, making a drink. The music was playing loudly, a soulful Bob Seger song, and he had slipped behind her, whispered something sexy in her ear, and worked his hands up around her round breasts. She moaned a little at his touch and felt his rigid member grinding against her butt.

The next second, she pulled down his hands and wriggled free of his grasp. Pushing him back, she told him in no uncertain terms that she would never cheat on Jack while they were together.

She had rejected him, all right. But it wasn't an outright blow-off. She had let her guard down a bit.

Robert remembered that encounter well. He was close, but no cigars. This time around, he felt sure she would be ready.

"Becky, I'll always have compliments for you, regardless of the circumstance," Robert said.

"That's sweet of you, Robert. I'm just a little jittery tonight because of Jack," Becky said in a rare admission.

"We'll get you some food, and you'll feel all right," Michelle said.

"I'm not that hungry, Michelle. I'm sorry," Becky said.

"How much of that coke did you do?" Michelle asked.

"About six lines, maybe 10. Who's counting?" Becky said with a laugh.

"You still should eat a little," Michelle insisted. "I'll get you a drink, and then we'll eat. The food is ready. Michael, can you help me in the kitchen?"

"I can take a hint," said Michael, winking at Robert.

"I saw that, Michael. Don't encourage him. It's dangerous," Becky teased.

As Michelle and Michael walked out of the dining room, Robert took Becky's hand and placed it in both of his.

"I want you to know tonight's entirely your call," Robert said, his voice low and controlled. "As for me, what happened last time...that was more about my lust than anything else. This time will be different. I promise."

He continued in his soft, practiced voice, the one that never rushed or rose. Becky didn't move or respond. She didn't want to have this conversation—not now—but she also didn't want Robert to mistake her silence for rejection. There was a difference between hesitation and disinterest, and she wanted him to know it.

Robert had a way of making her feel seen without pressuring her, admired without being cornered. He listened. He didn't lecture. Unlike Jack lately, he wasn't trying to fix her or warn her about consequences she didn't want to face. With Robert, everything felt lighter. Easier.

"Robert, I've got to ask Michael for a favor," Becky said, cutting him off before he could say more.

"I'm sure it won't be a problem, whatever it is," Robert replied, confidence flowing easily. "Tell me what it's about. I'm sure I can persuade Mike it's a good idea."

"Well, I'd like to go on a short vacation," she said. "Just until I can sort a few things out."

"Fair enough, given your situation," Robert said, his tone calm, understanding—almost intimate. "Mind if I suggest something?"

"No."

"Why don't you come stay at my place in Jamaica for a couple of weeks?" he said smoothly. "We'll put you up in a private suite. Better than any holiday you've ever had, I can promise you that."

The offer landed exactly where he intended.

Becky felt the pull immediately. Sun, distance, anonymity. A place where no one knew her as someone's wife or someone's problem. Robert made it sound safe. Luxurious. Temporary. Her expression didn't change—still playful, still guarded—but inside, the decision tempted her more than she wanted to admit.

"I'd like to think about it," she said carefully. "I don't know if I'd want to go there alone."

"Well, what if Michael and Michelle came along?" Robert said, leaning back, smiling as if the answer had been there all along. "Michelle's always keen on a spur-of-the-moment trip. Same setup as before—only this time, you'd go instead of keeping an eye on the restaurant. The day manager can handle things for a bit."

Becky studied him, curiosity mixing with relief. Robert didn't lecture her about money, the law, or what she *should* be doing with her life. Lately, Jack had become all rules and worries—counting expenses, watching the clock, warning her about police scrutiny, and the danger of being in the wrong place at the wrong time. He talked about saving, planning, and careers. Robert spoke about escape—about sunlight, space, and time. With him, she didn't feel judged or managed. She felt admired. And in that moment, that was enough.

She brushed her wavy red hair back, tilted her head, and felt a grin spread across her face despite herself. She nodded slowly.

"If only I could," she said. "It would be perfect."

"Consider it done," Robert said, already certain.

"Only if I can leave whenever I choose," Becky said, her voice firm now. "I need to know I can do that."

"Of course. No problem," Robert said without hesitation.

"It's settled. We'll leave first thing in the morning on my private plane. I'll take care of everything tonight."

"That's pretty quick."

"Don't you want to go?"

"Yes... I suppose," she said. "But I have to ask Michael."

"You already did," Robert said evenly. "He's said yes."

Becky looked at him, surprised. Robert met her gaze and smiled, calm and unreadable. She wondered—briefly—what kind of understanding existed between the two men, but she didn't press it. She didn't want to slow things down.

She agreed.

They sealed the trip with a kiss—easy, confident, and full of promise.

Jack was already a million miles away.

Chapter 16
Mackey's Unfinished Business

Tuesday, July 8, 1980

Michael read the morning newspaper and shook his head. "Did you see the story Becky's husband wrote about Tolbert's suicide?"

"Yeah, very nice. Kendall's a decent writer, isn't he?" Robert said, his voice dripping with sarcasm. "All the more reason we need to get outta here quick. I don't want Becky finding out her loving husband was around when Tolbert offed himself. She might start feelin' sorry for him—and that'd only muck up our plans."

"Does Michelle get the paper?"

"Michelle?" Michael laughed. "Her source of news is the

afternoon soap operas. You don't need to worry about that."

"Good," Robert replied, his tone sharp and controlled. "You reckon Tolbert told Kendall about us before he blew his brains out? And with all that blow stashed in his place?"

"He might have. We have to assume Kendall knows about us and didn't include that information in the story for some reason," Michael said.

"I agree," Robert said, his voice low and measured. "He's a newspaperman. The cops have probably found the coke in the house by now—especially if Kendall spilled the beans to them."

"We're screwed."

"Maybe not," Robert said, his tone cautious but sharp. "If Kendall knew, he might've kept his mouth shut about where it came from. Could be he's workin' on another story for bigger headlines."

"I've been reading Kendall since I've been in Sarasota. He gets many scoops and has a reputation to live up to, so I wouldn't put it past him to withhold that information for the next story," Michael said.

"If that's the case, he's the only livin' witness who can tie us to the stuff," Robert asserted. "We might have to deal with him—quietly."

Michael grimaced. "I hate to bring it up, but Betty Tolbert also knows."

"We might have to sort her out, too," Robert suggested.

"But Betty doesn't know anything about you, just me."

"All the same, the fact she knows is a worry."

"What are you going to do?" Michael asked.

"Haven't made up my mind yet," Robert said. "Gordo's sussing out the bagmen and peddlers—seeing what the word on the street is."

"Gordo has done a good job of keeping them in the dark about the restaurant, but when word got out yesterday about Tolbert, I told Gordo to let all our street people know we shut down. No sales until I give the word," Michael said.

"But?"

"But this is a small town. Word gets around fast if the supply is cut. Users could talk, and word might get back to the police about our bagmen," Michael explained. "I estimate we have three days before people start talking. Word could get back to us. Then the shit will hit the fan."

Just then, the phone rang. Michael picked it up and listened. "Right, good job, Gordo," he said.

Michael turned to Robert. "Finally, some good news. That was Gordo. He was able to get a server to take the rest of the product out of the restaurant last night."

Robert breathed a sigh of relief.

"Gordo was worried the police might be watching him, so he had one of his bagmen pick it up from the server's car. Jorge will move it to Atlanta as soon as he can."

"You can fill me in on the details on the way to pick up the girls for the trip," Robert said, his voice calm but edged with authority. "Let's get movin'."

* * *

The two drug dealers drove off from Robert's million-dollar house on Siesta Key.

On his way to the airport, Robert used his car phone to speak with his pilot and confirm that Michael, Michelle, and Becky would be the passengers on his Cessna 210.

They would depart from Beach Aviation at the Sarasota-Bradenton Airport, refuel in Miami, and then continue to Montego Bay. By midnight, they would arrive at Robert's house in the foothills of the Blue Mountains.

"You aren't coming with us?" Michael asked. "Gordo will update us on everything once we're in Jamaica."

"Change of plans," Robert said, his tone controlled and sharp. "I'll be leavin' in a day or two. Got some unfinished business to take care of before I go, and Gordo and his men will be helpin' me."

"What do you have in mind?" Michael asked.

"You don't need to know right now," Robert replied menacingly. "I'll take care of two problems in one go." He stared icily at the traffic ahead. "This situation has ticked me off."

Michael glanced at Robert as they drove to Michelle's house, wondering what he meant. Robert had something planned, and since he was the boss and had made his decision, it wouldn't do Michael any good to ask him about it.

All Michael wanted to do was get out of Florida. He had made several recent mistakes and was feeling pressure from Robert. A short vacation would be a welcome change. He'd already informed the day manager and several key support staff. They could handle the restaurant business for the time being.

But if he were honest with himself, he would like to retire. He had been thinking that since he'd met Michelle. He had made enough money in the cocaine trade. She knew nothing about him except that he was a Vietnam vet and a successful restaurateur.

He wanted to tell Michelle the real story, but he needed to

wait for the opportune time. This vacation to Jamaica could give him a chance.

Michael needed to see how this Florida situation played out before doing anything. Either way, he knew he'd eventually have to talk with Robert about retiring before telling Michelle. For now, he was relieved to leave Sarasota.

"Let's not disturb the girls with any of our problems, eh, Mike?" Robert requested as he pulled up to Michelle's house.

"Not a word," agreed Michael. "How will you explain not coming along with us to them?"

"I'll just say somethin' came up, and I need to speak with a few of my American partners," Robert said ominously. "Now, go inside and help Michelle and Becky with their bags. I've got a call to make."

As Michael walked into the house, Robert dialed Gordo.

"I've got another little job for you. I want you to take out Betty Tolbert. She knows too much," Robert said.

"Sure, boss," Gordo said.

Chapter 17
Drinks at Foley's

Wednesday night, July 9, 1980

Jack sat on a stool at the bar in Foley's, slowly sipping his rum and coke with a slice of lime. Two overturned shot glasses of Jack Daniel's lay in front of him.

He didn't want to give up hope, but with no leads, he decided his best move was to head over to Foley's, a place on Main Street he and Becky used to frequent because it was near their apartment. He felt odd there, but in the back of his mind, he wondered if he would see her sitting on a stool, talking with the bartender like they always did.

It was now two days after she'd left. She still hadn't contacted him as she'd promised. He needed a drink to help him relax.

Sometimes, when he got tense before a sports game or to chill out after a long day, he'd use the popular yoga breathing technique. But in this case, yoga was way overrated as a calming device. Black Jack Daniel's was the only proper, quick remedy for such anxiety.

He couldn't believe what had happened since Monday. Ed's investigation so far had turned up nothing on Becky.

The one promising lead on how Michael financed the purchase of the High Seas restaurant, with no apparent source of savings or income, turned into a dead end—there were no bank loans. Michael paid cash for the building and the renovations. That's pretty nifty for a Vietnam vet with no pension.

Ed said it looked like Michael received a "private loan" from a wealthy, anonymous benefactor. Although suspicious, the gift was not illegal per se. Money laundering was more likely. That would've been difficult to prove without a whistleblower or a tax audit, which only the police or the IRS could conduct.

After Bagley's phone call on Tuesday morning, Jack hoped the police would find and speak with Becky as part of their investigation. But Bobbie had checked with Lt. Stevens several times and was told the police couldn't find Becky or Michael LeCare. Moreover, the police had nothing more to say about the cocaine found at Tolbert's house.

LeCare covered his tracks very well. Police informants said cocaine gram prices had increased in the past few days, indicating supply was down. Bagley said the price increase proved the High Seas distribution network had shut down. Score one for the good guys.

But Jack was frustrated; he couldn't tell Bobbie about the tip Bagley gave him about the High Seas and the promised search warrant. He thought that would've been resolved by now.

In addition to that problem, Bagley suspected Jack was looking for Becky. The chief had asked him to stop, saying the police were continuing to follow leads and gather information for the search warrant.

Despite Bagley's request, Jack didn't ask Ed to stop looking for his missing wife. He wanted to do something, anything. He didn't know what that was.

He couldn't understand why Becky hadn't called or tried to contact him through such mutual friends as Tom Justice's wife, Susan.

Becky could be complex, challenging to figure out, and flighty at times, especially when using a lot of coke. She wouldn't want Jack to know where she was if she were bingeing. But her disappearance was another reason to think she was either involved with the drugs or that LeCare had silenced her.

That last possibility worried him. He was tempted to drive over to the High Seas for dinner or drinks, to ask around and see for himself. Bobbie had already offered to help. They could both go and make inquiries. Maybe a staff member knew something.

But Ed's police source told him that Becky and Michael hadn't been seen at work all week. It was unusual for both Michael and Becky to be out at the same time during the week.

It was a puzzling situation. Jack thought the cops were preparing to search the restaurant and interview everybody involved. Why they hadn't done that yet was a mystery. They must have had enough probable cause. As Ed suggested, maybe the feds slowed the investigation to get more evidence for a bigger bust.

Jack needed a new plan. Waiting wasn't cutting it. Having two shots of JDs and a few rum and Cokes was one thing, but it wasn't getting him any closer to finding Becky. He hesitated because of Bagley's warning and Becky's promise to contact him once she was settled.

It was enough to make him scream. Tomorrow, he thought,

tomorrow I'll go and question Chief Bagley, maybe get an on-the-record interview about the High Seas investigation.

He took another sip of his rum and Coke and pondered what else he could do to find Becky. He was conflicted about her involvement. Was she in on it, or wasn't she? If she wasn't involved, why hadn't she contacted him as promised?

Frustrated with the same thoughts, he finished the rest of his drink. He scanned the bar for Frank, the bartender. He needed another JD.

Out of the corner of his eye, he saw a vaguely familiar face sitting beside him. He was so engrossed in himself and his problems that he hadn't noticed the man.

"Say, your name is Steve, right? You used to work at High Seas?" Jack asked.

"How do you know my name? I don't know you," replied Steve Ferro, a burly, dark-haired man of about 27.

"Relax. Let me buy you a beer. I used to know someone who worked there with you," said Jack, pretending to be someone else to glean information from the man.

"Yeah, who's that?" Steve said.

"Becky Kendall."

"Yeah, I knew Becky. A really sharp lady. You know her?"

"I used to. I lost track of her. Does she still work there?" Jack said, continuing to press Ferro. He thought this man might have clues about what happened to Becky.

"As far as I know. I don't work there anymore. I quit," Steve muttered.

"When?"

"Couple of weeks ago."

"Oh," said Jack. "Got a better job?"

Steve took a sip of his Budweiser and didn't answer.

Jack looked him over for a second and decided to push his case. "Do you mind if I ask you a question?"

"What's that?"

"Did you notice anything unusual about High Seas when you worked there?"

"Say, are you sure you know Becky?" Steve asked. "You aren't no cop, are you?"

"Now, why would you say that?"

"Tell me who you are," Steve said as he started to get up from his seat.

"Okay. I'm Becky's husband. Okay? Does that explain everything?"

"Yeah, it sure does. You're that reporter, aren't you?" said Steve, sitting back down. "I heard she left town. No wonder you're here, drinking whiskey."

Jack stopped sipping his drink at that bit of news. After a moment, he closed his eyes and then gulped down the entire drink.

"Why did you think I was a cop?"

"You were asking many questions."

"So? Does that bother you?"

"So, I don't want to get into any trouble. I don't want to answer any questions about that place," Steve said.

"You mean High Seas?" Jack asked.

"Yeah, that place," Steve said as he got off the stool again. "Thanks for the beer. I've gotta go now."

"One minute, Steve," Jack said. "Relax. Sit down. Why did you quit?"

Steve hesitated and then looked at Jack.

"I know how you reporters work. I'm going to say something because I liked your old lady. She was very nice to me, and I was just a cook. Don't print what I said. I'll deny it. Let's say she was very close to management. I hope nothing happens to her," Steve said. "She's mixed up in something way over her head."

"What the hell do you mean?" Jack asked, grabbing Steve's arm and then patting it reassuringly.

In a softer voice, Steve said, "Hey, I understand. I know you want to find your old lady. Let me say that something's fishy about that place, and it isn't the tuna they sell, if you get my drift. The owners are mixed up in something I don't think is all restaurant business. Get the picture, bub?"

"I think so," Jack replied. "It's illegal."

"I'm not sure what it is, but I have my suspicions," Steve explained. "That's why I quit."

"Did you hear or see anything?"

"All I'm going to say is they take in too many boxes of food and supplies for a 25-table restaurant, even with a big bar," Steve said. "Watch them unload the trucks. Then, they have a room inside that is padlocked. Nobody can get in. One time, I asked about the extra boxes and the room, and they told me not to worry; it was for expansion plans."

"Do you think the room was to hide cocaine or pot?"

"Oh, I don't know or care. I know it is not food," Steve said. "I quit and am staying far away from that place. They paid me pretty well when I left. It'll keep me unemployed and drinking for three months."

Jack sat back on his stool. He'd finally received eyewitness confirmation of his suspicions. But why hadn't the police gotten something like this from other employees? Steve had mentioned truckloads of supplies and a locked room.

Still, it was just as Jack suspected. Becky worked for a

drug smuggler, probably from South America. The restaurant served as both a front and a convenient means of laundering money. The secret room was likely a lab for crack cocaine or a transfer station, and the extra supplies were probably fillers used to cut the cocaine into saleable street stuff.

"I hope you find your wife," Steve said. "Like I said, she was decent. Please, don't tell anyone I told you this."

"I won't. But why didn't you go to the police?" Jack said. "You sound like an honest guy."

"Ha! I've got a criminal record. I stay as far away from the cops as possible," Steve said. "Don't print my name, and for Christ's sake, don't tell the police what I said."

"I won't. I understand. Thanks for your help," Jack said.

After Ferro left, Jack ordered another drink. It was time to act. Ferro had said Becky was involved in something she didn't understand. If he'd told the truth, she must have known about the drug trafficking because of the room, the extra supplies, and the comings and goings.

Jack quickly formed a plan. He had been waiting for Becky to contact him for two days like a dope. Sure, he had asked Ed to investigate her disappearance. But he had put the High Seas off-limits because of the police's cocaine investigation.

During that time, Becky had vanished, a man had killed himself, drugs had been found at his house, and the place where Becky worked had become the center of a drug-smuggling ring.

He glanced at the clock; it read 11 p.m. It was time to head to the High Seas and see what was happening. He didn't care if the police were watching the place. He needed to find Becky, and if that meant disregarding Bagley's request and getting personally involved—even risking arrest—so be it.

Chapter 18
Siesta Key

After Midnight, July 10, 1980

Jack looked at his watch. It was now 12:30 a.m. He peered over the dashboard from his reclining position in the front seat of his car. The hotel parking lot across the street from the High Seas provided a good lookout spot.

He wasn't sure what he would discover by watching the High Seas after hours. He knew he was taking a chance, but he didn't see any marked or unmarked police cars. Maybe they had finished their investigation. Or perhaps he'd hear about it tomorrow from Bagley.

The restaurant closed at midnight on weekdays, and the parking lot was nearly empty. The servers and kitchen staff had already left. There was a light on inside the restaurant. Maybe cleaners, but it could've been drug dealers at work.

Suddenly, the light went out. Jack saw a man in a white suit come out. The light was faint, but it was enough for Jack to recognize he was the mysterious man at the stakeout. He'd looked out of place at the time, so he was connected to the restaurant and the drug trafficking ring.

The man in the white suit quickly walked across the parking lot to a black BMW. Jack waited until his target pulled out of the parking lot before starting his car. He saw no other vehicles around, so he followed the BMW.

The black car turned onto Midnight Pass Road and headed toward the south side of the key. Wherever the man was going, Jack hoped he'd take him to Becky. Jack had to be careful not to raise suspicions by getting too close, since there weren't many cars on the road in the middle of the week. He also checked his rearview mirror for anyone following him. Clear, so far.

Five minutes later, the car pulled onto a private dirt road on the bay side of the key. Jack drove past the entrance to the gated driveway and parked on a side street about 100 feet past where the black BMW had gone.

It was a dark, moonless night. A light breeze was blowing warm wind through the trees. It always seemed a little cooler on the Keys than on the mainland, especially at night.

Jack got out of his car, closed the door quietly, and walked back to the entrance road. A car slowed and passed him. He saw the car's brake light as it pulled into the next driveway. He wondered if it was an unmarked cop car. If it were the cops, he'd have to explain why he was there. Despite the risk, he decided to press on.

When Jack reached the private driveway, he noticed the electronic gate was slightly ajar. Odd, he thought. Is this an invitation? He had no choice. After coming this far, he needed to see for himself.

He quietly pushed the gate open and started walking down the driveway. Halfway down, he saw lights at a house. He wondered if it was LeCare's. If so, the police could've been watching this place as well.

Already on alert because he was on private property with the gate strangely open, Jack decided to be extra careful by moving off the driveway. He walked the rest of the way through the brush and trees, just in case it was a trap.

Someone had cleared most of the scrub to make the walk through the underbrush manageable. About 100 feet from the house, Jack saw three cars.

One of the vehicles was the black BMW, and the red sports car was Michael's. It must be his house. He couldn't make out the third car closest to the house.

He moved a bit closer and spotted it—Becky's green Buick Century. "Oh my God!" he exclaimed. Her car was here.

But was Becky here too? Excitement coursed through him as his heart began to race. He could feel his fingers tingle at the thought of barging in, finding her, and taking her home. He had to get closer to the house to get a better look.

Then he sensed something was wrong. Yesterday, Ed had said he had checked Michael's house, and Becky's car wasn't there. He would have reported seeing it. Maybe this wasn't Michael's house.

Inside, all the lights were on. Jack crouched and zigzagged his way across the lawn toward the residence. He knew he would be spotted if anyone looked outside. He took the chance anyway.

His heart beat madly. Sweat beaded across his brow.

He reached a window at the side of the house and looked inside. It appeared to be the living room. He didn't see anyone, but he heard music.

Somebody was home.

Suddenly, from behind the bushes, Jack heard a rustle. As he turned, someone grabbed him by the neck in a half-nelson hold. Another person seized his arm from behind and pressed a wet rag to his face.

Struggling against them, Jack could smell chloroform. As he began to lose consciousness, he glanced at the ground. One of the men wore red Converse sneakers, while the other wore white pants. The night grew darker around him.

As he felt himself getting sleepy, he heard a voice, "Hold him a second longer, Steve." Then he felt a blunt object strike his head.

Chapter 19
Drugged and Out

Thursday, 6 a.m., July 10, 1980

Jack's back burned like someone had spread hot plastic on his shoulders.

He was awake—but what had happened? Jack fought his nearly paralyzed mind to remember. It was all blank. He tried to get up, but he felt like his body weighed 1,000 pounds. It took all his strength to move his arm a few inches. He heard a loud ringing that sounded like a referee's whistle.

Oh my God, what am I going to do? Jack thought with growing panic. I can't move.

He closed his eyes and tried to relax, but the pain wouldn't let him. His head felt like it was splitting. Although groggy, he had to get up and get help, or else he would burn up.

But where was he? He was lying on a bed. He tried to look around the room, but his vision was blurred. He saw a phone on the table. With great difficulty, he concentrated on moving his arm.

Sluggishly, with his body shaking, he extended his arm to the table, reached over, and grabbed the cord. He slowly pulled the phone onto the bed beside him with enormous effort.

Who to call? He couldn't think of a name or a number. He struggled to punch in a zero as he lay on his back.

"Help. I need help," was all Jack could whisper. He heard a voice saying, "Can I help you? Hello?" His eyes became heavy, and he couldn't keep them open any longer. His energy was sapped. The darkness engulfed him, swallowing him, and his eyelids fluttered and slowly shut.

*   *   *

Mrs. Kendall woke up to a strange feeling.

She turned on the light and looked at the bedside alarm clock. It was 6 a.m. The room was quiet. Outside, the sun was rising. She decided to get up, make tea, and consider her day.

How's Jack doing? she wondered. I haven't heard from him since Tuesday afternoon.

Sipping her tea, she immediately decided to call him. She didn't want to worry too much, but Jack had been on her mind the past few days.

She dialed his number and immediately got a busy signal. Strange. He wouldn't be on the phone this early. She put her tea down on the kitchen table, sensing something was wrong.

Laura Kendall was very calm in most situations. She prided herself on being able to handle any problem with a cool head, a skill she'd learned as a high school teacher many years ago.

But this time was different. She decided to dress and drive over to her son's place. Something was wrong.

When she arrived 15 minutes later, Jack's apartment was

pitch black.

Mrs. Kendall found the door slightly open and stepped inside. "Jack!" she called out. "Jack!" Are you all right?"

She heard a beeping sound from the phone—off the hook in his bedroom.

Mrs. Kendall quickly passed through the living room and went straight to his bedroom. Jack was on the bed.

She ran to his side and shook him. He didn't respond. She felt his forehead; he was very hot and barely breathing. His lips were parched. Blood stained his shirt. She found the source at the back of his head.

Mrs. Kendall hurried over to the kitchen sink and dampened a cloth with cold water. She rushed back, sat beside him, and wrung the fabric over his head. The water trickled over his face. She dabbed the cloth across his cheeks, turned his head slightly, and pressed the fabric on the patch of blood on his head.

He started to stir.

"Jack, you've got to wake up," she said. "Wake up. Wake up!"

He slowly opened his eyes. His vision was blurred. He saw a woman sitting beside him.

"I'm hot," Jack said in a dreamy whisper.

"What happened, Jack?" Mrs. Kendall asked.

"I don't know," he mumbled.

"We need to get you to the hospital," she said. "I'll help you up."

"Who are you?" Jack asked in a hoarse, soft tone.

"Who am I?" Mrs. Kendall said. "Why, I'm... You don't know?"

Jack didn't answer. His head was spinning. His back wasn't burning as much as when he'd first woken, but he was still hot.

She helped him stand up and walk to the car. The early morning sun was starting to break through. The fresh air gave Jack energy, but he still felt weak and dizzy. She helped him to the backseat.

Mrs. Kendall quickly got into the front seat and started the engine. A tear welling in her eye, she guided her car to the hospital without a word.

Jack fell asleep. A few minutes later, they arrived at the hospital emergency department entrance. She beeped her horn, and a nurse and an orderly came out.

"Wake up, Mr. Kendall. Time to wake up, Mr. Kendall," the tall, burly orderly said.

Jack heard voices, but he couldn't see people. He was completely wasted and exhausted.

"Stay awake, Mr. Kendall," said the emergency room nurse. "You've got to stay awake."

He couldn't.

Chapter 20
Jack Who?

Four Days Later, Monday, July 14, 1980

Jack awoke in a private room at Sarasota Memorial Hospital. At first, he could only hear people walking and talking outside his room. When he opened his eyes, everything he saw was blurred and distorted. The rectangular window that let in sunlight seemed crooked and uneven.

He blinked and then noticed a nurse sitting in a chair at the foot of his bed. She was reading a book and hadn't seen him waking up. He looked past her and around the tidy white hospital room.

"May I have a drink of water?" Jack asked in a dry, parched voice.

As the nurse heard his words, she twitched in surprise and immediately set her book down. "Certainly," she said. She got up, walked to the nightstand, and picked up a pitcher. "How do you feel?" she asked soothingly, pouring the water into a plastic cup.

"Oh, not too good," Jack said. "I'm hungry, and I feel tired and weak."

"For a while, we didn't know what to think," the nurse explained. "Your family has been coming to see you every day. They hired me to watch you. They're very worried."

"My family? Every day? How long have I been here?" Jack asked.

"I think the doctor should tell you that," she said. "I'll be right back."

"How long?" he asked again as she neared the door.

She turned. "Well, I suppose it won't hurt to tell you. It's been five days."

"Five hours, you mean," Jack said, rubbing his head.

"No, five days," she insisted. "You've been in a coma. Just relax. Don't try to move. I'll get the doctor."

"No, wait," said Jack, not understanding what had happened. "How did I get here?"

"You don't remember?" she asked. "Your chart shows that you had quite a time. Cocaine, heroin, barbiturates, PCP."

"I don't understand," Jack muttered.

"That's what the lab test showed. It was in your bloodstream."

Jack truly didn't understand.

"You shouldn't do drugs, young man," said the nurse with all seriousness. "I'll be right back."

"I don't remember doing any drugs," Jack whispered with a puzzled look as the nurse rushed out to get the doctor. He became very sleepy again. "I'm feeling a little tired," he added, rubbing his eyes.

Jack closed his eyes and fell back to sleep.

*　*　*

Five hours later, Jack woke with a start. He opened his eyes, and a picture flashed through his mind. He had been walking through a strange city to the base of a mountain.

Then, he climbed to the top with a group of men dressed in battle gear. Startled at a familiar sight, he reached for the call button beside his bed and rang for the nurse.

"Nurse, nurse, nurse!" Jack called out with as much volume as he could muster.

"I'm sorry, Mr. Kendall, I was talking with the doctor on the phone. What can I get you?"

"Nothing. I just had a strange dream. I was on a mountain. Am I a soldier?"

"The doctor is on his way," the nurse said. "Try to stay awake this time."

Chapter 21
The Hospital

Wednesday afternoon, July 16, 1980

Sarah was applying chalk to a pool cue tip when Jack walked into the game room at the hospital unit. Standing beside the pool table, she expertly worked the chalk, observing Jack with a calm, expressionless face.

The tall, athletic-looking man with light green eyes and short, dark hair seemed somewhat out of place to Sarah. She noticed him enter the room tentatively, scanning his surroundings. She felt awkward and a bit off-balance when his eyes met hers. Not many men looked at her with such probing yet gentle, reassuring eyes.

Still, she had enough self-control to show Jack nothing but indifference.

Jack noticed a split second of indecision in Sarah's eyes and smiled. Surprised, she looked away, not wanting to appear too interested. Her dark eyes were fixed on the number seven ball she was preparing to sink.

The room was primarily filled with adolescents, and the pool table drew many to watch Sarah play Rob, a loud, cocky 14-year-old who had a penchant for poking holes in the ceiling with his pool cue whenever he missed easy shots. In the past three weeks, he must have made 80 small holes in the white acoustic tile.

Sarah was winning, as usual, and Rob was taking it out on the ceiling. The other kids were smoking, laughing, and bragging about "breaking out" of the hospital ward, how many drugs they were going to do, or how many rock concerts they were going to see when they were released. It was mostly talk.

The kids in the ward were notorious exaggerators, but not everyone knew it. Some hospital professionals—the psychologists, the social workers, and the nurses—knew they were being used in some grandiose children's game. But they didn't take it personally; as long as private insurance covered the care, the kids would be treated for various drug addictions and mental health problems.

Some workers cared about the kids, but they usually didn't last long. The job paid little, the hours were long, and the work required high physical and mental strength.

Jack watched Sarah, noticing she was older and more mature than the other kids, most of whom were in their early teens. She ignored him for the rest of her game. After she won, she approached him for a game.

"Care to?" Sarah asked, expressionless and unemotional. It was as much a challenge as an invitation.

Jack nodded and said, "Sure, if I can find a cue stick."

"There isn't much of a choice," Sarah said.

He walked over to where Sarah was standing and said, "Do you mind if I use yours?" Jack looked deeply into Sarah's dark green eyes, a shade lower than his own.

Sarah was about 21 or 22, Jack guessed. She was beautiful in a rugged, understated sort of way. She was dressed in a baggy, dark blue jumpsuit that downplayed her full figure.

She stared at Jack, who was dressed in an unflattering light-blue hospital smock, then walked over and picked up another cue stick leaning against the wall.

"Use this one," she said. "I don't like to share."

She then began to rack up the balls.

"I'll break," she said.

Jack nodded.

"You're new here, aren't you?" she asked after scattering the balls in a crisp break.

"Yes," Jack said. "This is my second day."

The six or seven kids watching suddenly burst into applause.

"Don't mind those morons," Sarah said. "You haven't been around, though, have you?"

"No, this is the first time I've been out of my room," said Jack, looking around with a firm stare to see if the smart-aleck kids watching them had any comments.

Nobody said anything.

"This place isn't so bad once you get used to it," Sarah said.

She knocked in her fourth straight ball.

Jack watched her closely as she moved around the table with great confidence. He thought he'd like to get to know her. She was different from the others here; he could tell from her eyes. He wondered why she was in the unit. Maybe she was thinking the same thing as him.

Besides the teens, the recreation room was filled with people of all ages, sizes, and races. Some were playing cards, reading, and talking in small groups. One woman playing the piano was dressed like a Native American in a bright red-and-yellow dress. Jack couldn't make out the tune, but it seemed pleasant.

Sarah finally missed her fifth attempt, a formidable bank shot down the rail. That made it Jack's turn.

He picked up the cue stick, sized up an easy, straight-in corner shot, and drilled it in with a powerful thrust.

Jack noticed an old lady sitting in a chair, watching him rather intensely. He looked at Sarah, who was coolly eyeing him. He sank the 10, the 12, and the 14.

The game was tied.

As Jack was preparing another shot, a girl screamed in the cafeteria across the hall from the rec room. Everyone stopped what they were doing and listened. A couple of the kids ran into the hall to see what the commotion was about.

"Get out, get out, get out of here!" screamed a heavyset girl. Her voice echoed quite clearly in the rec room.

"What's going on?" Jack asked.

"That sounds like Belinda," Sarah said. "I figured something like this might happen. Her boyfriend is visiting."

Belinda suddenly burst into the rec room. Her broad face was red with anger, and her chest was puffing.

"Can you believe that guy?" she asked, waving her arms around. "He just proposed to me!"

"That doesn't sound too bad," said Jack in a soft voice to himself.

"Who are you?" Belinda asked angrily.

He stared at her for a split second and said, "You can call me Jack."

"Well, Jack, I wouldn't marry him for nothing," Belinda said. "He thinks I'll marry him because I'm pregnant. He's not even the father."

Jack looked at Belinda quizzically, but he didn't dare ask who the father was. He'd said enough on his first day in the ward.

Sarah interrupted. "Do you mind, Belinda? We're trying to play," she said.

"Some friend you are, Ms. Whore. Fuck you and your boyfriend," said Belinda as she turned and stalked out.

Sarah glared at Belinda's back, but she held her tongue.

She nodded to Jack. "It's your turn."

"What was all that about?" he asked.

"I'll tell you later. Let's finish the game."

The old lady continued to stare at Jack. She didn't seem disturbed by the commotion. She looked mesmerized.

Jack noticed her staring and then looked around the room. Besides the kids, who appeared to be average juvenile delinquents, the people quietly sitting in chairs or slowly walking around the room seemed severely depressed and listless.

A middle-aged man sat still and upright in his chair, staring at the floor with a blank expression. His short black hair jutted out from his scalp like he had been hit by lightning or frightened by a ghost.

"Do you mind shooting?" Sarah said.

Jack's eyes moved back to the pool table. As he began lining up a difficult rail shot, he realized he was among some very sick people. Then he heard it.

"Help... Help... Help... Help..." The cry was faint yet clear.

Jack raised his head, straightened his backbone, and spun around to the sound.

"Help... Help..." said the old lady, staring at Jack and calling out in an ever-louder voice.

Jack pointed to the old woman and said excitedly to Sarah, "She needs something."

"Don't bother with her. She's always doing that, especially when new people are around. She wants attention. The orderlies will deal with her later," Sarah explained.

The old woman continued to stare at Jack and ask for help. He felt a little uncomfortable ignoring her calls.

"Please. Continue," said Sarah, motioning toward the table.

Jack took a deep breath and tried to tune out the sounds. Down the hall, he could hear Belinda screaming that she didn't want to take her meds. Everything seemed to be going wrong, and it wasn't very clear to him why. He wished he could remember things, but thinking about the past made his head hurt.

So, he looked at Sarah, who was staring at him demandingly, and wondered about her. Who was this good-looking, impatient girl? What was she doing here?

The bigger question, of course, was what Jack was doing here. He had spent most of yesterday dwelling on himself, wondering who he had been before he awoke in the hospital with a group of strangers around him. He could remember yesterday, but he couldn't remember the day before. Maybe thinking about someone else, like Sarah, would help him remember. But what was there to remember?

Chapter 22
Talk with Sarah

Wednesday night, July 16, 1980

Jack lay his head on a pile of three pillows stacked on his bed and stared out the hospital window. It was a little after 9 p.m., and the floor was quiet. Most of the others had gone to bed. His two teenage roommates were in the television room. He could hear the drone of programmed laughter from down the hall.

His first full day on the floor was better than he'd expected. After resting quietly for two days, with only brief interruptions from the medical staff and his roommates, he'd dreaded going to the breakfast room. But the doctor said it was time.

There were plenty of characters at the hospital, some with severe mental problems that were probably incurable. Those were the people Jack instinctively avoided. They acted strangely, but at least they knew—or some of them knew—their past, Jack thought.

After trying very hard to remember the people who visited him each day and said they were his family, he decided to stop trying. He was just tired, and his head still hurt.

A dull pain radiated across his forehead. Nurses had removed the bandage around his skull that afternoon, but his head still throbbed when he moved it too quickly or bent over to put on his slippers.

But what bothered him more than the pain was the strange, lingering sense that he should be doing something else—something important.

When his family visited, he asked them for information, hoping something might jog his memory. They told him his name was Jack Kendall and that he was a newspaper reporter. He asked them what had happened to him and why he was in the hospital. It was strange that they said it was too early to talk about how or why he had been injured. Maybe tomorrow, they said, when he was stronger.

Their little evasions only made him more anxious. The doctor said he had suffered a severe concussion from a head injury and a drug overdose. But with his diagnosis of post-traumatic amnesia, no one could tell him when he'd regain his memory.

His doctor thought staying in the hospital for a few days would be a good idea. X-rays showed his brain was still abnormally swollen, and he had stitches at the back of his head where they said he had fallen or possibly been hit with something heavy. He had no memory of anything.

Everything was confusing. For one, why was he in a mental health unit? His doctor thought it would be more "therapeutic" for him than lying in a general or medical-surgical unit. He would get more attention here. His doctor was right about that.

He wanted to leave the hospital, but to go where? Maybe if he returned to where he lived, he'd begin to remember things.

Or maybe he was nuts like the rest of the people here; perhaps he had spent his whole life moving in and out of loony bins, alternating between broken and functional periods. Maybe he was crazy and just "thought" he was normal. He had no clue.

But then there was Sarah.

Sarah. She was the only person he could relate to and liked right now, but he didn't know why. That was strange. He could have met hundreds of people before last Thursday morning when he was admitted to the hospital. But now, he only knew a handful. Still, he didn't feel alone when he was talking with Sarah. Admittedly, he was excited when he was with her.

Sarah reminded him of somebody. Somebody he knew once. Somebody very close. He felt it, but he couldn't remember.

At 22, Sarah was mature and knowledgeable beyond her years. There was no doubt she stood out here. Maybe Sarah could help him sort out things.

Jack decided he'd take a stroll to her room.

He was told not to enter the women's rooms, but thought he'd do it anyway. What could they do? Kick him out? He didn't care. He slid out of bed and put on his robe and slippers.

Although it was summer outside, the air conditioning made the inside air feel like winter. Jack shivered as he walked down the brightly lit hall at a brisk pace. The cold air cut through his thin, blue hospital garments. He hoped there weren't any inquisitive nurses around.

He stopped at Sarah's slightly ajar door and listened. It was quiet. Jack knocked softly, and then he heard Sarah's voice.

"Who is it?" she asked with some trace of irritation.

Jack hesitated. Maybe he'd better go back to his room.

In a whisper, he said, "It's Jack. Can I come in?"

"Jack? Wait a minute," Sarah said, putting down her book and removing her glasses. She felt odd because she'd almost expected him. "All right, come in. Be quiet."

Jack entered the room, which was dark except for the corner of Sarah's bed illuminated by her reading light. Sarah's roommate, a woman in her mid-30s suffering from a somewhat volatile episode of manic depression, had fallen asleep.

"You shouldn't be here; there are rules to follow," Sarah said in mock fright.

"I won't be caught," Jack said.

"No? You can make yourself invisible if someone comes in? And if Margaret wakes up, she might have a fit," Sarah said. "She was in one of those moods where they had to give her meds."

"Let's go to the rec room, then."

"It's past nine; it's closed," Sarah said coldly. "Everything is off-limits now except the bathroom and the television room."

"That's not sociable," Jack joked.

"Sociable?" she asked. "Where do you think you are? The Ritz-Carlton?"

"What if we sit in the corner over here and pull the drapes so Margaret won't see us if she wakes up," Jack suggested. "We'll be quiet."

"What do you want, anyway?"

"I just want to talk, that's all. I can't sleep. I've been cooped up here for the only two days I can remember, and I'm getting a little antsy."

"I don't have anything to say right now," Sarah said. "It's

late, and I'm tired. Why don't you wait for the group tomorrow? Go get some sleep."

Her relaxed attitude took Jack aback. She was dismissing him. She was blunt, direct, and painfully honest about her emotions. Her reaction both repelled and attracted him. He didn't know why. Everything seemed difficult to understand.

"I was just wondering about Belinda and what happened with her this morning," said Jack, struggling for something to start a conversation. "What's her problem?"

"You couldn't sleep because of Belinda? Right," Sarah said with another mock laugh.

"All right. All right," Jack admitted. "I wanted to see you. But I'd still like to know about Belinda, since there are very few people I seem to know right now. You were there. You heard what she said about us. What do you know about her? Why would she say all that?"

A quick smile crossed Sarah's lips, then vanished. Then she looked at Jack with a knowing expression. "I'm sure I don't know. I'm not her doctor."

"Yes, but you seem to know something about her," Jack pressed. "You know a little about everybody here."

Sarah frowned. "You have to understand that she is like many kids here. She is just messed up. She doesn't get the right attention, and she gets too much of it. This is all a game to her, and she likes being loud. It makes her feel important."

Jack thought about that for a second and realized Sarah was smart, but she was evasive. He made a mental note about that trait. She didn't seem to want to tackle issues or questions straight on. He wondered if she was doing that to hide something.

"All right," Jack said, pausing a second before continuing.

"I give up. What does that mean?"

"Her stepdad raped her. Her baby's father is her stepdad. Her boyfriend doesn't know that. Is that what you wanted to know?" Sarah asked.

"Oh, Jesus," Jack whispered. "No wonder she yelled at me. I should know better than to say things to people I don't know."

"Uh-huh," Sarah agreed knowingly.

"Sometimes Belinda seems okay, almost sweet and friendly. Then, other times, she's out of control, like a raving lunatic," Jack said.

"She's on meds. They give her a mouthful every day," Sarah explained. "She's crazy like the rest of us here. Meds control lots of kids. It's easier for the staff to handle everybody that way."

"Are you on any meds?" Jack asked.

"Yeah, I take some to calm me down," she said, looking down.

"They wanted to give me some medicine, but I told them I didn't want anything but aspirin to stop this damn headache," he said.

Sarah didn't say anything and looked at her book on the table. There was an awkward moment of silence. Jack wondered if he should tell Sarah that he had lost his memory.

Finally, Jack said, "You're not curious why I'm here?"

"Not especially. Everybody has a reason. You're going to group tomorrow, aren't you?"

"I suppose so. They asked me, but I am not sure I will go. I don't have anything to say."

"You should. Then you'll get plenty of opportunities to tell your story."

"I don't know my story."

"Oh?"

"What I mean is I can't remember," Jack said sadly.

"Is that why you had that bandage on your head? Do you have amnesia or something?" Sarah said.

"That's what they think. They call it post-traumatic amnesia. I don't know if it's temporary or what. I also had a pretty bad concussion, and I was in a coma for several days," Jack recounted. "They said after the brain swelling goes down, I might start remembering things more clearly. My memory could come back in several days or weeks."

"Does it bother you that you can't remember?" Sarah asked. She appeared more interested after the admission that he couldn't remember his past. As she waited for Jack to respond, Sarah thought about her own past and shuddered. It was something she'd like to forget.

"I have been told who I am, what I am, but they haven't told me much about my accident," Jack said. "My mother is quite concerned that I am not told too quickly. She wants my memory to come back naturally. I don't know what happened to me, but it must be bad."

Sarah didn't respond. She just looked at Jack.

He smiled and wondered about her past. "Do you mind if I ask why you are here?"

"No." She didn't respond further. She put on her glasses and picked up her book. A few seconds passed. Jack didn't know what to say.

"Does 'no' mean you don't mind talking about it, or does 'no' mean you don't want to tell me?" Jack finally asked.

Sarah looked out the window into the night. She started to say something, then stopped herself.

"If you don't want to discuss it, I understand. We barely

know each other. But I don't know how much time we have." Jack cringed at that last remark. It was way too dramatic. Sarah would rip it apart, he thought.

She pulled back her black hair that hung over her left shoulder. Looking at Jack out of the corner of her eye, she motioned for Jack to sit in the chair by the table.

"You think you have problems? You don't even know what they are. You don't want to hear about mine," said Sarah. She hesitated, then added unexpectedly, "I don't know why, but I'd like us to be friends."

Jack nodded and then lowered his head in silence. Neither said anything.

"All right then. What do you want to know?" Sarah asked.

"How long have you been here?"

"About two weeks this time."

"This time? How many times have you been here?" Jack asked.

"Twice," she said. "Since I'm a voluntary, I can leave anytime I want."

"Oh," said Jack. "Why are you here?"

Sarah looked out the window again and said nothing. Jack wanted to know, but he held off until she became more comfortable talking to him.

"I'll be here until I remember something," he said. "When do you leave?"

"Probably next week," she said. "It depends on whether my mother joins my dad in North Carolina. He left about two months ago to open a new office. My mom didn't want him to go, but he did. My mom misses him, so she'll probably want to leave and be with him."

"Are they very close?"

"They love each other, if that's what you mean," Sarah said in a defensive voice.

Knowing he had touched on a sensitive topic, Jack changed the subject. "Were you born in Sarasota?" he asked.

"It's my hometown, and I don't want to leave it," Sarah said firmly. "But my dad moved, and I want to be with him too."

Jack nodded. "I think it's my hometown too. The doctor told me I was born at this hospital 30 years ago."

"Why are you here?" Sarah asked.

"I don't remember," Jack said. "All I know is that I was found at my home, nearly unconscious, with a variety of drugs in my system. My mother brought me to the hospital."

"You overdosed."

"Yeah, I suppose I was pretty stupid, taking all those drugs," Jack said. "They keep on asking me why I took so many. The funny part is that I don't remember any of it. I don't know why I did it. But they say they found a note by my bed."

"A suicide note," Sarah said in a low voice.

"That's what they said," Jack replied. "They won't let me out until I remember everything and confess my sins. Maybe I took the drugs, passed out, and hit my head on a table or something—a big crime. I'm not sure what they think I will do. Maybe kill myself. The funny thing is that I can't think of any reason to kill myself. But then again, I don't know anything about myself."

Sarah interrupted. "I tried to commit suicide. I was stupid, foolish, and naive."

"I don't think you're stupid," Jack said. "You must have had a reason to feel bad."

"It wasn't a good one," Sarah said. "It was over some guy, I thought... Well, I thought he and I... Well, like I said. It was stupid. It was something that didn't work out."

"Have you seen him since?" Jack asked.

"No, and I never want to see him again," she said. "If I do, I'll..."

"You'll do what?"

"Nothing."

"Well, why did you come back the second time?"

"Things just didn't work out on the outside," Sarah explained. "I like it in here. I'm a little afraid of staying outside with my dad gone. I'm not totally well yet."

"No need to rush these things," Jack agreed. "I wanted to leave the first day here, but I was too weak. Now, I realize I need to stay in this place until I get stronger and figure out who I am."

"Do you think you have a drug problem?"

"I hope not. Why do you ask?"

"Because when they brought you in, the word was that you had overdosed and were zoned out for five days," Sarah said.

"That's true. I was in a coma for five days. So, honestly, I don't know if I am a drug addict or not," Jack said.

"You don't remember doing drugs?" Sarah asked incredulously.

"I don't remember anything," Jack said. "All I remember is the last few seconds before I passed out."

"Why don't you tell me about it?" she asked. "Maybe you'll remember something. It will help you get started in group tomorrow. What's the last thing you remember?"

Jack closed his eyes and thought deeply for a few seconds. A vision began to form in his mind. It was strange—he had been asked by a doctor and a nurse before, but he couldn't recall any last thoughts. Now, with Sarah, he was beginning to see something clearly.

"I'm outside, standing. I'm hit on the head. Everything is going black," Jack said. "I remember darkness. Wait…I see a light. I hear someone talking. I can't remember much, Sarah."

"Be calm. Relax. Think," she said.

"I remember waking up, then passing out again. I lost track of time. I felt heat waves passing over my face and up and down my body. My arms became heavy. I couldn't move.

"Then I felt like I was being lifted into the air. It was cool. I suddenly felt happy and satisfied. The heat passed. I heard a voice calling me. It was soft, sweet, almost angelic. I remember waking up and the nurse telling me I was at the hospital."

Jack stopped. It was strange how he remembered all of that. Maybe it was this Looney Tunes place he was staying at. He wondered if he was exaggerating it for Sarah.

"That's all I remember."

"That's something," Sarah said. "Anything else? It may be coming back."

"The doctors told me I was in a coma for days. They had me on IVs. I wasn't dead, although it probably was pretty close," Jack said.

Sarah put her book back on the table, got out of bed, and walked over to Jack. She took his wrist and led him to her door. Gazing up at him with her dark green eyes, she lifted herself on the balls of her feet and kissed him on his lips.

"I'll see you in the morning," she said. "Go get some sleep. You'll need it tomorrow."

Jack smiled at her, nodded, closed Sarah's door, and walked across the hall to his room. He was getting sleepy. As he put his head down on his pillow, he wondered if he would have another one of those mysterious dreams about the mountain, the strange old town, and the soldiers. He thought about the dream and Sarah as he fell into a deep sleep. It had been a long day.

Chapter 23
Childhood Memories Return

Thursday, July 17, 1980

Jack's second day started at 6:30 a.m. It was the first time since he had been at the hospital that his head didn't ache. As he lay on his bed, eyes closed, memories from long ago flashed across his mind.

He was five years old, sitting on a wooden floor before a big record player, listening to records by Elvis Presley and Patsy Cline. He was seven years old and riding a bike—a red bike. He was eight years old, playing hide-and-seek in a bamboo jungle. He was nine years old, taking a long car trip with his family, sitting in the front seat between his parents; he couldn't stop talking and laughing about what he saw as they drove along. He was ten years old on a train with other kids going to summer camp in the North Carolina mountains; he was playing cards, listening to and telling funny stories, and laughing, always laughing.

He was remembering bits and pieces of his younger years. Distant memories, childhood memories. He tried to recall more, but that was all.

Still, it was exciting for him to remember anything. He wanted to tell somebody about it. Sarah. He went to her room. She was still asleep. He wanted to talk with her, but didn't want to wake her.

As he stood there by the door, his stomach grumbled. He felt satisfied for the first time in a long time and had an appetite. He wondered if the breakfast room was open. It was nearly 7 a.m. He walked down the hall and saw the food cart being wheeled in.

He was starting to feel normal. He drank some coffee and finished nearly two trays of bacon and eggs, then walked back to Sarah's room. She wasn't there. Maybe she was showering.

Jack returned to his room, shaved, and cleaned up for the morning group therapy meeting at 8 a.m. He was ready for it today.

When he arrived 20 minutes later, Sarah was already there. He was in a good mood and planned to share some childhood memories with her. But there were people in the room he didn't know. He decided to tell her about his memories later, in private.

"Hi, Sarah," said Jack, smiling at her as he sat down.

She nodded but remained silent. Everyone was quiet.

Suddenly, Jack became nervous. It was his first session, and Sarah had warned him that he would be asked to introduce himself and explain why he was there.

Sally, a nurse and group leader, entered the room and wasted no time loosening the somber mood.

"Good morning, everyone. We have a newcomer to our group. Jack, would you like to start things off?"

Jack hadn't prepared to say anything. He glanced around the room, looked at the others, cleared his throat, and muttered: "I'm not ready. Maybe someone else should start."

"No, you can do it," Sally said.

"How is this done? What do you want me to say?"

"Tell everybody who you are or anything you want," said Sally.

Jack looked at Sarah, who nodded approvingly.

"Okay. Well, I was going to tell Sarah this later, but I suppose I might as well talk about it now," Jack said.

"First, as Sarah and Sally know, I came to the hospital to recover from an accident. I can't remember anything. My doctor said I had a head injury that caused me to lose my memory. He called it post-traumatic amnesia.

"This morning, when I woke up, I remembered little things from when I was younger. I've had a headache for days, but I feel better today," he said positively.

"But, as I was walking here, I remembered some other things. While I still don't remember much about myself, I recalled a dream I had when I woke up in the hospital after being in a coma for five days. I saw myself with a group of soldiers walking toward a mountain. I'm not sure what it means. Maybe I should talk about this while it is coming back?"

He looked at Sally, and she nodded. "What happened?" she asked.

Jack closed his eyes and relaxed, and thoughts began to rush through his mind. "I'm climbing a tall mountain. The trail is very rocky. I have to be careful not to slip. The air is cool and misty.

"I'm part of some military unit. We march up a mountain together through the clouds until we reach a beautiful, grass-covered field. It's quiet, very peaceful. I feel safe and relaxed.

"I look up into the dark sky, and a small, soft light appears. The sky is suddenly dotted with yellow, red, orange and white stars. We stand there and gaze at the sky. It's very colorful.

"After a few seconds, the stars disappear, and we see a man dressed in a white gown floating in midair. He descends slowly, covered in a soft light," said Jack, stopping for a second to look around at everyone. They were watching very closely.

He closed his eyes again as more images flashed into his mind. "This man in a white gown begins to speak. 'You are brave men,' he said. 'We have decided. Some of you will go to another place. You will not return to your family or friends. Yet you will be with them. Do not be afraid. A ship is coming for you.'"

"'A ship?' I ask the floating man. 'Where are we going?'"

"'You will stay,' he said as the ship appeared.

"I say, 'Stay? What do you mean? Where are you going? Don't leave me here.'

"But the man dressed in white said nothing.

"I say, 'Wait!' He doesn't respond.

"There is a flash of bright light. I am blinded for a second. Then I find myself alone on the field. The ship is gone, and so are the man and my fellow soldiers.

"Then I see a girl far away. She is dressed in white, just like the man. She walks toward me. Without speaking, she leads me down the mountain."

Jack stopped talking. The room fell silent. No one in the

therapy group filled the space. He sat motionless with his eyes closed, retreating inward, aware of a sudden heaviness he couldn't explain. When he opened his eyes, he felt Sarah's gaze on him—steady, searching—and he knew she sensed that something had shifted inside him.

Suddenly, his eyes opened wide. More childhood memories began to surface. He smiled. Everyone stayed silent, dumbfounded by what was happening.

Sarah began to sniffle, and Jack watched as Sally slipped an arm around her shoulders. He understood the conflict playing out in Sarah's expression. Part of her was relieved that he had finally talked about what he was feeling, just as she had urged him to do. But beneath that relief was fear. Jack could see it clearly now—she was afraid his memory was coming back, afraid that once he remembered who he was and where he came from, he would no longer need her, or even want her as a friend.

Jack remained silent, looking straight ahead. He started to shake a little. Sally waited. She didn't want to interrupt whatever was happening to him, but she was concerned.

Jack kept remembering things. He trembled a little more. Something was happening to his memory. He was on the verge.

"Jack? Are you all right?" asked Sally, breaking the stillness.

He nodded. Was he having another seizure?

"Just relax," the nurse instructed. "The dream is helping unlock your mind. Don't try to force anything. Take your time."

Jack's back tightened as Sally spoke, and he sat stiffly upright in his chair. His eyes brightened again, and his mind began to clear. Sarah became anxious as she watched Jack's face change.

It was happening, just as the doctor predicted.

"Becky," he said in a soft voice, not knowing quite exactly what he meant.

Sarah gasped. She put her hand over her mouth, and Sally held her tighter.

"Becky," Jack said again, this time a little louder. His memory began to process a picture of her: a red-haired girl with sparkling eyes and a playful grin.

Jack wasn't aware of anyone else in the room now. Images of Becky flashed through his mind. Her light blue eyes. Her thick red hair. She had a wide mouth, full lips, and a strong chin. Walking in the rain. Key West. Talking. Becky. He remembered her. He was in love with her. He remembered their wedding. They had been together for five years.

Thoughts rushed through Jack's mind. What felt like minutes to Jack was mere seconds to the people in the group. There was a murmur among them.

"Please, quiet; let Jack process this," Sally said.

Jack was thinking of Becky. He was packing to go with Becky to Jamaica. Or was that last summer? She wanted to go last summer. Remember? You wanted to wait another year. Why? Ah, yes, you tried to save a little more money.

"Becky," Jack said a third time.

"Jack. Relax. Everything is all right," Sally said.

He continued to stare ahead. Memories flooded his mind. He remembered following a man in a white suit. He remembered hearing a noise. He remembered being hit on the back of the head. He remembered waking up in the hospital.

Becky. He remembered Becky. And through Becky, Jack found himself.

But something was wrong. She was missing. He was searching for her. He began to feel faint. Gasping for breath, he shook uncontrollably. Black-and-white dots covered his vision. He tried to stand up.

"Becky!" he shouted one last time as he lost his balance and collapsed. As he slid downward, two of the girls in the group broke his fall.

Sarah began to sob as she saw Jack lying unconscious on the floor, trembling slightly. Sally rushed into the hall to call for help. Sarah was taken to her room and given a sedative by a nurse. Two orderlies carried Jack to his bed, and a doctor was summoned.

Chapter 24
Jack Remembers Everything

Later Thursday, July 17, 1980

Jack awoke, opened his eyes, and discovered his head was clear. He smiled because he recollected what had happened to him in the group therapy meeting.

He was Jack Kendall, just as his family had told him.

His second thought was of Becky.

"Nurse," he said to the young woman sitting by his bed. "Can you help me?"

"Mr. Kendall. Thank goodness you are awake. Everyone was so worried. You had another seizure."

"I feel better now."

"Let me go get the doctor."

"It's okay. Tell him I have my memory back. And please call my family. Tell them I'm ready to go home."

The nurse nodded, then turned to go.

"Wait! Before you go…tell me, where's Sarah?"

"She's probably in her room. It's four thirty, almost dinner time," the nurse said.

"Can you ask her to come in?"

"I really should get the doctor, but I suppose it won't hurt. I know you two are close," she said with a kind smile.

The nurse walked down the hall and found Sarah in the rec room. A few minutes later, she slowly poked around the door and looked in.

"Do you want to see me?" Sarah asked weakly. She had recovered somewhat from the morning's unusual group session.

"Please come in," Jack said in a happy, welcoming voice. "I apologize for what happened. I couldn't help myself. I didn't know my memory would come back like that."

Sarah shrugged and looked quickly at him, then turned away.

"I just wanted to thank you. I don't think I could have recovered without your help," Jack said.

"Well, I'm sure I didn't do anything," Sarah objected.

"You did more than you know."

"No," she said. "Don't give me credit for that."

"I only want to thank you."

Sarah didn't respond. Jack could see she was still shaken by the morning's events, her silence heavier than words. He sensed her fear—not just about what had happened, but about what was coming next. He would be leaving soon, and whatever fragile bond had formed between them was ending.

He realized she had liked him better when he didn't know who he was. Back then, he had felt harmless to her, anchored in the same uncertainty. As his memory returned and he began to sound like himself again, he noticed a shift in her eyes. To Sarah, his recovery meant abandonment, another man walking away, just like the others who had left her before.

"There's something else I want you to know," Jack said.

Sarah glanced at him quickly, then turned away as if she didn't want to listen.

"I thought about these dreams I've had the last couple of months. Only minutes ago, I woke up from another."

"Oh," mumbled Sarah, trying to seem disinterested.

"I want you to hear it."

"Maybe you ought to tell your doctor about it," Sarah said. "I'm surely not qualified."

Jack shook his head. "Sarah, just listen."

"All right, go ahead, tell me," Sarah replied. She admitted to herself that she was somewhat curious. Since Jack was leaving, she didn't have the foggiest idea.

He took a deep breath and began.

"One night, I dreamt I was walking with a group of eight other soldiers through a city that seemed to be controlled by some military force. Everyone was dressed in battle gear. We were marching as a unit. The leader commanded us to turn right and left, and we obeyed. We were very well-trained and professional. But there was a noise in my bedroom, and I awoke. I saw Becky walk to the bathroom and said, 'Are you all right?' Becky said, 'Yes, go back to sleep.' I remember it all perfectly clearly. I went back to sleep, but I didn't finish the dream. The next day, at work, a guy committed suicide in front of me. When I got home, Becky was gone."

"Becky?" Sarah asked.

"Becky," Jack replied, "is my wife. She and I have been

separated."

"Doesn't she love you?"

"I thought so. It isn't very easy. We had some arguments. I haven't been able to talk with her since she left," Jack said.

"Oh." Sarah had heard enough about Becky. "What did you say about someone committing suicide?"

"I witnessed a man kill himself while I was covering a story," Jack explained.

"Oh." Sarah nodded and waited patiently for the rest.

"We were marching through the city and toward a mountain. When we reached the mountain's base, the leader stood on a big rock and spoke to us.

"'Warriors,' the leader said. 'We are going on a mission. Not all of you are coming back alive.'

"As soon as he said that, I awoke in a cold sweat, breathing deeply. Now, I just had a third dream."

"Another like the others?" asked Sarah. She was trying very hard to understand him, for reasons she didn't know.

"Yes. I was marching with the platoon, just as in the previous two dreams. The leader took us outside the city to the mountain, just as before. He gave a speech about some of us not returning home alive. We marched up the hill and through the clouds."

"This is the new part of the dream. There was a battle above the clouds. I was separated from my unit. In the distance, I saw a ship descending from the heavens. I ran to reach it, but it was too late. The ship rose into a bright light. I was alone. I decided to try to make it down the mountain on my own. I felt like everyone had died, and I was the only survivor."

Jack paused. "Then a girl dressed in white appeared," he said. "She led me down the mountain and into the city. When

I woke, I was safe."

Sarah stood by the door in silence. She looked at Jack with a puzzled expression.

"Don't you see?" Jack asked.

"See what?" Sarah exclaimed. "Why do you constantly talk in riddles?"

"Why am I telling you this? You could be that girl who led me down the mountain."

Sarah looked around in panic. She couldn't accept it.

"No," she said, turning her back to him. She started to feel the kind of pressure in her chest that signaled an anxiety attack. She couldn't stand someone thinking about her that way; she didn't want that responsibility. She didn't do anything. She didn't deserve that.

"Oh, Sarah," Jack said gently. "I don't mean to upset you, but you helped me more than you know. I don't think I would have regained my memory without you. You encouraged me to finish the dream that brought back my memory. I fought that battle on the mountain. It's over. I know who I am."

The pressure in her chest kept building. She couldn't take it. She turned around and screamed at Jack: "No! It's not true! I am not the girl on the mountain. I wouldn't be her or do that!" She turned and ran out of the room and down the hall.

"Sarah, come back! I'm sorry!" Jack shouted as she ran out of the room. Then he said softly to himself, "You were that girl."

But Sarah was already in her room. She scrambled into her bed, pulled the covers over her head, and began to cry.

A nurse heard the commotion and ran into Sarah's room. She was still crying when another nurse entered and gave her a pill to help calm her.

Jack sat in his room, thinking. Maybe he shouldn't have told Sarah that story. She'd told him she had ups and downs and sometimes had anxiety attacks. But she'd seemed normal to him most of the time.

Maybe he just wanted the girl in white to be Sarah because he had come to know her and she had helped him remember who he was.

It probably wasn't Sarah anyway. After all, the dreams were of a girl with blonde hair, not dark hair like Sarah's, who had led him down the mountain. Besides, maybe those weren't the last of his mountain dreams. He didn't know.

The whole morning had been confusing. All these thoughts were flooding his mind. He didn't understand why he had these dreams—one after the other.

Poor Sarah, he thought. He now regretted laying it all on her. Hopefully, she would understand. Despite her problems, she seemed self-aware—a girl with great potential. She'll be all right. He hoped so, anyway.

But now that he had his memory back, his thoughts turned to Becky. He had been in the hospital for nearly a week and wondered if she was still missing.

Wait...he remembered seeing Becky's car at Michael LeCare's house right before someone hit him over the head. Someone had tried to kill him because he had gotten too close to Becky. Had she been in the house?

Strangely, he now remembered that Ed had told him he had checked out LeCare's house several times; it was empty, with no cars in the driveway. Why was Becky's car parked there? Someone must have put it there later, or it might have been someone else's house.

As soon as Jack left the hospital, he would return to that

house with Ed and his men to look again. He would also check with Bagley and Lt. Stevens about their investigation into the High Seas.

Maybe the whole case had been solved while he was in the hospital. He hoped his family would finally tell him what they knew.

As he walked to the nurse's station to ask them to call his family, he thought about Sarah again. He owed a lot to her. He realized his interest in her kept him going and helped him recover his memory.

He decided to talk to her one more time before he left the hospital, at least to say goodbye.

Chapter 25
Long-Awaited News

Thursday, 7 p.m., July 17, 1980

Jack, Ed, and Mrs. Laura Kendall were all smiles after the doctor told them Jack was well enough to leave the hospital.

"Jack, sorry about not telling you everything we knew right away," Ed said. "The doctor warned us not to bring you along too quickly, and Mom enforced his recommendation. I wasn't sure why those drugs were in you until I got the handwriting results back on the note."

"Note? Becky's note? You found something?" Jack asked.

"I don't think we should start this now," Mrs. Kendall said. "Jack is still recovering. You heard the doctor. Your brother has a higher risk of having more seizures because of his traumatic brain injury. He has to take it easy and come back for monthly checkups for the next year."

"Yes, but he did clear me, and I want to hear about the note," Jack insisted.

"Mom, I'm going to tell him. He's perfectly all right now," Ed said. "No, Jack, it wasn't Becky's note I'm talking about. It was the other one, the one Mom found next to your bed. It looked like a suicide note. It appeared authentic, but I didn't think so. I had it analyzed by a friend of mine in Tampa. It was forged, just as I thought. A good job, though."

Jack shook his head. "Those bastards."

"Jack, I was so scared. I didn't know what to think when I read that note," Mrs. Kendall said. "I found you at your apartment. You were so sick. After all you went through with that man killing himself in front of you and then Becky leaving, you were so distraught. I thought you were going to die. And then you couldn't remember anything because of the amnesia."

"That's all right, Mom. I understand. It's just not true," Jack said.

"I want to know who would want to do that and why," Ed snarled. "What were you doing that night you got attacked?"

"I was at Foley's, having a few drinks. I met a guy who said he used to work at the High Seas. I went to the restaurant to see if what he said was true."

"What was that?" Ed said.

"There was something about a coke lab at the restaurant. I thought I might see something I could use to find Becky. After I got there, I saw a guy I recognized from outside Charlie Tolbert's house the day he killed himself. I followed him to a house on South Siesta Key. Becky's car was there. I went for a closer look, and then I was ambushed," Jack recounted.

"You should have called me," Ed said.

"Yes, I didn't think of it. By the way," Jack said, "I want to take you there. I'm not sure whose house it is. There may be some clues we can pursue with the police."

"I have something to tell you about that later," Ed said. "But why would they try to kill you and make it look like a suicide? They went to a lot of trouble."

"I don't know—unless they thought I knew something about them. I'm going to find out," Jack replied determinedly.

"Do you know the name of the person you met at the bar?" Ed asked.

Jack flashed back to the instant he was hit on the head and chloroformed outside Michael's house. One of the men had said a name. Hold him, Steve.

"He said his name was Steve Ferro," Jack said. "I want you to find this asshole. He set me up, and he's probably still working for LeCare."

"I will, but you need to tell the police when you talk with them about the attack," Ed replied.

"Ferro said he worked at the High Seas. I am sure the police know about him. He said he has a record. I want him arrested. I'm sure he knows the name of the guy with the white suit," Jack said. "What about the note? Any fingerprints?"

"It was clean," Ed said. "I told the police everything. They know some things about that night but won't tell me. My source told me he believes the feds followed you from the High Seas to that house, but he isn't sure. With the feds involved, they're keeping information very tightly controlled."

"They followed me? Why didn't they help after I got knocked out?"

"My source said he believes the feds lost track of you after you walked to the house. I expect Bagley will call you about all this."

"I can't wait to hear Bagley explain that. But you told the police about the forged note?"

"Yes, they weren't too happy I withheld it, but they got over it," Ed said. He then motioned for Jack to sit down.

"Several things have happened since you've been in the hospital," Ed said.

Mrs. Kendall interrupted. "Ed, please! Not now. Let's get him home. You can talk tomorrow."

"Mom, I'm going to tell him everything," Ed replied. "Look at him; he's okay. He's got the old fire back."

Jack saw his mother shake her head, and he knew exactly why. She was afraid of the old fire in him—the one that flared whenever someone was being hurt or wronged. He'd lived with that fire his whole life. As a kid and into his teens, it had pulled him into more arguments and fights than he could count, usually in defense of smaller, weaker kids being bullied. His father had almost always been there afterward, steady and supportive, even when the trouble was messy.

That same instinct had followed him into adulthood. He'd felt it when he chose journalism over law, when exposing injustice mattered more than comfort or approval. Watching his mother now, Jack understood that she knew there was no stopping him or his brother from looking for Becky. When she finally sat in the soft chair and fixed her eyes on him, Jack felt the weight of her concern—and the certainty that his path, once again, was already set.

Ed turned grim. "The night you were attacked, Betty Tolbert was murdered, shot in the head. It was staged to look like a home invasion."

"What, Betty was killed? Why? What about her children?" Jack asked as he stood up.

"They were unharmed, but they must have heard the gunshots in the house and ran in to see her," Ed said. "My police friend told me they think it was related to the High Seas cocaine investigation. It seems you were right; Betty found out what her husband was doing, selling High Seas's cocaine, and wasn't happy about it."

Jack was stunned by the news. He paced around the room, trying to comprehend what was happening. His memory had returned, but some things were fuzzy.

"There is another important development," Ed added.

"Please, Ed, tell him later," Mrs. Kendall said.

"Let's get it over with. What else?" Jack asked.

"Becky is in Jamaica," Ed said.

"Becky? In Jamaica?" Jack exclaimed. He walked over to face Ed. "How do you know that?"

"Becky mailed six letters with postmarks from Jamaica. They all arrived together in one batch at your office at the newspaper yesterday. Wiseman called me," Ed explained.

"Did you read them?" Jack said. "Is she in danger?"

"No, I didn't. I was tempted, but I'd like you to read them as soon as possible."

"Is now too soon?" Jack said. "Let's go."

"Now, Jack, I'm not having you released from this hospital just so you can have another seizure or get hit on the head again by some gangster and wind up right back here," Mrs. Kendall interjected. "You are going to be careful. I don't care what Becky has gotten herself mixed up in. You let the police handle it."

"Mom, I don't want to argue with you, but there are things the police here can't do. Ed knows where Becky is. All we have to do is tell the police in Jamaica, and they'll take it from there," said Jack, knowing it wouldn't be that easy.

"But I don't want you to get involved in anything more than that," Mrs. Kendall insisted. "I know how you get when you're involved in something. You go gallivanting all over the place."

"Don't worry, Mom, Ed will keep me out of trouble," Jack said.

Mrs. Kendall rolled her eyes and said, "Bless them, Lord. I've done all I can."

Jack and Ed looked at each other and grinned. Their mom always said that after she had lost a debate with them.

It was like the two brothers were teenagers again, helping their late father, a medical malpractice and general practice lawyer, with an investigation. However, this time, it was more serious than doing amateur detective work to help their dad win a big case.

"I've just got to do one more thing before I leave," Jack said. "I'll be downstairs by the front entrance in 15 minutes."

*　*　*

Sarah was in the rec room, playing pool, when Jack walked in to talk with her.

"Do you have a minute?" he asked.

"I'm a little busy," she said, aiming at the six-ball.

"I'm leaving in a few minutes," Jack said.

Sarah looked up at him with a long face and sad eyes. She dropped her pool cue and walked over to the window, turning her back so he wouldn't see the tears running down her cheeks.

"I'm sorry. I've got to go," he said.

She stood there, motionless. He walked up behind her

and took her hand.

"Come with me," Jack said. She reluctantly walked down the hall with him and into her room.

"I've got to get back to my job. I'm a newspaper reporter," Jack said.

"I know. Sally told me about everything after you blacked out in the group yesterday," said Sarah, wiping away tears.

"She did? How?"

"Your brother, Ed, told her your story so she would be able to help you."

"That's okay. So, you knew more than I thought. I'm glad. But I've got to tell you something else. Do you want to hear it?" Jack asked, not knowing if she would break down further.

"I'm all right now," Sarah said. She sat down on the chair next to the bed.

"This whole thing started two weeks ago on a Monday morning," Jack calmly recounted as he sat on the edge of her bed. "I had been covering a story. A man had kidnapped two kids and was holding them hostage. He wanted to see me. So, I went in. Five minutes later, he committed suicide. I saw the whole damn thing."

Sarah didn't say anything. It was all overwhelming. She tried to keep her composure; she didn't like the feeling of losing control. This time, though, she was doing it for Jack.

"And then I get home, and Becky, my wife, is gone," Jack said.

"I said I know all that," Sarah said, her lip quivering.

"You know that I can't find her?"

Sarah's hands began to shake. "Jack, why are you dragging me into this?" she asked louder. "Becky is your wife. Why don't you go, find her, and leave me alone?"

"I'm sorry. Maybe I should go," Jack said and turned to leave. He took five steps toward the door before Sarah stopped him.

"I didn't think I would feel this way about you," she sobbed.

"I know. I felt close to you as well," said Jack, turning around.

"How long has it been?" Sarah asked in a soft voice, tears running down her face.

"What do you mean?"

"How long has it been since you've seen her?" she asked again, stronger this time, wiping away her tears.

"About a month."

Sarah turned away and said harshly, "Why do you need her now? After all she did to you? Why don't you forget about her!"

"I have a strong feeling she's in trouble and needs me. I can't turn my back on her. I've got to find her. Otherwise, I'll never know," Jack said.

"There are things you shouldn't know," Sarah said matter-of-factly. "I know about things like that."

"Maybe you're right, but I can't let it go until I know she is safe."

"Have you heard anything?"

"Not a word," Jack replied. "Ed has found some clues. We leave for Jamaica tomorrow."

"Jamaica?" said Sarah. "I know Jamaica. That's where the guy I knew... The guy that landed me here... That's where he lived."

"Is that right?" Jack asked. "You never told me about that guy. I didn't ask before, but do you mind telling me his name?"

"Robert Mackey," Sarah spat.

"Hmm, I never heard of him," Jack said. "How did you meet him?"

"In Sarasota. He owns a restaurant here. The High Seas."

Jack's mouth opened wide. "The High Seas? That's where Becky worked."

"Well, she must know Robert's friend, Michael LeCare," Sarah said.

Jack blinked. "Michael LeCare?" he said, gasping. "Why, he's Becky's boss. We thought LeCare owned the High Seas, but it's Robert Mackey?"

"Michael just works for him. They're close friends. I think they met in Jamaica," said Sarah, feeling better now that she was helping Jack. "Michael always goes to Robert's house in Jamaica for vacations."

"This is amazing," Jack said. "We've been trying to find out who owns the High Seas. And now you tell me it's Mackey? And you know both these guys?"

"Yes, that's right. It's a small town."

"Okay, so you say Mackey owns a house in Jamaica. Now everything's making sense..."

"What's making sense?"

Jack didn't respond. He knew Steve Ferro had set him up that night he was drugged, probably on orders from Michael LeCare or Robert Mackey.

"Jack, are you...are you all right?" Sarah asked.

"Hold on, Sarah, I remember something," Jack replied as he sat on the bed. "Let me think for a minute."

His memory was still a little fuzzy, especially about things right before he was drugged and knocked out.

He thought of Charlie Tolbert. He was selling cocaine for Michael LeCare and Robert Mackey through the High Seas restaurant.

Steve Ferro told him there was something wrong at the restaurant. He must have been telling him the truth.

But why would they attack him? There were two possibilities. One, they tried to kill him to prevent him from looking for Becky. Or two, they were worried that Charlie Tolbert had told him something before he died about their drug business. They wanted to get rid of him as a potential witness. The second possibility seemed more plausible, especially now that Betty had been killed. He thought Tolbert's wife knew something about the money and the cocaine.

Whichever the case, Robert or Michael had decided to kill him and make it look like a suicide to stop the police from suspecting Jack knew anything about the High Seas and Becky's whereabouts. They murdered Betty and staged it as a robbery to keep her quiet.

Finally, the facts fit. The past two weeks' events didn't seem that strange to Jack anymore.

"Sarah, Robert Mackey is involved in drug trafficking. Becky is in Jamaica with Mackey and LeCare. That's why nobody can find her," Jack finally said. "They tried to kill me to cover their tracks."

"It doesn't surprise me. Robert is ruthless and will do anything to anybody," Sarah said. Still, she was confused.

Mackey had promised to marry her nine months ago. Then, without warning, he'd dumped her. She had been devastated.

"I tried to kill myself over Robert," Sarah confessed. "I couldn't go on. He promised to take me to Jamaica with him and marry me. All of that. He lied to me. I've tried to put it all behind me."

Jack nodded, but he was thinking more about what to do next.

"He was my father's friend," Sarah continued. "I met him when he came over one time. He's 20 years older than I am. I should have known better. I know one thing for sure: Robert always had a lot of cocaine, and he is capable of pretty much anything."

Jack listened carefully. He had heard enough about Mackey and knew what to do.

"Sarah, Becky is in Jamaica and in serious trouble," Jack said. "I'm going there to find her."

"Jack," said Sarah, thinking quickly, "I'd like to go with you. I can help."

"Thanks. You've already been a big help, but I don't think it would be a good idea."

"I can help," she insisted firmly. "Remember, you said I led you down that mountain. I'm supposed to go with you. You need me. Besides, I know what Robert looks like and where he lives."

"That's true, but you can't just leave here," Jack said.

"I'm voluntary, remember? I can leave whenever I want."

"I don't know. I'd have to ask Ed about it."

"What are you afraid of?" Sarah shot back.

"Nothing. I don't think it would be safe for you," Jack said. "Why do you want to go?"

"I'd like to be with you, just in case something happens."

"Don't say things like that. Nothing is going to happen. We are going there to find Becky, period."

"Oh, sure. Do you know what you're saying?" Sarah asked. "Robert can be dangerous. When I was there, I overheard him talking with people. His house in the mountains is built like a fortress, with guards and guns surrounding it. You can't walk up, ring the doorbell, and ask for Becky. If they're drug dealers, as you say, they'll stop you and shoot you before you even get close."

"A mountain fortress? Is that what you said?" Jack asked as he flashed to his dreams about climbing a mountain and getting into a battle.

"You're going to need my help," Sarah insisted. "I'm going."

Jack was out of arguments. Besides, she may be able to help. She does know quite a bit about Robert Mackey and Michael LeCare.

"We leave at dawn," Jack said.

"Don't act cute," Sarah snapped.

"No, I'm serious," he replied.

"Just pick me up. I'll be ready."

Chapter 26
Becky's Letters

Thursday night, July 17, 1980

Jack arrived at the *Herald-Tribune* at 8 p.m. The newsroom was nearly deserted except for several copy editors and the night editor, Sam Parks, quietly working on a story at his computer.

As he approached his desk, Jack offered Sam a brief greeting. Sam was so preoccupied with editing a story that he didn't notice Jack arrive. Just as well. Jack wanted privacy while he read Becky's letters.

He sat in the green chair in front of his workstation and gazed with trepidation at the pile of mail. On top of the foot-high mound sat a packet of letters. He recognized the large, rather descriptive handwriting on the first envelope.

The ink was blue, the writer—Becky.

At the sight of her familiar signature, he longed to see, touch, and call her name.

He took a deep breath, sighed, and gazed aimlessly across the newsroom. The fluorescent light from the ceiling cast an artificial glow over the collection of tables, chairs, books, computers, and papers that littered a dozen workstations and desks scattered around the large, rectangular room. It was a familiar, calming sight.

But seeing the letters on the table gave Jack hope, joy, and worry. What would they tell him?

His instincts told him she was in trouble, but that relieved him. At least she was safe enough to mail letters. With that in mind, he decided to open them.

His hands tingled as he picked them up. He took a deep breath and slid the rubber band off. He counted six envelopes in total. He looked for postmarks, all stamped by the Jamaican post office on July 14, three days earlier.

He carefully tore open the tops of each envelope and spread the letters across his desk. The dates on them were all different. They began two days after Becky vanished on July 7—ten days ago—and ended on July 14.

With the October elections, political violence, and rumors of civil war, Becky knew this was the worst possible time to be in Jamaica. Why did she go at such a time?

With those troubling thoughts in mind, Jack picked up the first letter, dated July 9, and began reading.

> *"Jack,*
> *"I'm so sorry about how I left, but I knew you wouldn't let me go if I told you I needed some time away from us. It was hard for me to leave. I think, in time, you will understand. I hope it's soon.*
> *"I can't tell you much about why I left except to say I need my freedom right now. I haven't been happy with us for the last six months. I've told you*

some of the reasons. I don't think you listened.
"If you did, you didn't do anything about it.
"I'll try to write again.
"Don't try to follow me. You'll only get hurt.
"Believe me, Becky."

Jack recalled Becky's original goodbye note. It was similar. There was nothing new here except the warning. It was nice, though, to see her handwriting again. She always took an honest approach to her feelings.

Exhaling, he picked up the second letter. He noted the date of July 10, which she had written on the top.

"Jack,
"How are you? I'm fine! Things are going well
here. I'm living with some friends. Everybody
gets along really well. The island is as beautiful
as ever. I'm fine. Don't worry about me. I wish
I had more time to write, but I'm so busy. I just
wanted to let you know everything is all right.
"Becky."

Still nothing new. At least she isn't in trouble. Why is she writing? Jack wondered. The third letter, dated July 11, explained much more.

"Dear Jack,
"I've been thinking about you. I suppose you
deserve a more thorough explanation of why I left.
"I didn't want to tell you at first because I
wasn't sure how you'd take it, but I've thought

Well, at least she said it, Jack thought. She'd met somebody
else–Robert Mackey, a drug-dealing scumbag. He wondered

if she knew who this guy really was. He didn't believe it.

He stared at the letter and nodded. He knew what she said was true, but she completely ignored the main issue: her increasing cocaine use. They'd never agreed on that. But maybe he should have listened to her ideas more and found a better way to compromise.

But there were more letters. He quickly began reading the next one, dated July 12.

> *"Dear Jack,*
>
> *"I'd be lying if I told you things are going well. Something is happening in Jamaica. Worse than I ever believed. I can't tell you where I live, but it's in a remote area of the Blue Mountains. I haven't been to any towns since the third day I arrived, and I'm out of touch with the news. I've been overhearing talk, and it sounds like the political situation is getting worse.*
>
> *"Robert says not to worry, but I am worrying. From what I've seen and heard around here, he's involved in politics and other things I can't mention.*
>
> *"I've talked with Robert about going back to Florida. He says it can't be arranged right now because of politics. He's not telling the whole truth. I know it. I want to come home. I don't feel safe here anymore.*
>
> *"Love, Becky.*
>
> *"P.S. A friend here has been smuggling out these letters. I hope she doesn't get caught. She told*

*me a little about the political situation. I can't even
leave the property anymore. I feel like a prisoner."*

Jack's slowly building hope for Becky's safety now turned
to concern. His frustration was gone. He hated that he was so
far away from her. She needed him, just as he suspected all
along. He quickly began reading the following letter, dated
July 13.

> *"Dear Jack,*
>
> *"I miss you, baby. I miss you a lot. After
> everything I've told you, I didn't think I'd ever
> be repeating this. It's been rough on me since
> I've been gone. You wanted things your way,
> and now I see that maybe you were right.*
>
> *"If you change a little, I'll change a little.
> You know how afraid I am, but we could
> talk about having children. Maybe that will
> be enough so we can work things out.*
>
> *"You are the most giving person I've ever met,
> and I am so glad I found you. I can see that now
> I've been away. I didn't realize how good I had it
> with you. Maybe we can get back together. I don't
> think it's too late for us if you'll have me back. I
> need a little more time to work things out here."*
>
> *"Love, Becky.*
>
> *P.S. With all the hugs and
> kisses I've been missing."*

Jack was stunned by this last letter. He reread it. Had she
changed her mind? His frustration and impatience suddenly

returned. He wanted to see her at once. Then he began to read Becky's last letter, dated July 14.

> *"Dear Jack,*
>
> *"If Robert ever found out I was writing you, he'd kill me. I'm sure of it. He's changed since we got here last month. It's his business. Things have really gotten bad. Why, I don't know.*
>
> *"I'm terrified, honey. Can you come get me? Right away!*
>
> *"Robert won't listen. I've asked him many times to leave. I said, 'Please take me to the airport.' He doesn't listen. He is keeping me a prisoner. He thinks I know too much about his operation here and at the High Seas and says it's a dangerous time for me to leave.*
>
> *"I didn't know before, but he's heavily involved in the narcotics trade and with some right-wing group that's trying to prop up the Jamaican government. I think his drug smuggling helps pay for the political activities of a candidate or official he's bribed. I don't know many details. He doesn't tell me much of anything.*
>
> *"Please come get me. Right away! I'm not sure exactly where I am. We landed at Montego Bay airport at night and drove at least five hours into the mountains. I think it is past GoldenEye.*
>
> *"You'll have to find me through Michael LeCare. He was here for a while. Now he's gone. Maybe he went back to Florida.*
>
> *"Please hurry. I don't know how long*

*I can last here. I've heard gunshots in the
woods that surround the house. Robert says
people are just trying to scare us. It worked.
I'm scared and want to come home.*
　　"*Love, Becky.*"

After he read the last letter, Jack knew he was right about what he had to do. He was going to Jamaica to bring Becky home; no matter what it took, he would do it.

But he was also upset with her for going there. First, it was Jamaica, a place they loved to go, where they had many friends and many good memories. Second, the coming election had made the country extremely dangerous. Political violence, spurred on by the election and drug gangs vying for dominance, had led to the deaths of hundreds of men, women and children. Jack knew Becky was in grave danger, especially being there with notorious drug dealers like Robert Mackey and Michael LeCare.

Jack looked at the calendar. It was already July 17. Becky's last letter, in which she feared her life was in danger, was dated three days ago. He didn't have any time to waste.

He picked up the phone and called Ed, who answered on the first ring.

"I read the letters. Becky's in big trouble, just like I feared. We need to leave now."

"This sounds very serious, Jack," Ed replied. "It isn't going to be a vacation."

"I know," Jack said. "I have no choice. I must go. She needs me."

"It could be extremely dangerous," Ed warned again. "You know about all the unrest over there and the fact that this guy, Robert Mackey, if he is dealing drugs, probably has an army or a bunch of drug-crazy and dangerous Jamaicans to defend him. You know what's happening there."

"True, true. I'm not going to argue with you about the danger. But Becky's there. She's in the middle of this. She wants me to help her. I've got to go and find out if there's anything I can do."

Jack paused, then said calmly, "I can't just sit here and do nothing. Are you with me or not?"

"I know, I know. You know I'll go with you," Ed said. "All I'm saying is you can't expect a miracle—and we have to prepare for the worst."

"I'm not prepared for anything except to find Becky," Jack said.

"I'll do my best to help you," Ed promised. "Before we leave, I'll tell Lt. Stevens what you told me about Ferro, Becky's letters, and where we are going."

"Thanks. Find out if he can tell us anything more about the High Seas investigation or Becky's involvement. Oh, there's one more thing," Jack said, pausing. "Someone else is coming."

"Oh. Who's that? Superman, Batman, John Wayne?" Ed quipped.

"Jesus, Ed, quit joking around. Her name is Sarah. She knows all about the High Seas and Robert Mackey."

"Is Sarah that girl at the hospital?"

"Yes, but don't worry. She'll be all right."

"Oh, boy. I sure hope so, Jack. It's awfully risky, taking a girl along—especially one that's a little unstable."

"I'll keep an eye on her. And don't worry. We're going to have some extra help once we get to Jamaica," Jack said. "Meet me at the airport at 6 a.m. I'll have our tickets."

Jack called the airport and made reservations for three on the early-morning flight to Miami and Montego Bay. He called Sarah, who had checked out of the hospital and was at her father's home. She said she was packing and would be ready in the morning.

Then he called an old friend in Jamaica. He needed local help.

Chapter 27
Arriving in Jamaica

Friday, 11 a.m., July 18, 1980

Jack Kendall stepped through the cabin door of Air Jamaica Flight 799 and immediately felt a rush of warm, moist Caribbean air on his face. He paused at the top of the stairway to take in the familiar scene.

Ahead, across the asphalt tarmac, he saw Montego Bay's aging terminal. Behind it, he could make out the hazy outline of the Cockpit Country mountain range, which rose and stretched above MoBay, as locals called it. It was a beautiful and serene sight.

Jack had traveled to Jamaica several times with Becky, getting off at airports in Montego Bay or Kingston, depending on where they wanted to go or whom they wanted to visit.

While Kingston was the nation's most populous

metropolitan area, accounting for nearly half of the country's 2.1 million people, Montego Bay, with a smaller population of about 70,000, had the busiest airport.

Jack wondered why Becky had written about landing in MoBay. Landing at the Palisadoes Airport in Kingston made it quicker to reach the Blue Mountains. Maybe it was because the political situation in Kingston was growing tense.

Landing in MoBay meant a longer drive to where Jack was going: the GoldenEye estate, a celebrity getaway once owned by novelist Ian Fleming, the British author known as the creator of superspy James Bond.

GoldenEye, located on the north coast shores of Oracabessa Bay in St. Mary Parish, was a 90-minute drive east from MoBay. Jack and Becky had spent many happy long weekends there.

Jack's first trip to Jamaica was to interview record executives and rising performers in Jamaican music—Bob Marley, Jimmy Cliff, and Peter Tosh—when he was a young reporter covering Sunday feature stories on music, restaurants, theater, and films.

GoldenEye was also in the same parish as the home of his Jamaican artist friend, Raleigh Lakes, who lived in Broadgate, a small hamlet in the Blue Mountains' foothills.

Luckily, Raleigh also lived about 15 minutes from where Sarah said Robert's house was, near Castleton, just south of Broadgate, in a higher-elevation area of the western Blue Mountains. At least Jack wouldn't have to search the entire country to find Becky. If Sarah knew where Mackey lived, Becky would be waiting for him there. =

He was closer to finding her. He said a silent prayer that he wasn't too late. Then he made a vow. Robert Mackey: If Becky is harmed, even in the slightest, you will regret it.

As he walked down the stairway, Jack realized he was here not only to take Becky home. He also had a score to settle with Mackey.

He took a step, then paused halfway down the stairs. Could he get her out? He had to succeed. If he found Becky, one thing would take care of the other.

*   *   *

Ed and Sarah followed Jack across the tarmac and into the terminal. Ed hadn't said much during the three-hour trip from Sarasota to Miami to Montego. He worried about what Jack would do after Sarah pinpointed exactly where Becky was staying. He knew Jack would take the most direct action.

Sarah told Ed and Jack all about Mackey's security forces and the firepower they had. If Sarah was telling the truth, there wasn't much they could do to rescue Becky from Mackey's compound.

Ed suspected Jack had considered several options to get her out. He hoped to persuade Jack to report Becky as a kidnapping victim to the police and the U.S. Embassy, letting them handle it.

Putting pressure on the police and diplomatic staff was the only logical choice, Ed believed. The problem, and he knew it, was that Jack probably had something else in mind–something much more violent.

After a short wait at customs, they hurried into the main lobby to have their bags checked and their entry passes approved. A horde of cab drivers was yelling out offers for their services.

"Hey, mon, need a ride? Fifteen dollars to downtown. Me get

you there quick if ya don't have much time," said one cabbie.

The commotion seemed to jog Jack out of his thoughts of Becky and Mackey. He brushed past the man without looking. The cabbie said, "No problem." He joined the other cabbies, offering their services to the passengers now entering the terminal. It was a zoo. This was Jamaica, the land of opportunity.

"I've got to make a phone call and go to the currency exchange," Jack said. "Ed, why don't you find a halfway decent-looking cabbie? Someone not too wild."

Ed wondered who Jack was calling, but he nodded and went through the airport's front door to the cabbie stand. He had found cabs before in LA and New York. But this was different. The cabbies here were much more competitive. There was no traffic control. It was every man for himself.

*　*　*

Sarah followed Jack and gazed at the vibrant scene with awe, her heart thudding with a mix of wonder and fear. Although she told Jack she had visited Jamaica before, it was actually her first time traveling abroad. She had lied so she wouldn't lose the chance to see Robert again.

As they walked through the busy airport, the people they passed wore lively, Hawaiian-style shirts with leis around their necks. However, this place definitely wasn't Hawaii. The most common clothing appeared to be shorts.

The colorful clothing contrasted starkly with the building's condition. She had never seen such a decrepit airport, with dirty floors and paint crumbling from the walls. It was a poor, third-world country with terrible poverty.

But the people seemed open and friendly. *If only this were a vacation with Jack instead of a mission to find Becky.* It would do no good to dream. Then, her face hardened. *I'm here for one reason and one reason only: to make Robert Mackey pay for what he did to me.*

With that thought, Sarah said out loud, "Yes."

Jack overheard her and said, "Did you say something, Sarah?"

She realized her faux pas. "Oh, I was just wondering whether I packed my sneakers."

"Did you?"

"Yes, Jack."

Jack grinned at her and said, "Just stay close to me, Sarah. I don't want you getting picked up by any of these romantically inclined fellows."

Sarah blushed, but she moved closer to Jack and looked cautiously around.

*　*　*

They walked to the currency exchange. With the favorable three-to-one exchange rate, Jack exchanged several hundred American dollars for more than a thousand Jamaican dollars.

Jack found a phone and dialed a number. A woman answered on the second ring. "Hi, Telly. It's Jack. How are you? Is Raleigh home yet? No, we're all right. Just let him know we're here and staying at GoldenEye, the usual place. Oh, really? He sent a cab driver out to pick us up? His name is Freddie? Great, we'll look for him. Thanks. See you soon."

As he was hanging up, Ed approached. "Jack, I've got the cab. Ready?"

"Oh? I just talked with Telly. She said a cabbie was sent

to pick us up," Jack said.

"I know. His name is Freddie," Ed replied. "He found me, said Raleigh sent him."

"Okay, we're all set. Here, take a couple of these bags," Jack instructed.

"Thanks," Ed said sarcastically.

"The cabbie knows where we are going. GoldenEye in Oracabessa," Jack said.

"You've mentioned that place before. Isn't that the retreat that Ian Fleming owned?" Ed asked.

"Yep, that's the one. It's got some history. We've got a cottage with two rooms reserved. Sarah, you'll like this place even if you don't know who James Bond is. Fleming bought it after World War II and wrote Dr. No and 14 other 007 books here," Jack explained.

"I know who James Bond is, Jack," said Sarah.

"Good. Well, the new owner of GoldenEye knows me and gave us a good rate," Jack replied.

Ed laughed. "Well, it is during hurricane season, Jack. I think everybody gets a good rate at this time."

Sarah smiled. "I'm sure I'll like it. I like everything about this place. It's exciting. James Bond! Wow!"

Ed and Jack looked at one another and grinned. Jack thought she'd be all right if she maintained this positive attitude. Ed still wasn't sure whether bringing Sarah along was a good idea. He didn't like the fact that she had a history of instability. After all, she'd once tried to kill herself with sleeping pills.

But she did know what Robert Mackey looked like and where he lived. That would help if the police were uncooperative. Still, Ed didn't trust her. Jack wouldn't listen to Ed's concerns, so he closely watched her.

They walked out of the terminal and into the cab station. The Jamaican cab driver had the trunk open and rushed out to greet them when he spotted the Americans.

"Good evening, people. Welcome to Jamaica. Hope ya had a good flight. Let me help ya with dem bags. Just put dem down. I'll take care of dem, yuh see? You're here on vacation, right, mon? Raleigh told me to treat ya right. You good people. So just let me do all the work. You enjoy our beautiful Jamaican weather," said Freddie, a pleasant young fellow in his early 30s.

Ed and Sarah got into the back seat of the 1967 gold Chevy Impala. Jack watched the cabbie load the bags and close the trunk. The man looked back at Jack and motioned for him to get into the car.

"Let's get going. No time to waste," Jack said.

He looked at the mountains and climbed into the front seat. On the radio, reggae music played Jimmy Cliff's "Many Rivers to Cross." Freddie slid in, humming the song, and started the car.

"How long a drive is it to the hotel?" Jack asked.

"Maybe two, three hours at most. It won't take too long. If ya want, we can stop at a place along the way for refreshments," Freddie said as he turned onto Highway A1 East, heading for Oracabessa.

"You know the hotel?" Jack asked.

"Oh, sure, my sister just started working there," Freddie said. "Raleigh helped get her the job, in fact, mon."

"Oh, they're hiring? I know they've doubled the number of rooms since they started the expansion," Jack said. "Is it still the best?"

"Oh, ya, for sure, mon. My sister says," Freddie replied. "I've never stayed there. Can't afford it. Got too many little ones to feed, yuh see?"

"Have there been any problems in the area because of the elections that are coming up?" Jack asked.

"Wee! Mon. Hey. Things not good at all in the political establishment. Wish they would get dem over. It's the longest campaign in history, it seems. Just stay along the beach and near the hotels, and ya won't have no worry. No problem."

From the backseat, Ed asked, "Is it as bad as we've heard in the States?"

"In Kingston, ya. Montego, ya. Other places, not so bad. You have to be careful not to go in the wrong place, dig?" Freddie said. "There have been a few problems, but dey don't involve Americans, just Jamaicans, especially those who vote or ask too many questions.

"It's sad, mon, the common people just want to live and be free, yuh see? Some have seen what has happened to the country in the past few years and are asking questions. But if ya ask too many questions or ask for too much change, bang, bang, you find yourself dead. It's hard to say who's right or wrong. But ya people can enjoy the beach, maybe take a ride in the mountains during the day, and ya be okay. No problem. Just enjoy the island and leave the politics to us."

"That's what we're here for," Jack said. "Might want to do a little rum drinking, too."

"Say, do you need anything else, mon?"

"What do you mean?" Jack inquired.

"Ganja, you know, herb?" Freddie replied. "It's good smoke."

Jack looked back at Ed, who smiled and shook his head.

"No, thanks, Freddie. We don't want to get arrested on

our first day," Jack said.

"No problem. But it's an awful good draw, mon. And there's plenty of it everywhere. It's one thing that has kept this nation of ours going," said Freddie, looking at them in the rearview mirror with a wink. "If you need anything else—a ride, a tour guide, or anything—call me."

The cabbie handed Jack his card. It said Freddie Rough, cab driver and guide. The card had a picture of a cab and what looked like a smiling Freddie.

"Very nice card, Freddie. Thanks. I'm sure we will," Jack said. "Do you mind turning up the volume? I like this song."

It was Bob Marley and the Wailers' "This Must Be Love." It was Becky's favorite. Jack recalled the first time she heard the song. It was at a Marley beach concert in Kingston, the first time they'd visited Jamaica.

It was about 1 p.m. The drive to the hotel along the winding ocean road was quiet, the radio filling the space no one wanted to. Jack stared out at the water, turning over in his mind how best to rescue Becky. Beside him, Sarah sat rigid, already imagining the moment she would come face-to-face with Robert again. Ed listened without really hearing, scanning every curve in the road, wondering whether any of them would leave the island alive—and knowing it would be his job to keep Jack out of trouble. In the back seat, Freddie did the math, calculating how much longer he could stretch his money to feed his wife and four children. The car kept moving, but each of them was trapped in their own thoughts.Top of Form

*　*　*

Finally, about 4 p.m., the cab pulled up in front of GoldenEye.

Jack paid Freddie 200 Jamaican dollars and thanked him for the ride. Freddie whistled, and a hotel attendant appeared to take the luggage out of the trunk. The attendant asked the three to follow him down the tree-lined path to the lobby.

"This looks nice," Sarah said of the hotel. "I didn't realize we were this close to the water."

"It's got real charm," Ed agreed. "You can feel it."

Halfway down the path to the hotel's front steps, a man stood in the shadows wearing a dark overcoat. Ed saw him first and tugged at Jack's arm. "There's somebody ahead," he said.

The attendant ignored the man and continued past him.

"Want to buy some hashish?" the man said in a hoarse voice with a strong Jamaican accent. "It's good stuff. Only 40 dollars American."

Jack shook his head.

"If you don't want it, maybe you need an extra girl. Call this number. Just ask for Cherry."

"No," said Jack, wondering if the hotel knew about Cherry and her drug-dealing brother out front. "We're not interested tonight. Maybe another time."

"No problem," the man in the dark overcoat said.

"Sorry about that, Sarah," Jack said. "That never happened before at this hotel. I suppose...desperate times."

"Hey, I'm not insulted," she said. "He did say an 'extra' girl, not a different one."

Ed and Jack chuckled. Then, they walked up the wooden steps to the hotel lobby.

"Can you believe these people?" Ed said. "We're here less than one hour, and already people want to sell us drugs and prostitutes."

"I think it's exciting," Sarah said. "You'd never see this at a Sarasota hotel."

"All I want to do is get a room before we start breaking any laws," Jack said.

Ed and Sarah laughed. "I'm serious," Jack said. Then he laughed, too. He was feeling good for the first time in a long while. Maybe it was a relief. He knew Becky wanted him. And even though he understood she had turned to him out of desperation, all he wanted to do was find her. He was convinced everything would be all right and they could solve their problems.

They walked into the lobby, which was very well kept. Antique tables and chairs adorned the large room with high ceilings, and oversized Persian rugs graced the floors.

"Welcome to Jamaica!" announced the man behind the desk.

"We have a reservation. It's under Kendall, Jack Kendall," Jack said with a chuckle.

"No problem. It's the offseason, you know. We'll give you our best cottage," the concierge said. "Let me check. Yes, we do have your reservation, Mr. Kendall. You've been here before, haven't you?"

Jack looked at the clerk and vaguely recognized him from when he and Becky had stayed there.

"Yes. It's been a while. Before this mess."

"Yes, sir, I hope it ends soon. Our business has been terrible. We just renovated the old section and added more rooms. We still have the classic, original rooms. You'll see some improvements," the concierge said. "Just sign here, sir."

"What's your name?" asked Jack.

"Ajani," the clerk answered. "At your service."

"Ajani, is the bar open?" Jack asked as he signed the

registration and handed his credit card to the man.

"Yes, of course."

"Could we have a bottle of tequila, three fresh limes, and salt sent to us as soon as possible?" Jack asked. "And a big pitcher of fresh water with lemons. Maybe a few fried plantains, chips, and three plates of ackee and saltfish?"

"No problem. It's done. I'll have the attendant show you to your cottage and bring your bags. He will bring your tequila and food shortly after."

"Thank you." Jack turned to Ed and Sarah. "Let's get settled. Then we have some planning to do."

"I didn't think the tequila and lime were for anything else," Ed said.

"No dancing?" Sarah asked with a smile.

Chapter 28
A GoldenEye Evening

Later Friday, July 18, 1980

It was late afternoon when the hotel bellhop escorted the three Americans to their two-bedroom cottage, one of the original huts by the water.

"We're lucky to have gotten this room," Jack said. "Chris, the owner, must have intervened. We've known him for years."

"I think it's great," said Sarah. "You can feel relaxation in the tropical air."

Ed laughed. "Let's get in. I want to try out that tequila and baked plantain. The salt air has made me hungry."

The apartment was spacious. As the bellhop put their luggage in the bedrooms, the room service attendant brought in their drinks and food shortly after.

Ed poured the first shots. Jack and Sarah tried some of

the plantain chips.

"We should eat the food first. That was a long flight and a long car ride," Jack said.

"I'd like to take a shot of that tequila, and then I'll have a plantain," Ed said. "I've got something I've wanted to tell you all day about the High Seas investigation. I didn't want to discuss it on the plane or in Freddie's cab."

"Wait a minute, what about a shot of tequila for me?" asked Sarah, feeling left out.

"Let me demonstrate," said Ed as he cut the lime into wedges. He licked the side of his thumb, then sprinkled some salt on it. After downing the tequila, he bit on the lime wedge and then sucked the salt off his thumb. He smacked his lips.

"Perfect match," he said. "Sarah, now you try it."

She followed Ed's example, then winced and nearly fell over.

"First shot of tequila?" Jack asked.

Sarah nodded. "Wow, that was strong!"

"Here, have some more plantain chips," said Ed as he passed the bowl to Sarah.

"Enough for now," Jack said, rubbing his temples. "Ed, tell me what Stevens said."

Ed sat on the edge of the bed, the ceiling fan clicking softly above them, stirring the warm Jamaican air. He lifted his glass, took a slow sip of tequila, then set it down.

"He told me to pass along that he and the chief were glad you pulled through and wished you luck finding Becky down here," Ed said. "They were sorry they couldn't do more after you were knocked out at LeCare's place. At the time, the feds were gearing up for coordinated busts—High Seas and several other cities where Mackey was running the same setup. Restaurants as fronts. Coke and money laundering."

Jack frowned. "Bagley and the feds knew I was unconscious and nearly dead at my apartment?"

"They said they didn't know," Ed replied. "Stevens told me the agent saw you walk up to the house—but never saw you leave. They think one of LeCare's men hauled you back to your apartment by boat. Someone must've driven your car back the next day. That's where I found it."

Jack shook his head. "So my beef's with the feds. They raided the High Seas?"

"Yes—but this is where it gets fuzzy," Ed said. "Stevens couldn't say much. They got a warrant and hit the place a few days ago. No large quantities of coke, but they found that locked room. Forensics turned it inside out. Plenty of trace evidence—clear signs it was used as a lab."

"Anybody arrested?" Jack asked.

"Several of LeCare's bagmen. They're talking," Ed said. "But they don't know much about the upper structure. There's a warrant out for LeCare. The investigation's ongoing. But there's more. It's about Betty."

Jack stiffened. "Betty? You found out more about her murder?"

"A lot," Ed said quietly. "You might want to sit down."

Jack glanced at the bottle on the dresser. "From the sound of that, I think I'll take a shot." He poured one, raked salt onto his hand, knocked it back, chased it with lime, and exhaled sharply.

"Stevens said Betty was home with her two kids when she was shot," Ed continued. "Police believe the shooter was Gordon Gecht—LeCare's man. Goes by Gordo. An evil bastard. He's the guy you spotted in the white suit at Tolbert's house."

Jack's head snapped up. "Gecht? He's the guy in the white

suit?"

Ed nodded. "They have an eyewitness. A neighbor—Loretta Smith. You quoted her when Tolbert took those hostages. She heard the shots and saw Gecht leaving the house. Police already had him pegged as an employee at the High Seas."

Jack stood and poured another shot, his hand shaking. "He murdered her. Left her kids without a mother—to protect LeCare and Mackey while they poison and ruin thousands of lives. I knew he was slime the second I laid eyes on him."

"It was worse," Ed said. "Gecht tried to stage it as a home invasion. There was evidence of sexual assault."

Jack winced. "With her children in the house?"

"I told you," Sarah said quietly from the chair by the window. "These people don't stop."

Jack turned back to Ed. "Anything else?"

"It's about Steve Ferro."

"Ferro?" Sarah asked.

"One of the bastards who drugged me," Jack said. "Put me in the hospital. I'd like to get my hands on that cockroach."

"I told Stevens about him," Ed said. "They arrested Ferro. He talked. He said Gecht was the one who drugged you."

Jack exploded, pacing the room. "That scum-faced, dope-peddling animal tried to kill me *and* murdered Betty?"

"There's a warrant out for Gecht," Ed said. "Murder, attempted murder, cocaine trafficking."

Jack stopped, his jaw tight. "We've got scores to settle with him."

"I also told Stevens what Sarah told us," Ed added. "About Robert Mackey, his mountain mansion, that he owns the High Seas. Stevens already knew about Mackey and his operations in Atlanta, New Orleans, Nashville, and other cities in the

Southeast."

"What are they doing about him?" Jack asked, forcing himself to drink water instead of tequila.

"No warrant yet, as far as Stevens knew," Ed said. "They're building the case."

"The sooner they cage that scumbag, the better," Jack said, pouring fresh shots for all of them.

He felt torn—rage at learning Gecht was behind both Betty's murder and his own attack and near-death, and grim satisfaction that Mackey was finally exposed, at least in the States.

Jack raised his glass but didn't drink.

"We can't wait for the law to arrest Mackey and LeCare," he said. "We've got to find Becky."

"That's why we're here. I'm ready to start our little meeting about how to do that," said Ed. "I think what we should do is quite simple."

"I know. You want us to go to the local police and file a missing person's report. You think they'll go to Robert's drug house and bring Becky to us?" Jack asked.

"Something like that. We also need to involve the American Embassy in Kingston. They can help, especially since Mackey could soon have a warrant out for his arrest in the U.S.," said Ed, downing another shot of tequila as he started sampling the ackee.

"Sarah, what do you think?" Jack asked.

"I don't think the police or the embassy can do anything. What were you telling me about hiring a private detective to help us?" Sarah asked Ed.

"I found a good agency in Ocho Rios. They can find out who works at Robert's house, and maybe we can learn more about Becky. They can help us stake out the place to find out how best to get her out."

"I understand playing it safe like that at first, and I might agree to that, but I don't trust the police here. They're corrupt, worse than some big cities in America," Jack said.

Sarah interrupted. "I want to remind you both how ruthless, deceitful, and awful Robert is. He's probably already bought off the police for 100 miles around, maybe down to Kingston. We should hire a detective to help us until we talk with Raleigh."

Ed poured another round of shots and passed them around.

"How much will this detective agency cost?" Jack asked.

"A hundred dollars per day per operative," Ed replied. "It's expensive but safer."

"How long will it take them to get results?" Jack asked.

"At least a week," Ed said. "I would have liked to have hired them before we left, but you wanted to leave immediately."

"A week is too long," Jack said. "I remind you, Becky said six days ago she feared for her life."

"I'm aware of that. I must admit there is no guarantee they can give us actionable information," Ed grumbled as he shook his head.

"Just a minute; I want to try Raleigh one more time before we decide anything," said Jack, picking up the phone and dialing.

"Telly, it's Jack again. Any word? No? Well, we made it to GoldenEye. We will probably drive to your place tomorrow afternoon. Do you mind if we wait for him there? Good. Call me here if he shows up. Okay, thanks. See you then."

"Jack, I know Raleigh is your friend. But why is he so damn important?" Ed asked.

"It's a fair question. I can't tell you everything now. I'd

rather he explains, but he has connections that the police, the embassy, and the detective agencies don't have," Jack said.

Jack was mysterious for a reason. In the early 1970s, the CIA had recruited Raleigh Lakes as a "confidential informant" because of his international reputation as an artist and his friendship with America.

The agency initially wanted simple information on the interaction between government and the arts, including the blossoming world of reggae music, which was increasingly coming under the influence of the socialist Jamaica Labor Party, a 50-year movement now led by Michael Manley that espoused some communist ideas.

Then, as poverty, the drug trade, and violence escalated after Manley won the very closely contested 1976 election, CIA operatives persuaded Raleigh to play a more active role in helping coordinate local resistance to Manley's coziness with Fidel Castro in Cuba, a communist island 50 miles to the north.

The Jamaican agreed after he was assured that the U.S. government's dual interest was in opening trade between the two countries and in minimizing communist influence, twin goals he fully supported.

"Jack, even if Raleigh agrees to help, what can he do?" Ed asked.

"First, he will give us honest advice about all our ideas," Jack said. "Just trust me. After reading Becky's letters, I'm convinced she's being held against her will. As Sarah says, I don't think the police or the embassy can do much against Mackey's money, influence, and firepower."

"Maybe so. I read that last letter as well, and I agree she wants to leave, and Mackey is a bastard to keep her," Ed said.

"Don't think he won't use Becky to get what he wants," Sarah interjected. "You will probably have to kill him to get her back."

That surprised Ed. "Kill him? I hope it won't come to that."

Jack, however, wasn't surprised by Sarah's comment. He sensed something was wrong with her. She had been eerily cheerful over the past two days. It was out of place. Jack thought she was just excited about coming to Jamaica with him. After all, she was only 22, and he knew she had a crush on him.

But now he wondered if Sarah had another reason for coming. He had set that thought aside because she offered valuable insight into Mackey. He needed to keep a closer eye on her from now on.

"Sarah is right," Jack said. "Mackey is ruthless. He has to be to survive in the international drug trade. To get Becky out, we'll need a very clever plan—and we'll need to be prepared to use violence, if necessary."

"Robert tried to kill you once," Sarah reminded him. "He will try again."

"I haven't forgotten," said Jack, pouring himself and his friends more tequila shots.

"I want to propose a toast to Becky's freedom," Ed said, raising his glass and downing it. Jack nodded and did the same.

"You joke around, Ed, but Robert is deadly serious," Sarah said as she downed the tequila.

"You're right. We can't just walk up and ask to take Becky home," Ed said. "I ask again. How are we going to do it?"

"I have one idea. Raleigh will have several. Let's wait until I talk with him," Jack said.

"I don't suppose he has an army to bust in and rescue Becky like John Wayne did when he rescued Natalie Wood from the Indian camp in the old movie, The Searchers. Does he?" Ed asked.

"Ed, how many shots of tequila have you had?" Jack asked.

"Four or five, but I'm serious. Does he have an army?" Ed said.

"He might," said Jack, pouring Ed a fifth or sixth shot and himself a third or fourth. He was losing count. "Sarah, would you like another?"

"If I have another, I'll be dancing on that big bed over there," she said with a straight face.

"Pour one for her. I want to see that," Ed said.

"I think you both have had enough," Jack said.

"I apologize, Sarah," Ed said. "Maybe it's the ocean air and beautiful surroundings. I'm getting quite a buzz drinking this tequila and eating this Jamaican food."

"It's okay, Ed. I thought what you said was quite funny. I would bounce pretty high on that bed," Sarah said with a smile. "I think I've had enough. I shouldn't even be drinking with my meds."

"What do you take?" Ed asked.

"Lithium. I don't think I told you this, Jack, but I'm being treated for bipolar disorder," Sarah explained.

"I wondered about that. Are you feeling okay now?" Jack asked.

"Yes, and the tequila helps. So does the fact that you two have been so accommodating and kind," she said. "I haven't been down in a week. I think it is because I met you, Jack, and now you, Ed."

"Jack, you never told me how good-looking your brother is," she added with a little smile at Ed.

"It's the tequila talking. But Sarah, you're the one who is

quite good-looking," said Ed, adding, "It's true, but I'd better stop drinking as well."

"Okay, enough, you two! Enough flirting. Let's get serious. Back to the business at hand," Jack said. "The bar is closed."

"Before I go to bed, I'd like to know your plan, Jack," Sarah asked.

"My preference, of course, is to wait for Raleigh and hear his ideas. Outside of that, my only thought is to stake out Mackey's house every day, maybe with a detective agency's help or Raleigh's, and wait for Becky to come out," said Jack. "If she does come out—which looks less likely now based on her last letters, and if there are only one or two guards with her—we could stage a diversion. Fake a traffic accident with them, take her, and then escape with Raleigh's help.

"It's high risk, but we obviously can't raid the house with all the firepower he has around it," Jack said.

"That's brilliant," Ed said. "I hope Raleigh has a better plan because that one sounds like a suicide mission against armed guards who would surely be expecting something. They would shoot us immediately."

"It's a long-shot idea," Jack confessed. "We need another plan."

"If it would help, I could trade myself for Becky," Sarah declared.

"Don't even say that, Sarah," Ed said. "You know what would happen. He would take you and keep Becky."

"I'm just saying I would do anything to help," said Sarah.

"I know you mean it. Thanks, Sarah. I don't think it will come to that," Jack said. "It's bad luck that Raleigh had to go into the mountains to meditate and paint."

"Short of sacrificing Sarah, what will we do in the morning?"

Ed asked.

"I'll try Raleigh once more in the morning. If Telly hasn't heard anything, we'll go to the police and talk with the embassy. I don't like it, but at least it's something besides sitting around. I don't know how long Raleigh will be gone," Jack replied.

"Agreed. Now, it's been a long day," Ed said. "Maybe we should get some sleep. We have a big day tomorrow."

"Good idea. We've gone as far as we can with our information," Jack said. "Let's go to bed. Sarah, you have the other bedroom."

"I know, Jack," she said. "Goodnight to you both."

After Sarah left the room, Ed excused himself to go to the bathroom.

Jack got ready for bed. He wondered why he had agreed to visit the town police in the morning. It was because he was tired, and Raleigh was in the mountains.

He also worried that asking the embassy for help might backfire. The embassy would probably call Mackey to inquire about Becky. This might work, but it could also make things worse for her.

He needed to find Becky. Her life was at stake. She was so close.

But for now, it looked like Jack had no other alternative than to go to the police and contact the embassy. He hoped Raleigh would return by the morning.

Chapter 29

Breakfast at GoldenEye

Saturday morning, July 19, 1980

The next morning, Jack awoke with a start. He hadn't slept well. All through the night, he tossed and turned, his head filled with thoughts of how to rescue Becky. How would he get her out? Plan A: the police? Or Plan B: Raleigh?

He looked at the clock. It was 9 a.m.

Turning over, he saw that his brother had already risen. Ed always got up earlier than Jack. He was probably getting coffee in the small hotel restaurant. Jack wondered if Sarah was up already.

They had talked for several hours, weighing the pros and cons of finding Becky and getting her home.

Just before midnight, Jack agreed to ask the police and the embassy for help. It was a long-shot chance. He felt the plan was wrong, but in the end, he decided to show Ed and Sarah that he would try the less-violent option first.

Before they'd left Florida, Jack had known he would have to use force to get her out.

Mackey's attempt to murder him was a revelation. Even if Becky were freed, such a vicious attack—a severe head injury and poisoning intended to murder him—meant to Jack that he had no other choice but to kill Mackey to protect Becky and himself from future retribution.

He didn't want to be constantly looking over his shoulder and worrying that some thug sent by Mackey was out to kill him. No, Mackey needed to be dealt with. Permanently.

The question was how to do it. Raleigh would find a way to give him the opportunity. But was Jack up to it? Did he still have the killer instinct? Admittedly, Jack's love for winning was great. He didn't like to lose.

One time, a rival newspaper challenged Jack's paper to a game of "Killer," a simulated war game that resembled the children's game "Capture the Flag"—except it was played with air guns, paint bullets, goggles, and camouflage outfits.

Jack took it as a personal challenge to win.

He'd learned military tactics from a longtime family friend, Col. John Hanks, and two ex-Green Berets he met at his father's VFW post. They'd joined Jack's team as ringers and quickly proved their worth.

After several days of practice, Jack's newspaper team won. They performed so well and had so much fun that they joined a Killer paintball league and won most of their games using the advanced strategies they learned from their Army friends.

The difference in this situation with Becky was that he had no ringers, and rescuing Becky wasn't a game. Jack knew he needed professional help, which was why he was so intent on speaking with Raleigh.

Before he showered and went downstairs for breakfast, Jack picked up the phone and tried Telly again. She told him Raleigh was still not home.

It was 9:20 a.m. when he headed for breakfast.

*   *   *

Ed had slept reasonably well, considering all the tequila he drank. He took a hot shower and silently dressed so as not to wake Jack, who was stirring quite a bit in his sleep. He left the room and knocked on Sarah's door.

There was no answer, though Ed thought he heard voices inside, so he went downstairs to have coffee and read the paper. He wanted to learn more about the unrest on the island.

Ed ordered Jamaican Blue Mountain coffee in the dining room. It was a rich blend, a little gritty for his taste. He drank it anyway because he knew the day would be long and he needed caffeine as both an antidote to the tequila from the night before and as a stimulant for the day ahead.

The server, a native Jamaican who was very friendly and cheerful, brought him the morning newspaper.

Ed scanned the headlines. "Campaign Headquarters Viciously Bombed!" screamed the lead item. The story was about Michael Manley's Kingston campaign office being firebombed. Three dead, four injured, and no clues.

Another story on the front page described how both Manley and Seaga, who were facing off again that year in a campaign for prime minister, were shot at while giving separate speeches. They weren't hit, but the incidents underscored the election's drama and seriousness.

The other stories in the paper covered politics, crime, poverty, and culture. The most fascinating stories were about music—reviews of bands playing a range of styles, including reggae, dancehall, ska, and rocksteady.

But even the music articles discussed opposition to political violence, drug overuse, prejudice, and rioting—all current events shaking the foundation of Jamaican society.

Ed read the news and shook his head. How could Jamaica, a naturally beautiful country with wondrous beaches and a laid-back lifestyle, have so many problems?

Other articles he read answered some of his questions. Jamaica had a 50% inflation rate over the last four years, its unemployment rate was near 20%, the police force was mainly corrupt, gangs ruled the streets, and drug lord criminals— like Robert Mackey—were allowed to run wild.

Jamaica would be fortunate if Manley and Seaga survived this fall's election. Ed also thought he, Jack, and Sarah would be lucky to leave this island alive.

For a fleeting second, Ed wished he were there on vacation with Jack and Sarah. But he knew they were there for only one reason: to rescue Jack's wife, who was being held at a drug trafficker's house protected by a small army of violent men. What could go wrong with this rescue?

While he had a slight headache from the tequila he'd shot down the night before, the thought of what was about to happen was enough to give him a bigger headache.

He realized he was hungry. Time to order breakfast. He had been waiting long enough for Jack and Sarah to come down. Where was the server? He needed steak and eggs.

*　*　*

Sarah woke up, stretched, and looked in the mirror on the dresser. Her dark, thick hair was wild from a night of tossing and turning.

Despite her restless sleep, she felt good this morning—even better than yesterday morning, when she woke up joyfully thinking of cleansing herself of the horrible feeling of rejection that had permeated her soul and mind since Robert Mackey had abruptly left her.

Months of therapy still hadn't dented the hurt and betrayal she felt toward Mackey. She knew there was only one way of ending her daily torment: by killing Robert Mackey.

With a smile, Sarah went into the bathroom, stared at the mirror, and began her morning ritual of talking with herself. It was a habit she'd developed as an only child of constantly quarreling parents. As her mother and father had argued, Sarah would go into the bathroom and talk to herself, pretending she was talking with an older sister.

This morning was essential. She was going to show Jack where Robert lived.

She knew she needed to keep up her cheerful attitude so Jack and Ed couldn't guess she had a deadly motive for coming along with them.

She didn't know how to get close enough to kill Robert. All she needed was an opportunity. She'd improvise.

As she talked to herself and drowned out the world with her thoughts of revenge, she didn't hear Ed knocking on the door.

*　*　*

Jack casually walked out of the cottage and across the lawn to the main hotel building and dining room. The morning was warm, even with a light breeze off the Caribbean Sea. The day would be much hotter than in Florida this time of year. That was good. Because it was August and hot, there weren't many tourists.

Still, it felt good to be here, doing something. Maybe today, he'd have a definite plan to rescue Becky.

Ed was sitting at the table, reading the newspaper, as Jack entered the dining room. Only two of the 15 other tables were occupied by guests.

As Jack took a seat, Ed looked up.

"Good morning, stranger," Ed said.

"Ready to go to work?" Jack asked.

"Whoa, boy. I'll be ready only after my last meal."

"Very funny."

"Not intended to be. Have you seen the paper? There is so much turmoil in your island paradise that I don't know how long we'll last, even if we mind our own business," Ed said with his characteristic sarcasm.

"Are you backing out?"

"I didn't say that."

"Good, because we have much to do."

Ed nodded in agreement. "Have you seen Sarah?"

Jack motioned his head upstairs. "She was up. I told her to come down and that we needed to eat breakfast and go to the police station. She said she wouldn't be long."

"Good. I already ordered. Let me call the server. I'm sure she'll be here soon," Ed said.

Just then, Sarah walked into the dining room. She wore a white jumpsuit and a wide-brimmed hat.

Jack greeted her and waved to the waiter.

"This hotel is wonderful!" Sarah exclaimed. "It's like we own the place. Everyone is waiting on us like slaves."

"You're not too far off," Ed said. "Two hundred years ago, these people were slaves. Africans were kidnapped in the Congo, captured and sold by their own people, and brought here by English slave traders. From reading this paper, it seems some are still fighting to be freed—this time from their socialist leaders."

"Well, I'm sure there's a reason for their behavior. I feel..." Sarah paused and groped for a word.

"Say it, Sarah," Ed teased.

"Wonderful," she blurted out. "I know I'm saying that too much, but I can't help it. I'm so glad I came."

"Are you hungry, too, Sarah?" Ed inquired.

"Famished."

"Let's eat, because we're going to pay a visit to the police department as soon as we're done," Jack said.

Ed breathed a sigh of relief. He'd worried that Jack might change his mind about the plan they'd agreed on the night before. But he knew the only reason Jack had opted for the police was that he still couldn't reach his friend, Raleigh Lakes.

Chapter 30
Jamaican Police

Later Saturday morning, July 19, 1980

After breakfast, Jack ordered a cab to take Ed and Sarah to one of Oracabessa's wonders, a small stretch of sand near GoldenEye known as James Bond Beach.

It was a short five-minute ride to the famous peninsular beach, which was also very close to the local police station, where they would ask for help finding Becky.

Jack still wasn't sold on calling in the cops. He was still trying to decide whether to call off the plan, return to the hotel, and wait for Raleigh to contact him.

While he mulled over what to do, he decided to take Ed and Sarah's minds off the dangerous mission ahead. He could tell they were uneasy about what Jack was planning.

On the way to the beach, Jack told them a brief story he had heard years ago about the small beach. It was featured in the first Bond movie, 1962's Dr. No, with Sean Connery and Ursula Andress.

"This beach was called Laughing Waters Beach before Dr. No became famous," Jack began.

"Ian Fleming fell in love with Jamaica after spending time here in 1943. He was a British naval intelligence commander during World War II. After the war, he asked a friend to find a nearby beachfront property to build a house. The legend is that a friend spotted a girl swimming out in the water at Laughing Waters. He saw that she was naked when she came out of the sea."

"A naked girl? Is that your story?" Sarah exclaimed.

"I'm not finished," Jack said. "At that sight, he knew it was an excellent place for Fleming to build his home. The friend then found a nice 14-acre property for sale; Fleming bought it and named it GoldenEye, a tribute to his wartime intelligence assignment in Jamaica."

"Wow, the naked girl must have brought Fleming luck. He wrote a lot of Bond novels here, didn't he? Featured a lot of naked girls as well," Ed said with a chuckle.

"Yes, he did. One of the theories is that it inspired him to write the scene in Dr. No where Ursula Andress rises out of the water in a skimpy white bikini and discovers Bond watching her," Jack said.

"I can't wait to come out here for a swim," Sarah said. "I even packed a bikini."

At that thought, Jack and Ed looked at each other and smiled at Sarah.

"Is it a white one like Ursula's?" Ed quipped.

"You'll have to wait and see," she teased.

"I can wait, but not long," Ed said with a wink.

They all laughed. "We all brought bathing suits, Sarah. Let's see what the police say before we make swimming plans,"

Jack said.

It was a lovely summer morning, with a warm, gentle breeze blowing onshore from the north. The three continued walking along the beautiful beach.

Maybe because of the light-heartedness the group felt under such a beautiful sky and mild temperature, or because he couldn't reach Raleigh, or perhaps simply because Jack was impatient and wanted to get closer to finding Becky, he decided to take the chance and ask the police for help.

As they continued along the beach, panhandlers and street merchants approached them to sell their handmade trinkets and artifacts. The three bought a few souvenirs to support the local economy. They weren't collector's items. It was like running a gauntlet to get through the group.

Jack picked out one young kid who nicely asked if they needed a guide.

"What's your name?" Jack asked.

"Teddy," the boy replied.

"All we need is for you to take us to the police station," Jack said. "Can you do that?"

"Sure, mon. You follow," Teddy said.

Jack handed the boy two Jamaican dollars. They walked 10 minutes past the beach, through trees and vegetation, to an ancient building with a sign reading POLICE HEADQUARTERS in large letters.

After thanking Teddy, the trio entered. One police officer was inside the decrepit-looking office, and several others were standing around.

Jack and Ed, with Sarah trailing close behind, approached the front desk.

"May I see whoever is in charge?" Jack requested.

"Do you have something to report?" the desk sergeant inquired.

"Yes, a missing person. May I talk with the captain?"

"Dee, the captain isn't here. He's in Ocho," the sergeant said. "You can talk with Lt. Renault. Lieutenant?"

A young man in his late 20s, with a thin mustache and short-cropped hair, came out of a nearby office. "I'm Lt. Renault," he said. "I'm in charge here. What you three doing in Jamaica in this troubled time? Eh?"

"May we talk with you in private?" Jack asked, taking a step toward the lieutenant.

"Oh, ya, come in," Renault said.

Jack followed the police officer into his office. Ed and Sarah trailed behind.

"Lieutenant," Jack said quickly, "I'm Jack Kendall from America. We need help. My wife has been kidnapped."

"Your wife? Is that so?" Renault asked without sincerity. "And how did you come by this information?"

"Long story, but she wrote me several letters. She said she wants to leave but can't because she's being held against her will."

"Oh, a kidnapped woman can send letters out?" Renault said with a challenging smirk. "The letters are free, but she isn't. Very interesting."

"Listen, Lieutenant. This is serious. She's been missing for nearly three weeks. I'm her husband, and I'm telling you the truth. I know from her letters that she is in danger. I can give you any information you want about her: name, a description, anything.

"I can even tell you where she is," Jack added. "Will you help us?"

"I might be able to help you, but a lieutenant makes only a small amount of money, and there is so much work to do. With such a small salary, it is hard to make ends meet," Renault said. "Do you understand?"

"I have some money if that is what you want. But there is a crime of kidnapping involved here in Jamaica," Jack said, raising his voice. "We've already called the American Embassy in Kingston for help. I could call them again."

"Yes, you could. But that would take time, and you don't have it. Am I right?" the lieutenant said.

Ed interrupted, "Lieutenant Renault, how much do you want, and what will you do for it?"

"Two hundred American dollars to run a background check to see if she is in Jamaica. More will be needed if we determine a crime has been committed and if we need to pick her up," Renault replied.

"Pay him," Jack said to Ed with disgust. He turned to Sarah, flushed with anger. "I knew this was a bad idea."

She whispered, "Let Ed handle this. Let's go outside."

Jack nodded, and they exited the station.

Three minutes later, Ed came out of the lieutenant's office.

"Strange. I showed him the pictures of Becky and the one of Robert Mackey that Sarah had. His eyes seemed to flicker a bit when he saw Mackey's picture. Like he knew him."

Jack wasn't surprised. "I'm sure he did."

"And he didn't ask to keep the photos. I told him we have extras."

"Did you ask him anything about Mackey?"

"No, once I suspected he recognized Mackey, I didn't want to let on that we knew much about him. He didn't ask any questions either," Ed said. "He just told us to go back to the hotel and that he'd contact us later this afternoon."

Sarah looked concerned. "The police will tell Robert we're here and do nothing to help us."

"We stuck our necks out, so we'll just have to wait to see what the police do," Ed replied. "If they don't help, I will tell the embassy. If they do help, it will be just a matter of paying an official visit to Mackey. If she's there, they'll use their authority to get her out if she wants to leave."

"At least, thanks to Sarah, we already know Becky is with Mackey at his mountain house," Jack said. "I have a bad feeling. I don't trust that lieutenant."

"That's putting it mildly," Ed muttered.

Chapter 31
Shocking News

Saturday, p.m., July 19, 1980

After they returned to GoldenEye, Jack suggested they change into bathing suits and lie on the beach in lounge chairs under one of the giant umbrellas.

"Jack, we should be careful. What if those cops tell Mackey where we are?" Ed cautioned.

"I've asked security to make sure we don't have any surprise guests. We are safe here," Jack said with a smile. He wanted to do more, but they needed to wait for the police and, hopefully, for word from Raleigh.

Hours passed without a word. The sun was hot, and the large umbrellas shielded them from its direct rays. The last thing Jack wanted was a sunburn.

Even though the concierge had promised to let them know if the police called or came looking for them, Jack wanted to be doubly sure. Every 30 minutes, one of the three would walk from the beach to the hotel lobby to check for calls and get fresh water.

Later that afternoon, the lieutenant called the hotel and said he was sending someone over with information. A bellhop went to the beach to tell Jack that the police were on their way.

Five minutes later, two police officers walked into the hotel lobby. Pacing around like an expectant father, Jack spotted the cops and quickly headed toward them.

"Where is she?" he asked anxiously.

"We found the red-haired girl," said the younger police officer.

"Where? Is she safe?" Jack quickly asked.

"Hey, mon, I've got some bad news."

Jack froze, not knowing what to expect.

"She's dead."

Jack closed his eyes, dropped his head, and slumped forward. Even if the police were lying, Jack didn't want to hear anyone say his wife was dead. Sarah and Ed, coming up from behind, grabbed his arms to steady him.

"What do you mean she's dead?" Ed demanded. "How did she die?"

"In a fire," the older cop said.

"Are you sure? There must be a mistake," Jack said.

Ed led Jack over to a nearby chair, and he fell into it.

"Tell me what happened," Jack mumbled. "I want to know everything."

"There wasn't much left," the young cop said. "It was quite a blaze. Burned the whole house down."

"Who else was killed? The house was full of people," Sarah pressed.

"We are investigating. We don't have much information. We think the owner died with the house staff and several other people," the older cop said.

Sarah also sat down, looking shaken and upset, her face grim and tense in a way Jack hadn't seen before. She stared at the floor, her jaw clenched. Was she distressed about the fire? He tried to focus on the news he was hearing.

"When did this happen?" Jack asked.

"Three nights ago," the older cop said. "I'm sorry, mon. That's all the information we have to tell ya."

"We'd like to know more about this fire," Ed said. "You haven't given us much information. Did you report it to the American Embassy? There were U.S. citizens in the house."

"Like I said, we are investigating. Lt. Renault's advice is to leave Jamaica on the next flight," the older police officer said. "We will contact you in Florida and tell you what is needed."

Jack sat in the chair and said nothing as the police officers left the hotel bar. He was stunned and quiet.

"It's time for us to go to the Kingston embassy. Freddie can drive us. I called this morning and left a message. Once they learn about this, they should be able to confirm what happened, if anything, to Becky," Ed said. "It may not be real. They can pressure the police in Ocho Rios to investigate and send out a team to look into it."

Jack didn't respond. He sat in the chair with his hands over his neck.

Ed and Sarah looked at each other. Sarah began to speak, but Ed motioned for her to keep quiet. He knew Jack was planning his next move.

A few moments later, Jack said in a loud, determined voice, "She's not dead. They're covering up for somebody, probably Mackey. It's just what Sarah said: Mackey paid off the cops. We're going to find her, just as we planned."

"If she's alive, that means Robert is alive and knows we are coming," said Sarah.

"Sarah's right," Ed said. "If Becky is alive and this fire story is a lie, we can't get close to her now. They won't let her out of the house until they know we're gone."

"My rescue plan of using a diversion to get her out wasn't realistic anyway. We can't do it ourselves. I've got to get a hold of Raleigh. He's the only one who can help us. I should have waited for him," Jack said. "I was too damned impatient."

"Jack, don't blame yourself. It was probably my fault. I was following police procedure," Ed said.

"Now, both of you guys are to blame?" Sarah asked. "That's great. But what are we going to do? Call the embassy or your friend?"

"We should call the American Embassy and tell them what happened. They'll be able to find out about Becky," Ed said.

"No more official channels, not at least until we talk with Raleigh," Jack said. "The police will tell Mackey they told us Becky died and that we should leave. If we contact the embassy to confirm the fire, they'll try to contact Mackey, and he'll know we didn't believe the police. Let's pretend we're leaving."

Ed decided to keep quiet. After all, Becky was Jack's wife, and he should be calling the shots.

Jack excused himself to try Raleigh again. He wondered whether his visit with the police hadn't put Becky's life in greater jeopardy. After all, he'd made the mistake of telling the cops about her letters. He prayed Renault hadn't told Mackey everything.

His hand shook as he dialed Mrs. Lakes to tell her they would be driving out shortly. Whether Raleigh was there or not, they needed to leave GoldenEye and find a secluded place.

Jack also wanted Sarah to show him where Mackey's house was, so they could see if it had burned down.

But Jack knew it was all up to Raleigh now. Becky's life depended on it.

*   *   *

While Jack was on the phone in the hotel lobby, Ed went to the window and peered out. There, the police were right out front, waiting, just as he'd feared. He surmised that Renault must have ordered the officers to stay and follow them out of town to ensure they left.

Although Ed didn't want to believe Jack's scenario about the police faking the news of Becky's death, he now began to see the situation in a different light.

Maybe this is a cover-up, just as Jack said. Becky must be alive. Why else would the police want us to leave so quickly? But more importantly, who gains the most by Jack leaving Jamaica? Mackey, of course.

"Ed, what are you thinking?" Sarah asked. "Do you think Becky and Robert are dead?"

"I don't care about Mackey, but I agree with Jack. She's still alive," Ed said. "They asked us to leave and are waiting outside. They want to make sure we do."

"What do you mean?" Sarah asked with a touch of worry in her voice.

"Well, at the police station, Lt. Renault recognized Mackey's face in the picture I showed him. There was a flicker," Ed said. "Based on how the police acted, it seems reasonable that these boys are working for Mackey."

"I think you're right," said Sarah, relieved that Ed thought Robert was still alive.

*　*　*

Jack finished his phone call and walked over to them as they talked.

"Everything is set. We are going over to Raleigh's house now. I'm sure he can help us. I'll call Freddie to drive us over," Jack said.

"No can do. Jack, did you know those cops are waiting outside?"

"They are? Those slimy motherfuckers," Jack growled. "Oh, sorry, Sarah."

"That's okay. Probably a good word to describe them," Sarah said without a smile.

"Jack. We can't go to your friend's house. We can't go anywhere without these bozos following along," Ed said.

"All right. All right," said Jack. "Here's the plan. Let's go back to the room and change. Then we can get our bags and check out. I'll call Freddie and explain the situation. He can drive us to Raleigh's."

"What about the cops?" Sarah said.

"We need to give them another bribe. Can you handle this, Ed?" said Jack. "I've got some money in the room."

Thirty minutes later, they were dressed, packed, and checked out.

Jack looked out the lobby window and saw the two Jamaican officers sitting in their old squad car.

"Go find out what they want," Jack said.

"Be careful, Ed," Sarah said.

Ed walked outside and approached the two police officers watching the hotel. They seemed surprised at his directness.

"I've got a favor to ask you two officers," Ed said. "We'd like to do a little sightseeing before we leave. You know. We just got here last night. The lady wants to see the Blue Mountains and Port Antonio. It's a long mini-bus ride there. How about giving us until tomorrow night before we leave? How about it? Your boss won't mind. And here's a little something to help you pass the time."

Ed handed the younger officer $100 in U.S. bills. He took the money but didn't respond. "That's not enough? How about this?" Ed handed him another $100.

"Is that all right?" Ed asked. "You boys taken care of? We'll be seeing you," and he waved goodbye to them.

Ed knew he had taken a chance. The police could keep the money and still follow them.

As he stepped back, the older one nodded and nudged the younger one to start the car.

"Hey," said the older one to Ed. "You go see the sights. We'll come back tomorrow night. Be gone by then. Don't cause no trouble. And don't go deep into the mountains. There's trouble up there, yuh see, and not even American money can help you."

Ed waved goodbye and watched the squad car pull away from the hotel.

That was an expensive visit to the police, Ed thought. Four hundred dollars, and we're in worse shape than when we started. Mackey knows we're here and about Becky's smuggled letters, and we're running from the local law.

When Ed walked into the lobby, Jack breathed a sigh of relief.

"I don't know what you said to them, but it sure worked," Jack said.

"Two hundred bucks buys a lot of ganja and Red Stripes. I don't think they wanted the duty anyway. Let's go. We don't have much time," Ed said.

"Our ride should be here any moment," Jack said.

"You called the cabbie?"

"We can't leave Jamaica without Becky."

"Let's find her," Ed said. "I'd like to get the hell out of this country. It gives me the creeps."

*　*　*

Freddie's cab screeched to a halt before the GoldenEye, and he jumped out with the motor running.

Jack was out front, by the street. Ed and Sarah were waiting down the path.

"You said fast," Freddie said with a broad grin.

"I'm glad you could make it," Jack said. "Do you mind helping with the rest of the bags?"

"No, sir," Freddie replied as he left with a spirited trot down the lane. Jack tucked his bags into the trunk.

As they were leaving, something caught Jack's eye on the road in front of the hotel. It was a black jeep with a fire-red lightning bolt airbrushed down the side, driving very slowly.

There were three men in the jeep. Strange. They weren't looking his way, but why were they driving like that? He looked for the police and didn't see them, then glanced back at the jeep and made a mental note. Maybe it was paranoia, but the Jeep looked suspicious because it was new, and all the other vehicles were old.

The cabbie came back with Ed and Sarah.

Jack was already in the front seat with another $100 American bill in hand. After Freddie loaded the bags in the car, he slid into the front seat and stared at the century note.

"What is this, mon?" Freddie asked with a big grin. "We going far?"

"To Raleigh's house."

"Oh, sure, been there many times," Freddie said.

"It's only 50 miles, but I want you to provide an extra driving service," Jack instructed as he waved the bill.

The cabbie's eager eyes followed the bill. "No problem. Tell me, boss."

"Do you have a full tank of gas?" Jack asked.

"We can get one pretty quick," Freddie said.

"Here's the thing," said Jack, turning toward Freddie. "Some guys might want to see us cut our vacation a little short. We don't want to go just yet. I need you to ensure we aren't followed to our next stop: Raleigh's house. For that, the $100 is yours, plus expenses."

"Are you gangsters or something from Chicago? Bang-bang!" the cabbie said with a laugh.

"Not by a long shot," Ed piped in from the backseat. "No bang-bang, please."

"We're here on a rescue mission," Sarah added enthusiastically.

"My wife was kidnapped, and we're trying to find her," Jack explained, taking a chance in confiding with Freddie. He knew Raleigh, after all. "Will you help us?"

"So that's it. Raleigh said you might be in trouble and to do anything to help you. I expected something like this. What about the police? What do dey say?" Freddie asked.

"We went to the police," said Ed with disdain. "They weren't any help. They might be trying to cover up something. We don't know. Maybe they want to shake us down."

"That sure not right. Some police are very bad, very bad," said Freddie as he started to drive away from the hotel.

He continued. "Me keep you safe and help you, but you first must come with me to a place I know. It is near Raleigh's house and where you want to be. To be sure, it will take us a little while to make sure no one is following us. It's a real Jamaican reggae bar. Most tourists never get a chance to see a place like this. You'll have fun. Relax. You'll be safe. Me do the driving."

Freddie looked in the rearview mirror and saw a black jeep following behind.

Jack looked back at Ed and Sarah. They shrugged. Sarah laughed. "A party! What a wonderful idea," she said.

"All right," Jack said, exhaling. He hoped Raleigh was right and that Freddie was one of the good Jamaican guys. He had to trust Freddie. Now that Mackey knew he was in Jamaica, he had little time to find Becky.

Chapter 32
The Silver Spoon

Saturday night, July 19, 1980

After filling the tank with gasoline, Freddie turned east on a road that led away from town along the coast to Port Maria. Soon, he turned south and up into the mountains toward Highgate. The road wound around lushly foliated emerald valleys and alongside peaks that grew steeper with each turn.

Every 10 miles or so, Freddie pulled over at scenic viewing stops. But it wasn't to show his passengers the beautiful views. It was to find out if the black jeep was still following. A few cars passed, but they didn't appear interested in a beat-up old cab.

"Doesn't look like your friends in the jeep are coming," Freddie said. "Maybe dey don't like mountains."

"Let's be safe and stick with the plan," Jack said. Ed nodded in approval. The cabbie gunned the engine, and the car lurched back onto the road.

An hour later, Freddie pulled his cab into the nearly full parking lot of the bar—the Silver Spoon.

It was getting dark outside, but the lights were bright inside, and the music was blaring with the two-chord sounds of Jamaican reggae.

"This is the place I tell you 'bout. Very close to Raleigh's," said Freddie. "You will get the full flavor of the island inside, my friends. Just be calm, relax, and enjoy."

"Is it safe?" Jack said.

"Don't ya worry one bit, mon. Many inside are friends of Raleigh's. Ya find out. If your friends still follow us, dey find out too."

Jack felt better as they walked into the bar. It was filled with the pungent aroma of ganja. Dreadlocked heads turned. The band stopped in mid-song. Deep black faces stared at Jack, Ed, and Sarah with profound yet curious expressions.

Freddie, who led them in, smiled and whispered to Jack, "No problem. Just buy dem drinks."

Jack took one look at the Jamaicans, at least 50 strong. Some men were bearded with long dreadlocks, and others were clean-shaven or wore mustaches and goatees. Most were dressed casually in T-shirts and blue jeans. Some wore vests over their backs, with gold chains and ornate necklaces. The women wore colorful bandana skirts with white or light-colored shirts. Their hair was pulled up in a turban-style scarf of the same fabric as the skirt.

Jack glanced at Ed, who shook his head. "Nice group. We may run out of money tonight," he said out of the side of his mouth.

Sarah was scared. "Do something, Jack. Offer them two rounds," she whispered in his ear.

Jack kept a straight face for five seconds, looking around directly at many in the crowd. The room became heavy. No one seemed to breathe. Then he smiled and said in a loud voice: "We're just passing through with our friend, Freddie, and we want to honor the real Jamaica! Down with oppression! Up with freedom! Long live Jah! Red Stripes and rum for everyone!"

At first, the crowd seemed stunned. Then came a roar of approval, and the band picked up right where it had left off.

"I told you there would be no problem," Freddie said. "I hope you have cash. No credit cards accepted here. We might be here awhile."

While swigging a Red Stripe, Jack phoned Mrs. Lakes again to let her know where they were and that a suspicious black jeep had followed them.

"Hi, Jack. Raleigh just got home. I will tell him to come to you as soon as possible. He has to make a quick stop first, then he'll be there," Telly said.

"Does he know where this place is?"

"Oh, yes, it's not too far from our house," said Mrs. Lakes with a chuckle.

"Not far? Freddie drove us to this reggae bar on purpose."

"Of course. Raleigh and Freddie's late father were good friends."

"Ah, yes, I see, it would be safer if he picked us up here."

"Yes," Mrs. Lakes said. "It would be safer if people followed you."

"We'll wait for him."

"He will be there soon," she said. "Don't worry."

They spent the next 30 minutes talking with Freddie and several of his friends about how Jamaican politics and music often meshed so tightly they became indistinguishable.

Some Jamaicans were interested in life in the States. Jack told them how many Americans loved Bob Marley and reggae music. He told them about sports. They seemed to love American football.

As Jack talked about America and his love for Jamaica, Sarah asked Ed to dance. "Follow me!"

Ed looked at Jack, who shrugged, then nodded. She took Ed's hand and led him to an open spot on the dance floor. They joined the group, which was rhythmically moving around the center of the bar, to hear "Legalize It" by Peter Tosh.

She began sashaying back and forth from left to right and clapping her hands in time with the beat. Ed was a little reluctant to relax, but he liked the music. Sarah smiled at Ed, who began to get into the groove, nodding, snapping his fingers, and bobbing. They stayed on the dance floor for 10 minutes until the band decided to take an herb break.

As they left the dance floor, Jack, watching the parking lot out of the corner of his eye, spotted the black jeep with the red thunderbolt pull into the lot and park out front. Three men got out of the jeep and began talking. Jack saw the one who appeared to be in charge pointing to the cab. Uh-oh, Jack thought.

One of the men stayed by the jeep while the other two walked toward the bar. Jack motioned for Ed to come over. "Ed. That jeep is here. It looks like they're coming in."

Sipping a beer, Freddie overheard the warning and said, "Me take over. As soon as things get loud, hop out the back door."

The cabbie quickly approached a group of men. He pointed to Jack and then to the door. The men nodded and spread out to tell others. Jack, Ed, and Sarah moved to the back of the bar, near the rear door. Several Jamaicans stood as shields in front of them.

Jack paid the bartender $200 U.S. for the beer and rum and an extra $50 as a goodwill tip. He smiled and wished them well.

One of Freddie's friends, Marcus, a sizeable Rastafarian, began giving a political speech.

As the two men entered the bar, Freddie nodded to Jack, and the diversion began.

"People, there is concern about what is happening in Kingston and our country. This election is causing too much hurt. It is prophesied that change must first come from within oneself before it can be passed on to one's brother.

"Chapter 21 says, 'Jah shall wipe all tears from their eyes; and there shall be no more death, neither sorrow nor crying, neither shall there be any more pain; for the former things have passed away.'

"We must stop blaming our government and political leaders and accept that we have not made ourselves worthy of Jah's love. There needs to be changes, yes. But it needs to be done from within. Put away your swords and open your hearts to Jah. Good things will follow. Our country will be saved."

The two men stood by the door, looking around, wondering what they had walked into.

Marcus's words were intended to stir up a commotion among the mix of Rastafarians, many of whom supported the positive aspects of Manley's socialist government, and among the more anti-government or paramilitary Jamaicans.

Heckles started to erupt from the crowd. It was an ingeniously spontaneous diversion.

"You dare to make a political speech here, you coward? Now we know who wears the skirt in the family," said one Jamaican.

Marcus pointed and gestured at him. "Is it a coward to want the bloodshed to stop?" the big man asked.

"It is a coward who does nothing while the American CIA takes over our country. They paid assassins to shoot Bob Marley," said another Jamaican. "We know who de real enemy is."

Jack was hoping they were play-acting. It seemed very real. They were using strong words.

"They are only here to help keep the Communists out," Marcus said. "See, people, this is the danger; we must not let others divide us. We must unite to solve our problems from within."

While Marcus spoke, several Rastas working with Freddie in the diversion took up positions by the two men at the door.

One Rasta asked one of the men if he agreed with the speaker. The man shrugged and started to move away.

"You not believe in peace?" the Rasta asked as he turned to face the man aggressively.

"No, mon, me not believe in it. Back off," the man said.

He tapped the Rasta lightly on the chest to make his point. As the two men began looking for Jack, several other Rastas blocked their path.

"You lookin' for something?" said one of the Rastas. "Me don't know you. Maybe tell me 'bout it."

The two men couldn't get around the group of Rastas. One reached inside his shirt for a gun. Before he could pull it out, however, two Rastas grabbed his arms and twisted the weapon away.

"Well, what have we here?" said one Rasta as he held up a .38-caliber revolver.

Marcus stopped speaking, and the band started to play

again. With the local boys firmly in charge, Jack, Ed, and Sarah escaped. As they ran out the back door, another man appeared from the shadows—tall and lean with heavy dreadlocks, a calm, watchful gaze.

"Jack," said the man. "Do you need a ride?"

Jack froze for a second until he recognized the newcomer. "Raleigh? Jesus, you've got good timing."

Raleigh smiled and nodded. "We'd better get out of here. Follow me. My Jeep is back here."

Jack turned to Freddie. "Thanks, you've been great," he said, digging in his pocket for a tip. "You'd better get out of here now. We'll be in touch."

"Sure, mon, anytime. I hope you find your woman," said Freddie. "Be seein' you."

* * *

Driving on the mountain road without lights, Raleigh expertly guided his dark green Jeep Cherokee through the road in the lushly vegetated countryside. "As a child, I played in these woods," he said. "It doesn't change much."

Ed and Sarah held on to the backseat crash bars as the Jeep bounced over the rocky road. Jack filled Raleigh in on Becky and her disappearance.

Five minutes later, Raleigh pulled into his driveway and parked his Jeep in the garage. "Go on in, Jack; I'll be there soon."

The small mansion sat high in the Blue Mountains, a weathered yet elegant structure of stone and wood, softened by flowering vines and wide verandas that wrapped around its upper floors. Below it, a lush green valley rolled outward in layers of mist, dotted with banana trees, coffee plants, and the distant glint of a narrow river cutting through the land. The air was cool and scented with rain and earth, and from the doorway, the world felt hushed, as if the mountain itself were keeping watch.

They walked to the mansion's front door, where Telly Lakes—graceful and calm, with warm brown skin, expressive eyes, and long dark hair wrapped in a colorful headscarf that gave her a quiet, regal presence—opened it to greet them. "Jack, welcome. Do come in," she said.

"I'm so glad to see you again, Telly," said Jack, who hugged her. She held the door open as Jack introduced Ed and Sarah.

"Welcome to you all. Come in," Telly said. "I prepared the guest bedrooms. I've got one for Sarah. The other is the one you and Becky stayed in when you came last time..." She paused, holding one hand over her lips.

"I remember. Even though Becky is a city girl, she loved staying in the country and being around so much nature," Jack said.

"This is a lovely house—so many beautiful paintings on the walls. I will never forget it," Sarah interjected. "But if you ask me, Becky missed the point about nature."

Jack sighed and said, "Becky missed a lot of points."

"I'm so sorry, Jack," Telly said. "I can't believe Becky is in trouble. Why don't you get settled and join Raleigh downstairs in the music room?"

"Thank you, Telly. You're a real angel," Jack said, kissing her on the cheek. She blushed and hurried off to make brandy nightcaps.

"Those Rastas, Freddie, and Raleigh bailed us out," Ed said.

"If only more people on the island were like them, this

place would be a real paradise," Jack said.

The three went upstairs to put their bags away. Raleigh came in from the garage and joined his wife in the music room. He gulped down a brandy and left to wash up. A few minutes later, the three came downstairs.

"Raleigh is taking a shower," Telly explained. "When Raleigh paints, he sometimes stays in the mountains for days. We have a little hut that he uses. No electricity. We have a two-way radio for emergencies. When he comes home, this is how he looks and smells."

"Believe me, Mrs. Lakes, with those two thugs on our tail, Raleigh looked pretty good to me," Ed said.

"Call me Telly, please, Ed," she replied. "Raleigh always looks good to me," she added with a twinkle in her eye. "Come on in, and I'll give you some drinks."

Sarah yawned. "I'm a little tired. Do you mind if I go to bed? Can you show me where to go, Jack? A little too much excitement for me tonight."

"How about if you go put Sarah to bed?" Jack asked Ed with a smile. "It's upstairs, three doors on the right."

"Now, don't think I'm a baby," Sarah teased. "I'm just tired."

"Go ahead, Ed, tuck her in," Jack said. "I need another drink. I'll wait down here and talk with Telly."

Ed and Sarah climbed the tall wooden stairs. The house, solidly built at the turn of the century, had weathered many tropical storms and hurricanes. Ed looked down the hall as they reached the top of the stairs. The electric lights were dim. He led Sarah to the room Telly had prepared for her.

"Will you be all right, Sarah?" he asked.

"Yes, Ed. You are so nice. I want to lie down and relax for a while and then get some sleep," said Sarah, adding, "I wish we had more time."

"We have tomorrow."

"Oh, yes. You go down and make your plans. I'll be fine."

"Okay. Sleep tight."

Sarah squeezed Ed's hand and said, "Thank you—and Jack—for everything. Tell him thank you for bringing me here and for allowing me to be part of this. It means a lot. Meeting you meant a lot as well."

"The feeling is mutual. Just go to sleep. We have a lot to do tomorrow," Ed said, thinking of her goodnight wish and the strange look on her face—a tight, unreadable mix of gratitude, relief, and secrecy behind her eyes.

Sarah nodded and closed the door.

Ed walked down the stairs and returned to the music room, where Telly had put on the Wailers' latest album, Exodus.

Sleep was the last thing on Sarah's mind. She locked the door, took off her clothes, folded them, and put them on the table. She lay down on the bed and began to rub her vagina slowly until it became moist. After a few moments, her legs began to twitch, and she convulsed.

"Oh, Robert. Oh, Robert," she moaned as she finished, holding her legs tight together.

"You sweet bastard...you're going to die soon," she said.

Dressing quickly, Sarah began to carry out her plan for revenge.

Chapter 33
Raleigh Lakes

Later Saturday night, Aug. 19, 1980

Jack and Ed talked with Raleigh for several hours. The artist told them that Jamaica's problems were far worse than they had imagined from news reports back in the States.

Since the beginning of 1980, when socialist Prime Minister Michael Manley announced that elections would be held this coming October, more than 700 people had been killed, either by political hit teams inspired by both sides or in violent riots, mainly in Kingston's ghettos. The economy was in shambles, with shortages of food, oil, and other essential supplies.

"I was wondering why Becky flew into Montego Bay instead of Kingston," Jack said.

"Mackey has supporters in Kingston but also enemies," said Raleigh. "He probably didn't want to risk getting caught up in that. It is a dangerous time in my country right now."

Raleigh told them about the older women who were shot in their beds in the middle of the night because their sons supported Manley, and about the children who were killed because their parents supported Edward Seaga, head of the opposition Jamaican Labour Party.

Bands of young shooters attacked each other with M-16s. One of the bloodiest confrontations occurred at a JLP dance. Dubbed the Gold Coast Massacre, dozens of paramilitary troops landed at the waterfront dance in water rafts. They opened fire, and a dozen teenagers fell.

Raleigh stated that Manley and Seaga were competing not only for control of the government but also for Jamaica's soul.

Jack shook his head in disbelief. He hadn't realized how polarized the country had become, with murder replacing debate for political discourse.

"You know I'll do my best to help you find Becky. But you must understand what Jamaica has become since you two were last here. Some Jamaicans like myself have tried hard to win the support of Americans, even though our leaders have chosen to ally with Castro, Grenada, and ultimately, the Soviet Union," Raleigh said.

"What you are seeing now is a nation torn apart by poverty, drug wars, and a lack of investment. Manley has a good heart, but is aligning himself with the wrong people. He's got the support of most of the Rastafarians, mainly because they're a religious cult that grew up revering Manley's father, who created the People's National Party in the late 1930s," Raleigh explained.

Jack and Ed soaked in all the information, growing concerned about what lay ahead in rescuing Becky and getting out alive.

"So, who does the average Jamaican support?" Ed asked.

"Hard to say. I reluctantly support Seaga. But Manley has

received support from Bob Marley, who is also a close friend of mine. Bob wants peace and believes these campaigns are killing innocent people," said Raleigh, shaking his head.

"But Bob has been getting weaker and weaker from the cancer and doesn't have the strength to take sides, even if he wanted to," said the artist. His voice turned sad. "He's on his last world tour now. I don't know how he does it. I don't think he has much time."

He sighed and took another sip of his brandy. "Even though I suspect Seaga is a bully and behind much of this violence, I cannot stand idly by and watch my country turn its back on our friends in the United States. Once he gets past this election, I believe Seaga will crack down on drugs, turn away from Cuba, and attract more investment from the U.S. It is a gamble, but for us, right now and long-term, it is the best option."

"I take it you believed in what Manley was doing for most people. How did things get so bad that he had to go to Castro for help?" Ed asked.

"It's been a slow process. Since 1972, when Manley became prime minister, he and his party, the People's National Party, have moved Jamaica closer to communism. He thought he could do here what Castro began in Cuba—take away power from the few and give it to the many.

"Of course, Castro became power hungry. He betrayed the people and democracy. Once you gain control, as Castro did, it can often lead to authoritarianism and the elimination of political opposition.

"I once thought Manley could do what Castro initially intended. It was a worthy goal, and it might have succeeded.

"But oil prices started to rise in 1974. And we must buy

oil. We don't have any. When prices rose, we ran out of money. Manley imposed high tariffs on exports to American companies, such as bauxite used to make aluminum. That hasn't worked. Jamaica has, for all purposes, spent all its money reserves on oil."

"But that was a few years back. What's happened since then?" Ed said.

"Inflation has been terrible. Then, the shortages came. First, it was cooking oil, then rice, then soap, then everything. I'll tell you this: if it weren't for the ganja trade and cocaine distribution—which I believe Manley tacitly allows and may even encourage—most of the factories would be shut down.

"Without proper police enforcement, Manley has allowed ganja to be grown and traded openly to bring in American dollars. It has helped to prop the country up financially, but the trade has further strained relations with the U.S. and led to much violence."

He paused, took a deep breath, and said, "The little money the drug trade has brought us isn't worth the tradeoff: an explosion of drug dealers, traffickers, gangs, and open warfare over territory and a share of the profits."

Jack interrupted in a low voice. "Do you think Mackey has the support of the Manley government? I mean, how else could he operate?"

"It seems very likely. There are several drug lords like Mackey operating in Jamaica," Raleigh said. "But from what I know already about Mackey, he is one of the country's biggest traffickers, an international drug dealer who does business with Escobar in Colombia. It is going to be extremely dangerous to deal with him."

"But can we do it?" Jack asked softly.

"Honestly, I don't know if we can get Becky out."

Jack was stunned at Raleigh's statement. "We have to get her out."

Ed shifted in his seat and whistled. "Jack. You heard what Raleigh said. He doesn't know. This is going to be pretty hairy."

Jack stood up, walked by the window, and looked into the darkness. He took a long sip of his brandy.

"What can we do, Raleigh?" he finally asked.

"I'm having some friends check on Mackey. We monitor all the major drug traffickers and their deals. I should know soon," he said.

"Who are these friends?" Ed asked.

"They can be trusted," Raleigh replied. "We will find out about Becky very soon."

"Damn Robert Mackey," Jack said as he kept staring out the window. Becky was alone out there, being held by a criminal with no principles who cared only about selling cocaine and making money.

He remembered how Mackey's henchmen had clobbered him and then tried to kill him with an overdose of drugs. He had told Raleigh about it.

"I know how you feel, Jack. Just be patient. Don't do anything on your own. It's much too dangerous. There are things we can do to help," Raleigh cautioned.

Ed shook his head. "I know you want to help, but what can you do? It seems as if Mackey holds all the cards."

It was Raleigh's turn to interrupt. "There are things that can be done, and they will be done. I can say now that you came at the right time, but I cannot say any more. It's getting late, Jack. Do you mind if I turn in? It will be a busy day tomorrow."

Raleigh excused himself and went to bed. His steps were

heard down the hall. A door closed, and there was silence.

"What do you make of that?" Ed asked.

Jack shook his head. "He has something in mind. He did say we came at the right time. Not sure what that meant, but he knows we have little time."

"But what can he do? Can he call out the army? Because that's what we'll need to free Becky, especially if Mackey has guns and the support of the police and government and half the people."

"No, I don't think Raleigh has an army," said Jack. "He has something better."

"What do you mean, something better? Now you're talking like him, in riddles."

"I didn't want to tell you before because I thought it might come out when we talked with Raleigh. You should know now. Raleigh is CIA."

"The CIA?" Ed said. "Raleigh is a CIA agent?"

"He works with them. He's never told me directly, but he's given enough hints that I know he is. They're everywhere in the Caribbean. The CIA is always where America has big interests—and we have a big interest in keeping Jamaica away from Cuba and communism," Jack said.

"Yeah, I suppose so. It figures," Ed said. "That makes me feel a little better about this mission. At first, I thought it was hopeless. Now, less so. Maybe we can do it. Get her and ourselves out of here."

Chapter 34
Mountain Dream No. 4

Early Sunday morning, July 20, 1980

The soldiers stood at the mountain's peak, gazing at the sky. A man in a white robe was floating high in the air, looking down. The soldiers gathered close together.

Jack heard mumbled words from the man's mouth, but couldn't make out what he was saying. As before, he knew where he was: in Jamaica's Blue Mountains, having another dream.

Suddenly, the words became louder and clearer.

"My friends, you have been summoned to a great mission that will test your courage, strength, and resolve," said the floating man. "Do not fear the coming battle. Whether you live or die, you will be rewarded for your great deeds against evil."

The soldiers raised their arms and began a hoarse murmur

from deep within their guts, growing louder and louder. They banged their swords and axes on their shields and shook them high to support their leader and to show great defiance of the enemy.

Even though Jack knew he was dreaming, he became excited by his fellow soldiers' growing enthusiasm for battle.

"You will be rewarded when you are finished. Now, go forward; free yourselves and your loved ones," said the floating man. "Go forward and fight. Fight for what you know is right!"

A bright light filled the sky as the floating man disappeared. Jack woke up, mumbling, "Fight, fight, fight."

Chapter 35
Sarah's Obsession

Sunday morning, July 20, 1980

Jack slept until mid-morning. In the mountains, the nights were cool, peaceful, and calm.

When he awoke, the mountain dream flashed into his mind. He hadn't had one in several days. Before, the dream had disturbed him. Now, it relaxed him.

On his way downstairs, as he thought of the dream—and the message from the leader to fight for what's right—Jack stopped by Sarah's room and knocked on the door.

"Sarah?" Jack called. "Time for breakfast."

There was no answer.

"You awake? Sarah?"

The door was partly open. "I'm coming in," he said, pushing through. He looked around. She wasn't there.

Something felt off. Everything was tidy. Then he saw that her bed was untouched. On top of the sheets was a note.

"Oh, Jesus," Jack said. He took two giant strides to the bed and picked up the handwritten letter.

> *Dear Jack, I've got a confession to make.*
> *While I wanted to help you at first, I found*
> *myself driven to see Robert one last time. I*
> *hope to see you again someday. If not, I cannot*
> *thank you enough for bringing me here. You've*
> *been a real friend. I hope you find Becky.*

That was it. Jack crammed the note into his pocket, raced out of the room, and bolted down the hall. When he reached the top of the stairs, he yelled, "Sarah's gone to find Mackey!"

Ed and Raleigh emerged from the den with quizzical expressions.

"Jack, what the hell are you talking about?" Ed shouted.

Flying down the stairs, Jack said breathlessly, "She left a note explaining it. She doesn't know what she's doing. She will tell him everything about us, about Raleigh, and put Becky's life in danger."

"I knew she'd be trouble," Ed said flatly.

Telly came out of the kitchen at the sound of the commotion. "Everybody, please, be calm," she said. "There's nothing you can do right now. Raleigh, tell Jack everything will be all right."

"Jack," Raleigh said. "Let's sort this out in the den."

"I'll bring more coffee," Telly said. "And Jack, you can't do anything until you have your breakfast."

Jack couldn't believe Sarah had left. He paced back and forth in the den, clenching and unclenching his fists. He bared his teeth and ground them together as he tried to decide what to do. How could she have done this? He had trusted her, even though Ed was suspicious.

But now, everything started to make sense. She'd pretended to be over Mackey. She'd said she never wanted to see him again.

Despite her anxiety, Jack thought Sarah had gotten over Robert. He was wrong. He realized he didn't really know her. She must have suppressed her true feelings all this time.

When she recognized the opportunity to visit Mackey on his home turf, she must have devised this half-baked plan. That was why she'd been so sweet for the last two days. She'd been setting him up, trying to ease his worries about bringing her. He'd sensed her joy and sweet behavior were out of character, and he should have questioned her about it.

All he had thought about on this trip was finding Becky and making the mission less scary for Sarah and Ed. He sometimes went out of his way to make it seem like a vacation. Deep down, he'd known the danger and accepted the probability that things would turn deadly.

Now, he understood Sarah's plan.

"I know what Sarah is going to do," Jack said, calming down and beginning to see things more clearly. "I don't think she'll talk about us. That would spoil her plan."

"Which is?" asked Ed.

"She's going to kill Mackey."

"Do you think?" Raleigh asked. "Murder?"

"No way," Ed said. "She wouldn't know how."

"Yes. Sarah really hates Mackey. Just think about it. She kept this plan to go to Mackey a secret and fooled us completely," Jack said.

"You're right; she did talk about how we'd have to kill Mackey to get Becky out," Ed recalled. "When she talked about how ruthless and deceitful he is, I took that as a warning for us. But she was saying that out of bitterness."

"Yes, it was all a ruse," Jack said. "Still, I don't think she can do it without a clean opportunity. I'm worried that she could mess the situation up enough to make things worse for Becky."

Just then, the phone rang. Raleigh put his finger to his lips and motioned for quiet as he picked up the receiver. The two brothers looked at one another.

Was it Sarah calling to say she had changed her mind? Was it Mackey calling to say he knew everything?

Then, the worst thought crossed Jack's mind. What if Mackey tried to use Sarah as a bargaining chip to force Jack to leave the country? He couldn't do that with Becky. Sarah was expendable.

"Yes, this afternoon will be fine," Raleigh said. "The party is on for tonight? That's wonderful. Will everyone attend? Yes, that's just right. I'll be over later to make the arrangements."

"Everything okay?" Jack asked.

Raleigh hung up the phone and sighed. "That was my contact about Mackey. It's just as I'd hoped," he said with a smile. "If everything works out, we'll have a chance to take Becky out tonight. We can also rescue Sarah if she's there."

Chapter 36
Jack Confronts Michael

Sunday afternoon, July 20, 1980

The afternoon dragged. There was nothing to do except rest and wait. Jack was relieved when Raleigh told him something would be done.

But his worry about Becky's safety grew with every passing hour. He also worried that Sarah would be forced to talk, which could complicate everything. If she tried to kill Mackey and failed, her actions could make it harder to rescue Becky.

In the early afternoon, Raleigh said he was going to town to talk with someone he described as a sympathetic former police officer who had quit months earlier because of corruption. Now, as a private detective, he specialized in protecting political officials.

Sounds like the CIA, Jack thought. Ed agreed.

Thirty minutes after Raleigh left, the phone rang. Telly picked it up. "Oh, hi, Freddie. Yes, he's here."

"Thanks, I'll take it," Jack said quickly. Telly handed the phone to him.

"Was it you?" Jack asked.

"Me picked up de girl last night. She told me you all were staying at de house and that she needed a ride somewhere, mon," Freddie said nervously. "The girl said it was an emergency and part of the plan, eh? Me asked why you didn't call, and she said you were busy and not to worry. This morning, thinking more about it, me became more uncertain. She was all nervous, so me called to let you know where she went."

"Where?" Jack said.

"Da big house. Me can show you if you like," Freddie offered.

"Come right over, but don't be followed," Jack instructed, then hung up.

"Did I hear you right?" Ed asked. "Are you thinking about paying a visit to our local drug dealer?"

"No, don't be silly," Jack said. "I think it would be good for us to find out exactly where Becky is. We'll gather as much information as possible and then return here to let Raleigh know."

* * *

Freddie said it was only 15 minutes south and up the mountain road toward Mackey's mansion. Ahead, they saw a small roadside bar and food store.

"How much farther is it?" Jack asked.

"Da house is up the road. No more than five minutes," Freddie said. "She asked if I knew where dis big house was that they had all dem guards. I thought it was part of the plan to find it. I so sorry I did this."

"I wish you hadn't, Freddie, but there is little to be gained going over it now," Jack said, wondering how he would turn this fiasco into an advantage.

"Let's stop for a minute before we get closer. We need to talk about this," Ed said, sensing danger ahead.

"Just for a few minutes. I want to check out Robert's house," Jack replied impatiently.

As Freddie pulled the cab off the road and into the dirt parking lot next to the bar, Jack spotted someone familiar coming out of the store.

"That's Michael from Sarasota, Becky's boss from the High Seas. We're going to find out a few things—right now," Jack declared, excitedly opening the door.

He didn't recognize the American woman walking beside Michael. She was tall, suntanned, and beautiful. Had he seen her at the restaurant before?

"No, Jack, stay here," Ed called out calmly, not wanting the couple to hear him.

But it was too late. Jack slammed the cab door shut and walked briskly to meet the pair. His heart was pounding, and his blood was boiling.

Ed closed his eyes briefly and said, "Keep the car running, Freddie. We might have to get out of here fast. Talk about blowing our cover..."

"Here we go again," Freddie said. "You two sure know how to find trouble."

"Where's Becky?" Jack snarled at Michael as he approached.

"Everybody, it seems, is in Jamaica this time of year. Kendall, I'm going to pretend you aren't here...for your own good,"

Michael replied.

"Are you Jack?" the woman asked in surprise.

"Michelle, stay out of this," Michael said softly. "I'm going to give you some friendly advice, Kendall. We've given you a little slack, but you're starting to upset Robert."

"Who's Robert? Is he your boss? The big man with all the coke who took Becky and is destroying countless lives in the States? And for what? Money?" Jack said in a fast, angry tone, itching for a fight.

Jack took another step forward. "You and he are going to have to answer for the awful things you've done in the name of avarice and greed," he said loudly enough for everyone in the parking lot to hear.

Jack's harsh words took Michael aback. He paused, then said menacingly, "Kendall, get off this island. Now."

"Not without Becky. Now, I've got some advice for you. Let Becky go, and you won't have any trouble from me," said Jack, pointing at Michael.

"Let Becky go?" Michael said. "What the fuck are you talking about? She's perfectly happy here. She doesn't want to go. You've got to get a hold of yourself. It's over between you and her. If you don't know that, you must be delusional."

That was all Jack could take. Rage consumed him as he lunged at Michael, using his 6-foot-4, 220-pound frame to push Michael back with a forceful shove.

"You son of a bitch!" Jack shouted as a surprised Michael fell into the dirt. "You don't know anything about her or me. Get up! C'mon!"

Shaking with rage, Jack loomed over Michael as the similarly sized drug dealer lay still on the ground.

Seeing the fray, Ed, 6 feet 3 inches tall and 210 pounds,

jumped out of the car and took up a position beside Jack, fists clenched and ready for a fight. Michael's two men followed suit.

"Get up, you bastard!" Jack roared. "I'll at least give you a chance to fight, unlike the cheap shots you gave me when you had your men drug me, knock me over the head, and send me to the hospital for a week."

Michael just sat on the ground, furious. "What are you talking about? If I wanted you killed, I'd do it myself! You're lucky I don't do it now after that cheap shot."

"Michael, stop talking like that," said Michelle. "And you, Jack, stop it too. You don't know me, but I'm Becky's best friend. She's all right. I promise. Please, go home."

Jack stared at Michelle, the words taking a second to register. Becky's best friend? He hadn't even known she had one, certainly not one hidden from him in Sarasota. The thought that she had another secret from him stung more than he expected. How many other things had she kept tucked away, pieces of her life she'd kept hidden?

He pushed it aside. This wasn't the moment to unravel Becky or himself.

"If she's all right," Jack said evenly, forcing his attention back where it belonged, "then help her come back to me. She made a mistake. She must have told you."

Michelle didn't know what to say. She looked over at Michael, who, throughout Jack's tirade, stayed on the ground. He was angry, but he didn't make any threatening moves.

His instinct was to jump up and mix it up with Jack. But he didn't want to cause any trouble, not in front of Michelle or with the big drug deal later that night.

Jack simmered down a bit, seeing Michael wasn't going to fight.

In a calmer voice, Jack said, "Listen, asshole, if she's all right, let me see her. Let me talk with her. Give her a chance to make a choice."

What happened next surprised everyone. Michael got up, dusted himself off, smiled at Jack, and walked toward his car without speaking a word.

His two men stared at Michael in disbelief as their boss walked away from the fight.

Still trembling with rage, Jack also didn't say another word as Michael opened the door to his car. The

Before he got in, Michael turned around. "As I said, I'll just pretend you aren't here. It's best this way, Kendall. You don't believe me, but it's best for Becky that she doesn't know you're here."

Jack just glared at Michael. He had made his point.

"She doesn't want to see you again," LeCare continued. "And I'm warning you: if you're seen anywhere near the house, I'll personally make sure you'll never see Florida again. If you won't leave, fine, enjoy the island. Get some sun. But forget about her. She's not worth it."

Jack was still shaking with fury as Michael drove off with Michelle. Approaching Michael like that had been a calculated risk, but his gamble to draw information about Becky and Sarah had paid off.

At least Jack knew Becky was still alive, and Sarah hadn't told Robert anything about their plans. He was now confident Becky was safe with Robert. But would Raleigh be able to find a way to get her out—and Sarah, too? He would find out later tonight.

Jack's thoughts were interrupted as the black jeep with lightning stripes drove past. The two thugs with Michael had parked behind the store and sped off to catch up with their boss.

"Isn't that the jeep that followed us the other night to that reggae bar?" Ed said.

"And that's the same one we saw patrolling in front of our hotel," Jack added, shaking his head. Everything was coming together.

"Michael said he's known about us for two days. They've been following us all along," Ed said.

"Yes, that's my hunch too, but they haven't done anything about it other than come into the Rasta bar," Jack said. "Let's give them a couple of minutes and follow them up the road. I want to see this mountain fortress Sarah talked about and get a look at exactly where Becky is staying."

"Jack, that's crazy; after what Michael just told you, we should stay away from the house," Ed advised.

"I just want to drive past to see what it looks like," Jack said. "We won't stop. No one will notice."

Chapter 37
Michelle Decides

Later Sunday, July 20, 1980

As Michael drove away, he glanced in his rearview mirror and saw Ed talking to Jack. As the heat of the moment faded, he shook his head slowly. He now knew that everything Becky had said about Jack's unwavering determination was true.

But he didn't think Jack would be crazy enough to follow him back to the house. That would be suicidal. He had made it clear to Jack that he'd never see Becky again if he did so.

Besides, after tonight, they'd all be gone, including Becky. Michael knew he'd done the right thing by not escalating the encounter. Still, he was disappointed he hadn't had a chance to test Kendall.

"Michael, what was all that about?" Michelle asked.

"It was nothing. He is nothing."

* * *

Michelle saw it differently. What she had just witnessed in the fight was Jack risking everything because he loved Becky and wanted her back. As for Michael, Michelle felt a chilling clarity settle in: whatever hold he thought he had over her was gone, replaced by a quiet resolve to survive him.

Becky was right about Jack. He was everything she had said he was. Strong, fearless, principled, determined, handsome.

Michelle wondered why Becky had left him. It wasn't because he didn't love her enough. It was clear he was crazy about her.

Then Michelle looked at Michael and wondered whether he would chase her to a foreign land if a similar situation arose.

Michael noticed Michelle was staring at him. He glanced over, and their eyes met for a brief moment. She had her answer. She knew he wouldn't do the same. He was upset, but he had a cold look in his eyes. He wasn't going to reassure her.

She turned away and looked out the side window. Jack was a romantic. Michael? Well, he was simply a businessman with muscles and a high sex drive.

"Michael, what's going to happen next?" she asked.

"With Jack? He'll be on a plane in a couple of days," Michael said.

"I don't know. Becky said the one fear she had in leaving him was that he never gives up something once he starts it."

Michael didn't respond right away. He was thinking about the pending drug deal that night.

"Michael," Michelle prodded, exasperated.

"Oh, sorry. It's admirable that he doesn't quit. I'm sure it serves him well as a journalist. But it's different here. He could get killed trying stunts like that," Michael said.

"Killed?" Michelle said. "This is getting worse and worse.

When you told me about your 'real' business last week, you also said you'd be getting out. I told you then, and I'm telling you again: either you stop, or I'm leaving you. It's not what I bargained for. I want a normal life. You promised."

"I told you, Michelle, this is the last big deal. We have to do it. That's all, and then we can leave," Michael said.

"I agreed to that, I know, but what was all that about with Jack?" she said. "I don't want to be around if you're going to kill somebody."

"That's just talk. Kendall won't bother us anymore," Michael said.

"You don't know him at all."

"Oh, and you do?"

"No, but Becky told me all about him. I told you he's a hothead, but he also isn't a quitter. He won't stop. He knows where she is, and he will try to get her out."

"That's suicidal."

"Stop saying that. Michael, something bad is going to happen. I feel it. For my sake, why don't you ask Robert to let Becky go? She wants to go home; you know that. Robert is practically kidnapping her."

"It's for her safety that she stays. We've talked about that. Besides, it's impossible right now," Michael said. "Robert doesn't want to take any chances until the next deal goes down."

"Please listen to me, Michael. Let Becky and me catch a plane this afternoon before anything happens. You can escort us to the airport with your bodyguards. Then you can tell Jack that Becky has left the island and show him the proof. He'll be gone tomorrow."

"That doesn't fit into Robert's plans. I've talked with him

about it, and he will not change his mind about keeping Becky here until this is all over. We need another day to do this deal, Michelle. Can't you wait?"

"No, not anymore," she said. "You've got to let Becky go."

Michael was trying to be patient. He had been patient with Kendall and Michelle, but they were amateurs.

"Okay, I'll talk with Robert once more, but there's something you have got to understand," Michael said.

"I'm listening."

"Hold on." Michael turned into the compound's driveway and stopped the car. About 20 feet from the road, a 12-foot-high iron gate barred their entrance.

A large man with dreadlocks peered out from behind the gate. The tip of the barrel of his semi-automatic weapon peeked out between the bars.

Michael waved. The man pushed a button, and the big gate swung open. Michael guided the car past the gate and down the driveway toward the large white house on the hill.

Between the sprawling mansion and the fence stood a smaller building that housed the 30-odd men who protected Robert. Michael drove past the guardhouse, stopped the car again, and turned to Michelle.

"I didn't want to tell you this because I feared it might scare you, but I suppose you should know. You and Becky are in great danger if you leave the compound alone—at least right now. I shouldn't have taken you to the store to get cigarettes. It was risky."

"Oh, Michael," she said fearfully.

"You are safe here, thanks to the security we have around the house. Robert has done everything he can to keep us safe. It won't be long; this deal will be done, and we will all leave this island. But Robert can't be sure that if he lets Becky go, she wouldn't be killed or taken hostage by our enemies," Michael explained, pausing to look her directly in the eyes. "That's why he can't release her now."

"But why doesn't he tell her that?" Michelle said. "She might understand a little more. Right now, she thinks Robert is being controlling for no reason."

"Two reasons. One, Becky isn't part of all this, and Robert wants to keep it that way, for now. She doesn't know about the business, and he doesn't want to complicate things by telling her until the deal's over, and he's sure about her. And two, Robert doesn't want to frighten her unnecessarily. It's for her own good."

"Why did you bring us both here, Michael? This is crazy. It doesn't make sense!"

"Ah, yes. Don't think I've considered that. We didn't realize the situation in Jamaica would deteriorate this much. As the election draws near, the political climate worsens. But I can't discuss it now. We need to get inside the house. I have to talk with Robert about a couple of issues. I can tell you this, though: we suspect a security breach, and we're on high alert. That's why today is so important. Afterward, I'll be glad to leave."

"I just wish we could all leave now," Michelle said.

"It will all be worth it. Just wait. Remember, we have that joint bank account in Colombia. There's enough money to tide us over for life. This is my last deal. It's icing on the cake. I promised Robert, and I can't let him down. Besides, you don't cross Robert. He has friends I don't even know about.

"Just another day. That's all I ask. Then we can fly to Bogotá. Okay?"

"I'll think about it," Michelle said. But she had already

made up her mind that he was lying.

Michael shrugged, started the car, and drove ahead. Several men were walking about the yard, each toting an automatic weapon. He nodded at several of them as he passed the guardhouse and drove up the path to the mansion.

"Don't say anything about this to anybody," Michael said. "And please don't tell Becky. You've been good about that so far."

Michelle didn't say anything. She didn't trust Michael anymore, and she had decided to tell Becky everything and leave tonight, if she could, regardless of the danger. She wasn't exactly sure how she'd pull it off, but she'd find a way. It was the only thing to do.

After what Michael had told her, something was going to happen—maybe tonight—and she didn't want to be around to see it.

Chapter 38
Sarah and Robert

Sunday morning, July 20, 1980

During the night, Sarah left for Robert's house. Freddie dropped her off on the road a half mile from the house. She found a soft spot on the ground in the woods and slept for a few hours.

In the morning, she approached the large gate and asked the guard to let her see Robert. The guard was surprised to see a girl alone and skeptical of her intentions.

Thinking it might be a clever ruse before an attack, he pressed a small button on the floor with his foot to call for help. They were already on alert. The compound immediately went on emergency alert.

A jeep carrying several other heavily armed men approached the front gate at top speed. They searched Sarah for weapons and explosives, then called Robert.

Twenty minutes later, Robert drove up to the guardhouse, where his men interrogated her to find out why she was there.

The police had informed him that a young woman was traveling with Jack and his brother, but he was shocked to learn that the woman was Sarah. He hadn't seen her in nearly a year.

Robert met Sarah through her father, a friend and business associate. He liked her because she was intelligent, funny, and fresh.

Then, one day at Siesta Beach, when he'd seen her in her bathing suit, he asked her out. He dated her while he was in Florida. But over time, he realized how unstable and immature she was and left her.

"Sarah," he said, his eyes narrowing. "What in blue blazes are you doin' here?"

"I had to see you, Robert," she insisted. "Don't judge me yet. I've changed."

"Come with me," Robert ordered sternly as he led her to the main house. "You've got a lot of explainin' to do."

"It was all for you," she pleaded. "I can help you with whatever you're doing here. Just give me a chance."

"We've been over this—you and I are done," Robert said, his voice low and dangerous. "I'm not pleased to see you here. So, tell me straight: how d'you know Jack Kendall and his brother?"

Sarah had rehearsed everything she was about to say. She knew Robert would question her and that she had to tell the truth, mostly.

"I met Jack in the hospital, where he was being treated for a serious drug overdose," she recounted, trying to be as convincing as possible. "He had amnesia, and when he regained his memory, he learned from the police about the connection with Michael at the High Seas. Have you heard about that guy who committed suicide? He worked for Michael. That's how Jack got involved. He told me."

"I don't bloody believe it," Robert growled, his eyes narrowing. "What else aren't you tellin' me?"

"Jack told me the police are investigating the High Seas for cocaine and looking for Michael. Do you know about that? Several employees have already been arrested. The police know Michael has made several trips to Jamaica and think he may be here. When Jack told me he was coming, I told him I knew Michael and that I might be able to find him and Becky. I did all of this so we could be together again. I'm sorry. Jack doesn't know anything about us."

"But how the hell did you know exactly where to find me?" Robert demanded, his voice rising with controlled fury.

"Uh, you told me one night that you have a large house in St. Mary's near Castleton. Do you remember?" Sarah asked, hoping Robert *wouldn't* remember.

What Robert remembered was one drunken night when he stupidly invited her to spend a weekend with him. He knew he hadn't told her he owned a house in Jamaica. He always kept his business secret.

Maybe her father, who operated an international import-export trading company and occasionally provided him with business support, had told her where he lived.

Sarah was trying to deceive everyone. She'd lied to Jack about going to Jamaica with Robert and to Robert about how she'd found his address.

Her biggest lie to Robert was that she intended to be with him when she had a very different plan in mind.

"Does your old man know where you are?" Robert asked, his tone tight and suspicious.

"No, he went to North Carolina. I was staying with my mother," she said.

Robert listened, but he didn't believe her story. He decided to let her stay, at least until the drug deal was over.

"All right, come on then," Robert said, his tone cooling but still firm. "I'll get you some breakfast while I work out what to do with you."

He led her to the kitchen, where she ate under armed guard.

"When she's done, take her to the empty bedroom upstairs," he told the guard.

"Sarah, stay in your room," he ordered. "I'll talk to you later. Remember, I'm angry with you, so behave yourself."

She didn't want to go, but Robert insisted it was either that or he would put her on a plane home immediately.

*　*　*

Sarah had been asleep when she heard knocking on the door next to hers.

"Becky, it's me. Open up," Michelle said in a harsh whisper. "I've seen Jack."

Sarah opened her eyes.

"Jack's here," Michelle whispered again.

At the mention of Kendall's name, Sarah quickly rolled out of bed and went to the door to listen.

Becky finally opened the door and whispered, "He's here? Jack? Thank God. He got my letters."

"It's true. He's here. Wait until I tell you what happened," Michelle said.

When Sarah heard Becky's door close, she went into the hall outside the door to eavesdrop.

*　*　*

Michelle told Becky the entire conversation with Michael. "You let me come to Jamaica when you knew Robert was a drug dealer?" Becky asked, frustration in her voice.

"I didn't know what Michael was doing at first. When I guessed, he made me promise not to tell you or anybody else. Becky, he threatened me," Michelle said. "I was scared."

"Well, you still could have discouraged me from coming here."

"I'm sorry. I never expected our short trip to be so dramatic. I thought it would be fun for us. I didn't know the gang situation was so bad when we left," Michelle said. "There's a big deal going down tonight. I didn't know about that either. Michael told me it's one reason we must stay inside, where we're protected."

"Michelle, we have got to get out of here," Becky insisted.

"I'll call the airport and get us two tickets for the morning flight," Michelle said.

"Good. After you make the reservations, call this phone number. Ask for Louisa," Becky said.

"The maid, Louisa?"

"Yes. Just call her and ask her to send a car for us."

"A car? Will she do it?" Michelle asked, surprised. "Her brother works security for Robert."

"I know, but she's very sympathetic. She was the one who got word to Jack for me," said Becky.

"Really?" Michelle said. "You are quite the operator."

Michelle paused. "But how will we get out of the house?"

"Oh, Michelle, just call the airport," Becky said impatiently. "We'll figure it out later."

Michelle picked up the phone and listened. It sounded clear. She was a little nervous; she wasn't sure whether the phone line was monitored. She didn't think so, but she had to take the chance anyway. The two women held their breath and looked at each other.

Michelle dialed the number. The Air Jamaica operator answered.

"Reservations. May I help you?"

"Yes, I'd like two tickets for Bogotá."

Becky's eyes lit up in surprise. She'd expected the Miami flight.

"What time and day?" the airline representative asked.

"The early one, tomorrow," Michelle said.

"What are the names?"

"Michelle Talley and Becky Kendall."

"Just one moment."

A long few seconds passed. Becky paced around the room. Michelle tapped her fingers on the table.

"Hello. I'm still here," said Michelle. "What? To Bogotá? Are you sure? No. That's okay. Thank you."

Michelle hung up the phone and stared at Becky, mouth open.

"What happened?" Becky demanded.

"We have tickets to Bogotá in the morning. Somebody made the reservations for us," Michelle said. "It must have been Michael."

"Why Bogotá?"

"That's where the money is, silly."

Slowly, Becky asked, "What money?"

"Lots of money. Millions," Michelle quietly said. "It's drug money, of course. Michael and I have a joint account there.

If he survives this, we'll split it. If not, you and I will."

Becky didn't respond. She wanted to leave. She had intended to go to Sarasota to wait for Jack. But it wouldn't hurt to take a slight detour, especially for millions of dollars. She'd contact Jack later.

"I'll go, but why did Michael make the reservations?" Becky asked.

"I asked him to get us out. He seemed to want to help us but said he needed to talk with Robert first."

"We're so lucky. Michael will know how to get us out. I am not sure we could have done it alone with Louisa anyway," Becky said. "I think we're all set. Bogotá in the morning!"

Michelle returned the paper with Louisa's phone number to Becky. "I don't think we'll need a ride now," she said.

Becky nodded. "I suppose not. I could use a good night's sleep."

*　*　*

Sarah listened to the conversation and smiled, feeling completely satisfied. The upcoming drug deal tonight was exactly what she needed, offering her a perfect opportunity. She went back to her room and waited patiently for the right moment.

Chapter 39

Robert's Final Plans

Later Sunday, July 20, 1980

Downstairs, Michael and Robert met in the command center, a large room in the basement, custom-designed by Robert with thick concrete walls reinforced with steel and filled with survival gear, weapons and telecommunication equipment.

"I know you'd like to take Kendall out, but our information is that he is staying with Raleigh Lakes," Michael said.

"The CIA agent?" Robert said, brow tightening. "What the hell's he doin' with that jackal? Doesn't matter—the deal goes down tonight, and tomorrow we're off to Colombia."

"Becky won't like that. She wants to go back to Florida."

"I don't give a toss if she likes it or not," Robert growled. "We can't go back to Florida—Gordo reckons the cops raided the High Seas and nabbed a few of our bagmen. He's in Miami, waitin' on my word. Becky can wait too; I'll explain everything to her once this is over."

"When did you talk with Gordo?" Michael asked.

"Yesterday mornin'," Robert replied. "He's heard there are warrants out for us. Even though we did a decent job shuttin' things down, my lawyers say the cops found enough evidence to close the restaurant."

"So, my career as a restaurant tycoon is over? Why didn't you tell me yesterday?"

"I needed to talk with Gordo today about somethin' first, but couldn't get through—he's probably switchin' hotels again," Robert said. "Best I don't tell you everything right now. We've got enough to think about for tonight."

"What about this girl, Sarah?" Michael asked. "Is she going to be trouble?

"Sarah cooked up that story about why she turned up. She found out where I lived from her old man; I never told her," Robert said, his voice low and dangerous. "She must've told Kendall about the house. If it weren't for her old man, I'd feed her to the sharks."

"What about Becky?"

"She's been a right handful—a hot lay, but not what I expected," Robert lamented. "Once we're gone, she's got two choices."

"Oh? What do you have in mind?"

"She can marry me—or she can kiss her arse goodbye," Robert said with a cold chuckle. "Wives don't testify against their husbands. And dead women don't talk."

"You're quite romantic," Michael said with a sinister laugh. "Michelle will go along with our plan to lie low for a while. She already agreed to marry me. If she doesn't, she'll be dead as well. She's starting to get a little too demanding."

Michael knew that lying to Robert was a considerable risk. He was trying to have it both ways: first, by telling Michelle the truth about his business, and second, by following Robert's ideas. The truth was that he had fallen for Michelle and planned to quit the cocaine business. He didn't want to tell Robert about it right away.

"Becky'll have to make that choice—I'll say it a bit more gently," Robert said, pausing. "Things'll change once we clear out and she sees the money waiting for her. Reckon I won't have much trouble once she understands."

He added casually, "I've already told my supplier in Bogotá to keep her looked after if anything happens to us."

Michael looked stunned. "How's that work?"

Robert's smile turned thin. "Simple. I don't want her talkin'."

"She'll still be married to Jack."

"That'll be sorted once we're gone," Robert said calmly, his tone edged with menace. "He knows too bloody much."

"He's a smart-ass, too. I wouldn't mind if you gave me that little job of terminating Kendall with prejudice," Michael said, remembering the morning confrontation with Jack.

"Plenty to sort before then," Robert said. "Don't you go near Kendall—I've put Gordo on that job."

"What's going on with the deal? Are we on schedule?"

"The helicopter pickup is scheduled sometime tonight. I won't know the exact time until we get the coded message. I'm expecting that at any moment now."

"That's good. I told Michelle I'd talk with you about letting them leave. I made her think the drug deal would go down in a couple of days. She'll have a good sleep tonight, and by morning, this whole thing will be over, and I'll tell her we are leaving," Michael explained.

"I've got three plane tickets reserved for you, Michelle, and Becky for tomorrow morning's flight to Bogotá. I will take my private plane the next day," Robert said. "It's all gassed up and ready to go if we need to leave earlier.

"I hate to leave this place unprotected for too long, but the $10 million we make on this deal should be the icing on the cake for us."

"Are we closing up the shop permanently?" Michael asked.

"We're taking a break until the election is over. I will leave a skeleton staff here. I also gave word to close down operations in Atlanta and New Orleans. Escobar will take over our other shops in Nashville and Louisville," Robert said. "Besides, the election here is going to be close. If Seaga wins, he will probably shut us down because he knows I financially support Manley."

"It'll be good to relax after all these years," said Michael, thinking his resignation to Robert might not be so difficult.

"Let's not rush into retirement so quickly. I have more plans with Escobar in Colombia. I'm just starting to get tight with him," Robert said. "By the way, was there anything to that tip we got about the Rings posse hitting us?"

"I checked it out. There is a high probability, but we should be all right if we play the deal tonight. The rumor we planted is that the deal will go down tomorrow night. By then, we should be long gone, and the Rings will have made a trip to see us for nothing," Michael said.

"That's good. But as a precaution, I want the compound on alert when the sun goes down."

"Right. But what about Sarah? Do you have a ticket for her back to the States?" Michael asked.

"We leave her here."

"Won't she be a witness?"

"No, she'll be a corpse. I'll lead her on a bit, then send her on her way," said Robert.

"What about her father? I thought you wanted to protect her?" Michael asked, puzzled.

"Don't worry about her," Robert growled. "I'll tell her father she came unannounced and had an accident."

Michael nodded with a smirk.

The two men turned toward the row of TV monitors that scanned the property's perimeter. It wouldn't be long before nightfall. The security lights would soon come on. The last deal would be consummated, and they would make their getaway with $10 million.

Chapter 40
Planning the Rescue

Sunday night, July 20, 1980

Jack and Ed returned from their encounter with Michael long before Raleigh got home. They were resting in the living room when Raleigh arrived with his men.

Raleigh walked in with a group of 12 fighters behind him. Jack and Ed stood up and gazed in wonder at the group, an assortment of dreadlocked Jamaican men dressed in Army-style fatigues. They would blend perfectly into the surrounding jungle and forest.

"Jack, I'd like to introduce you to my friends," Raleigh said.

"It's a pleasure," Jack said to the steely-eyed soldiers. "I can't tell you how happy I am to have you men on the good guys' side."

Then Jack noticed Marcus, the big man from the Silver

Spoon, and several others who'd been there the night they narrowly escaped Mackey's men.

"Marcus, good to see you," Jack said. "Welcome to you all."

Marcus and the other men nodded but remained stoic. They would soon be going into battle.

Raleigh asked Jack to sit down. "Becky is safe," he said.

Jack nodded. "I know. I have something to tell you."

Raleigh smiled. "You're going to tell me you took a little afternoon drive to our local supply store and ran into Michael LeCare?"

Jack looked puzzled. "You know?"

"I've got eyes all over," Raleigh said. "Don't worry. It might have surprised them, but it's to our advantage that they think you're alone. At least you made it back in one piece."

"I wanted to find out for myself whether Becky is there and unharmed," Jack said. "What else have you learned?"

"We also know that Robert Mackey is involved with a larger group of terrorists who've been trying to keep Michael Manley in power. Their purpose, like that of many of these traitors, is to continue the highly profitable ganja and cocaine trade and keep the country in turmoil," Raleigh explained.

"What's the plan?" Jack asked.

"Our reports indicate a raid by the Rings on Mackey's estate tonight," Raleigh replied. "We will do nothing before then. Mackey has his compound on full alert."

"We plan to let the battle play out, then at the end, follow the raiders and eliminate all hostiles. Then we will take Becky out."

"Don't forget to look for Sarah," Ed interjected.

"We will take her as well, and any other innocents we find," Raleigh said.

Jack had always known it would come to this—a gun battle, with Becky and Sarah inside the house.

"Who are these raiders?"

"A rival drug lord from West Kingston, Lester Coke, whom we think has loose ties to Seaga, has decided to double-cross Mackey and cut in on his big drug deal, which is supposed to go down tonight," Raleigh said. "He's sending the Rings, a young mercenary group with whom we've had run-ins before, to do his dirty work."

"Do you think Becky will be safe inside the house?" Jack asked.

"Mackey will see to that. Of that, I am sure. Besides, there's nothing we can do except what we are already doing," Raleigh said.

"And you are sure of your intel?" Jack asked.

"Yes. We know Coke plans to kill Mackey, steal the cocaine and the money, and take over the drug trade in northeastern Jamaica," Raleigh said. "It is an aggressive plan, but one that could be very lucrative for Coke and the Rings. Once the money arrives for the drug purchase, the Rings will attack and kill everyone in the compound. They would then set fire to the mansion and burn whatever evidence is left."

"But what about Becky?" Jack exclaimed.

"It won't get that far," Raleigh said. "The Rings don't know Mackey has brought in reinforcements. The Rings will attack, and in the counterattack, be decimated. Mackey's men will be weakened, and then we will move in to mop up the survivors."

"It sounds hazardous for your people," said Jack, looking around at the Jamaicans.

"Jack, I don't believe you fully understand the motivation of my men here and what we want for our country," Raleigh said.

"No, I don't, not fully. I know you want a free, democratic Jamaica," Jack said. "Free from outside political influence, American or Cuban, and free from the violence the cocaine trade has brought."

"Yes, that is true. I underestimated you," Raleigh said. "Beyond that, what my men see here is an opportunity to eliminate two major drug gangs and one drug lord, Mackey, who has helped fund death, destruction, and political corruption in our nation."

"So, this is it," Jack said. "Is there no other way?"

"If we time this correctly and wait until both sides are exhausted, our plan could work perfectly," Raleigh said. "Besides, we've monitored the compound for the past several days. It's on high alert. You'd need the U.S. Army Rangers or Navy SEALs with air support to break in there now and succeed."

"I believe you," said Jack, with Ed nodding in agreement.

"If you had come to me a week earlier, maybe we could have surprised them with a night assault," Raleigh said. "But now we don't have any choice. We have to wait and do it this way. I'm sorry. It's our best chance to get Becky out."

Jack turned and stared out the window, wondering whether Becky would be safe during the battle. But Raleigh had conceived an excellent rescue plan, and his men looked fierce, brave, and dedicated to a larger ideal.

Chapter 41

The Mountain II

Shortly after midnight, July 21, 1980

It was an unusually bright, quiet night. The mountain air was cool. The stars were as big and plentiful as Jack had ever seen, even from the Blue Ridge Mountains in North Carolina, where he had gone to summer camp many years ago.

Jack and Ed sat silently on the front porch. Jack glanced up at the night sky, pondering what else he could do. There was nothing. The plan was set. It was just a matter of waiting for the signal. Then the raid would begin. He would finally find Becky.

Raleigh and his Jamaican fighters stood by their jeeps, checking their weapons and chatting quietly. Raleigh had stationed an advance team to watch Mackey's house. Once the team spotted the Rings, Raleigh would be notified, and everyone would move into position.

Suddenly, there was a commotion. Raleigh grabbed the walkie-talkie, listened for a second, then yelled, "Let's move out!"

The five jeep drivers started their engines, and one by one, they drove up a mountain trail toward Mackey's big house.

Jack and Ed looked at each other and nodded in mutual understanding. They raced over to Raleigh's Jeep and jumped in.

"What's happening?" Jack exclaimed.

"Our scout reported seeing a large group of vehicles approaching Mackey's hideout. They appear to be well-armed," Raleigh explained.

"Oh, fuck," Jack muttered. He began praying for Becky's safety.

"Jack, when we get there, I want you to wait by the jeeps with Ed and Oku. You shouldn't be directly involved in this until we clear everything," Raleigh said.

"Are you going in too? I didn't think this would be your fight," Jack said.

Raleigh just smiled, gunned the engine, and followed the other jeeps. "A wise Jamaican once said, 'But the stone that the builder refuse shall be the head cornerstone, and no matter what games they play, there is something they could never take away.'"

Jack listened and thought about it. The words sounded familiar, but he couldn't place them. "Who said that?" he finally asked.

"Bob Marley," Raleigh said.

"Oh, of course. What does it mean?"

"It means that what helps you, my friend, helps me and my country," Raleigh said, looking at a concerned Jack. "I will be careful. Don't worry. If she is there, we will find her. I promise. Have faith in the builder."

Jacked nodded and held on as Raleigh drove up the rugged mountain road. After 10 minutes, they rounded a corner, and Jack was jolted from his deep thoughts by a cacophony of automatic gunfire and explosions that sounded like cannon fire.

"Jesus, do they have artillery? I thought this was a Jamaican gang!" Ed screamed from the backseat.

The jeeps pulled off the road, into the woods, and went straight up the side of a hill.

"This is where we get off. It's about 300 yards from here down this hill and over the next," said Raleigh, jumping out and grabbing his gun.

Jack reached out and held Raleigh's arm. "I can't let you go alone. I'm going with you," he said.

"What? No, you can't. You aren't trained or equipped," Raleigh objected excitedly. "We've got no time to argue. We're going in. You wait here, Jack. Stay put."

Raleigh pointed to the ground to reaffirm his point. The Jamaicans, who had helmets, night-vision goggles, and bulletproof vests, were in position and ready to move out.

"Go then," said Jack, not wanting to get into an argument with Raleigh about whether he was capable of joining the battle to save Becky, "but be damn careful."

Raleigh smiled, nodded, then turned and barked a few orders.

"Gladstone, cover my flank! Marcus, I'm right behind you! Spread out!"

They vanished swiftly into the darkness. Jack and Ed stared after them, concerned. A full moon hung in the sky, and high above, beneath the stars, flashes of light and echoes of gunfire and explosions filled the air. The battle appeared to be intensifying. Jack and Ed stood motionless by the jeep.

Oku was sitting in the next vehicle. He held a walkie-talkie and appeared to be speaking into it. Jack looked inside Raleigh's jeep. On the floorboard lay another walkie-talkie. Jack reached in and picked it up.

"What are you doing?" Ed asked.

"I want to hear what's going on!" Jack replied. He turned on the walkie-talkie and adjusted the volume. At first, there was static, but then he tuned it to the right channel and heard Oku's voice.

"Dillinger is out for a stroll at the appointed hour. He will be there as planned," Oku said. "Over."

An American voice responded. "Enter the compound at Sector 12."

"Roger, Dillinger should be there, over and out," Oku said.

Jack quickly turned off the walkie-talkie and stared at Ed. "Did you hear that?" Jack whispered. "It sounded like Oku was talking with someone coordinating the raid."

"CIA. You were right. They're involved," said Ed, his eyes wide with excitement. "The CIA, the drug gang, the Jamaicans. They're all gonna kill each other."

"Ed! If the CIA is actively helping, Raleigh and his men have a better edge than we thought. But maybe they don't know Becky's in the house. We've got to get down there and see for ourselves!" Jack shouted. "C'mon, follow me!"

Jack took off running through the woods and up a hill toward the house. Ed glanced back at Oku. He was looking the other way, listening to the radio, and didn't immediately notice Jack's hasty departure.

"Oh, Jesus. There he goes again," Ed said softly, picking up the walkie-talkie, jumping out of the jeep, and taking off after his brother.

When they reached the hill, Oku spotted them and yelled for them to stop, but it was too late. A moment later, Jack and Ed were down the mountain and into the darkness.

As Jack ran up the next hill toward the house, a vision flashed through his mind of the crazy dream he had been having.

The mountain dreams!

He looked around wildly and realized he was climbing a hill. He was in the Blue Mountains of Jamaica. He heard gunfire ahead. He was living his dream—a soldier marching toward a mountain battle. He fought back the chill that swept through him and climbed the last few steps to the top of the hill. He had reached the peak. Ahead, the house loomed.

Then he remembered the end of that dream. A woman had led him down from that peak. He had thought the woman might be Sarah, but she had dark hair, unlike the blonde girl in the dream.

But the dream was fuzzy on that part. Maybe he had been mistaken, and the girl had red hair. Perhaps it had been Becky all along, and they would come down together.

Secure in that thought, his chest warm with confidence, his strength increased. He breathed deeply and intensely. He felt that the dream—the premonition, the vision, whatever it was—would protect him and help him find Becky.

Jack gazed across the top of the hill. It was a surreal sight. On the other side, he could see the house, partially on fire. The blaze's light revealed men rushing around, shooting each other and throwing hand grenades. Explosions, noise, screams, fire—chaos everywhere. People were dying.

A helicopter circled above and peppered the house with

machine-gun fire. A large rocket shot out from the roof and struck the helicopter. It exploded in the air and careened toward the ground, where it crashed and became a fireball. Another helicopter was burning in the field by the house.

Unbelievable, Jack thought.

He suddenly heard a scream from inside. It sounded like a woman's voice. Becky?

"Ed, I hear her!" Jack yelled.

"It's not Becky," Ed said, breathless and finally catching up to Jack.

"We've got to move and get closer to the house. She's inside," Jack said.

"Wait, Jack! Let's wait!" Ed screamed. "This isn't one of those stupid paintball games you like to play. It's real, with real bullets. Those are real dead people lying on the ground down there. This is a fucking war, brother."

But Jack didn't listen and couldn't wait. He broke into a run again, grabbed a machine gun from a dead Jamaican, and headed toward the house.

"Jack! Where the hell are you going?" yelled Ed as he ran after him, picking up an automatic weapon from another fallen warrior. He pulled the trigger to see if it was working—a stream of bullets shot from the barrel into the ground.

Jack glanced back at Ed and recognized the look immediately—the one Ed always wore right before acting on impulse. It was the same look he'd had since they were kids, whenever Jack dragged him into trouble without fully thinking it through. Back then, Jack started the messes; Ed figured out how to get them out of them. Different situation, same pattern. Same movie, just on a different channel.

Jack jumped over dead and dying men as he raced for the

back door of the house. He still hadn't seen any of Raleigh's men, who were dressed in green and brown camouflage. They must have already cleared this area, or maybe they were on the other side of the house, where he could hear gunfire.

As he approached the small back door, a man dressed in black and carrying an automatic weapon rushed out, clearly terrified. Jack didn't recognize him, so he quickly fired a short burst from his gun. He was surprised by his own instantaneous reaction to kill. The man fell dead at Jack's feet.

Jack looked at the blood oozing from the man's wounds. It was the first time he had killed anyone. It had happened so fast he didn't have time to think. He just reacted. It was kill or be killed. Jack's senses were operating at a higher level than ever. He was in a zone.

Stepping over the man, he stopped by the door and peered inside to see if anyone was following. The downstairs room looked empty.

Now, more screams and gunfire erupted from upstairs. Feet pounded quickly down the stairs. Jack listened for the female scream he had heard seconds ago, crouching at the foot of the stairs.

Two men in black military outfits turned the corner. Jack immediately pulled the trigger and shot the two Jamaican drug dealers to pieces.

Suddenly, from behind, he heard multiple gunshots. He turned around and saw Ed. His gun was smoking from the bursts he'd fired to kill a man who was aiming at Jack.

"Thanks, bro. Cover me here. I'm going up," Jack told his brother.

* * *

"Right," Ed exhaled. "I'll cover you down here."

Ed turned on the walkie-talkie he carried from the jeep and called for Oku.

"It's Ed. We're in the house. Send over some men to secure the backyard."

"Ed, this is Raleigh. What the hell are you doing in the house? It's not secure. Get the hell out!"

"We can't, Raleigh. It's Jack. He's gone upstairs looking for Becky, and I'm covering him."

"You get out of that house and wait for us to clean this up," Raleigh ordered. "There's still a hell of a battle out front between Mackey and the Rings."

"I'm telling you that the backyard is now clear. Send some men around," Ed insisted. "Everybody is dead around here. They're all fucking dead. Get some men back here and get us covered."

He heard a noise from the door they had used to enter the house. Someone was coming in. He crouched behind a chair and waited, finger on the trigger.

The figure emerged from the hall, and Ed prepared to shoot. It was Oku. Ed relaxed.

"Oku, get down," Ed said.

Oku dropped. "You, okay, mon?"

"Yeah. Why did you follow us?"

"Why did you leave? I was supposed to stay with you two."

"Ask Jack. He's upstairs, and Raleigh's pinned down out front. We must be in the back part of the house. Anybody out there?"

"No, everyone back there is dead. I saw some running away," Oku said. "They're done fighting."

"I'm going upstairs to find Jack. Cover me down here. If

you hear shots, come up," Ed said.

Oku nodded. He flicked on his walkie-talkie to call Raleigh and let him know where Jack and Ed were.

* * *

Meanwhile, Jack climbed the steps and walked over several other dead bodies. Sporadic gunfire toward the front of the house was heard, but everything was quiet upstairs.

Jack crept down the second-floor hall. He sensed he was alone. Was he too late? He looked into several rooms. No one was there. Where was Becky?

Continuing down the hall, he spotted what looked like the master bedroom. He slowly pushed the door open and looked inside. A man in a peach suit with bloodstains across his chest lay on the floor by the bed. He had been shot multiple times. Jack entered the room and examined the body closely. He looked familiar, but he didn't immediately recognize him.

Ed entered the room. "All clear up here?"

Jack motioned toward the man on the floor.

"That could very well be Robert Mackey," Ed said. "He looks like the guy in the picture Sarah gave us."

Ed scanned the room. It was shot up pretty badly. Then he spotted bullet holes in the closet door. He looked down and saw an arm sticking out of the closet. It looked female. There was a trail of blood running from the closet.

Jack also saw the carnage. He stood frozen.

Ed strode over the dead man and around the bed. He looked into the closet.

"Oh, my God," he said.

"Who is it?" Jack asked.

"Don't worry. It's not Becky. It's…"

"Who?" said Jack, hurrying over to where Ed was standing.

Jack looked down into the closet, and there lay Sarah, her eyes wide open above what looked like a smile. It was no use taking her pulse.

"Oh," said Jack, pausing to take a deep breath. "Sarah." He turned away, stumbled toward the bed, sat down, and ran his hand through his hair.

Jack was stunned. Sarah was dead. Jack's first goal was to find Becky. His second was to keep Sarah safe. It now looked like he had failed that goal.

He looked at the position of the two corpses; they'd faced each other across the room. It was clear what had happened.

Sarah must have been hiding in the closet when Robert entered the room. She fired the first shots, and Robert must have fired back. The exchange killed them both.

"Jack, we have to get out of here. It's not safe," Ed said. "Let's go. Follow me."

Jack wiped his eyes and stood up. "Why, Sarah?"

"I don't know, but I think she wanted it this way," Ed said. "I had an odd feeling about her from the start. She came to kill this guy, and she did it."

Jack nodded. "She hated him."

"That bastard deserved it. C'mon, Jack, let's go," Ed said. "This thing isn't over. We've got to get out of here."

"I must find Becky," said Jack, standing up. "She must be around here. Maybe she's hiding."

"She isn't up here," Ed said. "I checked every room. She probably left before the battle, or maybe she wasn't here at all. We have to regroup with Raleigh. He wants us out of the house."

"No, I want to look for her!" Jack yelled as he walked down the hall, looking into several other rooms and calling Becky's name.

There was no response. Everything was quiet upstairs. Two minutes later, multiple gunshots rang out in the backyard.

"Jack, Oku is downstairs covering us. Let's get him and get the hell out of here," Ed said. "We don't know whether the fight is over."

"I'm going downstairs," Jack replied as he rushed down the steps.

He searched the kitchen, dining room, and living room. No one was around. There was still sporadic shooting outside, but it was getting quieter.

"We gotta go, Jack," said Ed, following. "Oku said Raleigh wants us out."

"Wait. I want to see if there's a basement," Jack snapped.

He went to a side room that looked like a study, lined with full bookshelves. There was a door on the far wall. He opened it and saw stairs leading down. The lights were on.

"I found it! Tell Oku we found a basement we're checking out!" Jack shouted.

Ed followed Jack's voice to the study. "What is this?"

"I'm not sure. Let's go down and take a look. Might be a safe room," Jack said.

Just then, Raleigh entered the study with two men. "Jack, what are you doing? Let us look for Becky."

"I found Sarah. She's dead," Jack replied. "Everything else in the house is clear except for this room. Is the fight over outside?"

"Yes. I have my men guarding the house. We need to leave

before the police arrive," Raleigh said.

"Wait! Becky might be hiding down these stairs!" Jack shouted.

"Let Marcus and me check it out. You've done enough," Raleigh said as they took a few steps down the stairs.

"I'm right behind you," Jack said.

"I'm coming, too," Ed said.

The four men reached the bottom of the stairs and saw that the room was clear. Ahead of them, in another room, a steel-reinforced door stood ajar.

Raleigh walked over to it, pushed it in, and found a body on the floor.

"Looks like a communications center. Got a dead white man here," Raleigh said.

Jack walked over and immediately recognized him. "That's Michael LeCare, Becky's boss at the High Seas."

"Nobody else is here. Jack, Becky isn't here," Raleigh said.

"She probably got out before the shooting started," Ed suggested.

Jack looked around in disbelief. He was sure he would find her. After all this, she's not here?

"We can't do anything more. Time to go!" Raleigh ordered. "If she's here, hiding somewhere we don't know about, the police will find her."

Jack argued briefly with Raleigh, but reluctantly agreed to leave. As he walked out, he wondered whether Becky was hiding in another safe room or had already left, as Ed thought.

Jack felt empty as he climbed into the jeep for the ride back to Raleigh's house.

Chapter 42
Recovering

Two weeks later, Aug. 6, 1980

By now, everyone at GoldenEye knew Jack and where to find him.

He was either down on the beach, sitting in a favorite lounge chair near the water, where he spent hours writing about what had happened over the past month on a yellow legal pad, or in the hotel bar, alternating between daiquiris and Irish coffee.

He was in no hurry. From time to time, he would stare at the incoming surf, watching the waves roll in, one by one.

News reports warned of a major hurricane from the east—Hurricane Allen—with strong winds predicted to reach 190 mph, making it a Category 5 storm. Its track showed it heading toward Jamaica's north coast, where he was staying.

Jack knew he had to leave soon to avoid the dangerous storm. He grew up in Florida and remembered the big ones that hit Sarasota. Donna, in 1960, with 90 mph winds, had been the worst by far. Hurricanes Betsy in 1965 and Agnes in 1972 had also been major hurricanes, causing extensive damage and deaths along the coast.

Allen was going to make those hurricanes look like squalls. It was shaping up to be a monster. Jack knew he had to go, even though he still hadn't heard from Becky.

The horror he'd experienced in the battle on the mountain often flashed through his mind. He remembered shooting people, seeing dead bodies, and hearing screams and explosions.

But the things he remembered most were seeing Sarah's corpse and the emptiness he felt when he couldn't find Becky.

He thought about Ed, Raleigh, and Marcus leading him away from the house that night. It was a sensation of déjà vu, the same numb feeling he'd had when he'd walked away after Charlie Tobert committed suicide.

He'd looked everywhere in the house for Becky, searching as long as he could with Ed, before Raleigh and Marcus finally insisted they leave.

Jack hadn't cared whether the police found him there. He was looking for his wife. He would explain later. "Maybe they could help," he'd argued. Ed reminded Jack that many sided with the drug dealers; the police weren't necessarily on the law's side.

Ed and Raleigh promised they would continue the search. After spending the night at Raleigh's, Jack returned to GoldenEye, checked into a room, and waited for her to contact him.

But when the next day turned into the next day, and the next day into the next week, he began to worry that something might have happened to her.

Raleigh discovered she had a plane ticket to Bogotá the morning after the raid, but there was no record of her using it. Ed contacted the American Embassy in Bogotá, but they had no record of her entering the country.

In a letter, she'd mentioned a housekeeper named Louisa. Ed tracked her down. Louisa said she hadn't heard from Becky since before the battle and would contact Ed if she learned anything useful.

Ed traveled to the American Embassy in Kingston to request assistance. He was angry that they didn't seem interested in the case, so he demanded to see the ambassador.

The security officer in charge of missing persons met with him and admitted that their hands were tied. The drug gang battle had become a political flashpoint.

More than 60 Jamaicans had been killed. Rumors linked gang members to both Manley and Seaga. Suddenly, the U.S. Department of State, the embassy, and the CIA wanted to stay out of Jamaica's "internal politics." After four days of searching, Ed tried to persuade Jack to come home with him. There were no more clues to pursue.

Raleigh was equally frustrated with the limited information his CIA friends provided. He finally admitted to Jack that he had worked with them on the raid. He had risked his and his fighters' lives, yet they had nothing to share about Becky.

Jack suspected they knew something because they showed no interest in helping. He got the impression that higher-ups in Washington wanted the investigation into the drug battle quashed and anyone related to it forgotten. He guessed it had to do with the upcoming election.

Jack wanted to give Becky a few more days. If she were alive, he felt she would contact him at GoldenEye. Ed did all he could and left for home. He promised to

contact Chief Bagley for an update on the High Seas case. He would also continue to ask about Becky in Sarasota, Jamaica, and Bogotá, and let Jack know if there was any news.

Raleigh also had to leave for the mountains to finish a series of paintings for a client. He wished Jack well and invited him to return to Jamaica. He promised he would keep pressure on the CIA for more answers.

Jack held onto the slim hope that Becky was still on the island and hadn't surfaced because she was afraid Mackey's accomplices might be looking for her. He hoped she would come to him when it was safe.

Another possibility was that Mackey had arranged for Becky to leave the island before the battle. In that case, Jack wondered whether they planned to meet at a prearranged rendezvous. Since Mackey was dead, Jack wondered whether Becky was alone on some nameless beach, sipping iced fruit drinks and living extravagantly on illicit drug money.

Jack's thoughts were interrupted by a sudden change in temperature. The burnt orange sun sank into the ocean to the northwest, and the wind blew cool air onto the beach, turning the waves into whitecaps. It's time for daiquiris and some food. He picked up his papers and trudged silently back to the hotel.

He knew he only had a day or two left before he had to go ahead of the approaching hurricane.

But where to go? Home to Sarasota? Or south to Bogotá to look for her? Jack couldn't decide. Officially, he was on sabbatical and had permission to stay out the rest of the month, but time was tightening around him. The hurricane would soon force his hand.

Bogotá wasn't just unfamiliar—it was dangerous in ways he couldn't control. He'd be walking straight into cartel territory without a plan, backup, or legal protection, chasing rumors instead of facts.

Sarasota, on the other hand, was where he could regroup, dig for information, and force the story back into the light. From home, he could lean on old sources, work the phones, pressure the feds, and follow financial threads that might lead him to her faster than wandering blind through a city on edge.

One thing he learned in Jamaica was that finding Becky wasn't about motion; it was about leverage. And Sarasota was where Jack still had some. Still, going home to Sarasota felt, to him, like giving up, and he didn't like that option either.

Jack walked into the hotel, which was nearly empty of patrons except for workers installing storm windows and covering furniture with plastic sheeting.

On his way upstairs to his room to shower and change, he stopped by the front desk to pick up mail, as was his custom.

"Anything for me, Ajani?"

"Oh, yes, Mr. Kendall," the clerk said. "I would have brought it to you, but I've been so busy preparing for this hurricane. It will be a bad one. Yes, you have a letter."

Jack froze. He placed his hands flat on the old desk and stared at the clerk.

"Here it is," Ajani said, handing it over.

Jack quickly took it. He sensed it was from Becky.

"I hope it's good news, Mr. Kendall. You will have to leave soon, no?"

Jack closed his eyes, exhaled, and said, "I don't know, Ajani."

He just wanted some news, good or bad. He didn't recognize the handwriting on the envelope. He tore open the seal and immediately recognized the handwriting on the letter. It was from Becky. He didn't waste a second and started reading.

> *"Dear Jack,*
>
> *"I know you are probably wondering about me. I'm all right. So much has changed since I wrote to you in Florida."*
>
> *"We must be so careful because I don't want anyone to know where we are. Robert has enemies everywhere. Some may still be looking for us. I can't tell you everything. But as soon as the shooting started, Michael took Michelle and me out through a secret underground exit. We were so scared. He had a driver take us to a small airport where Robert kept his plane. They would meet us there when it was all over. They never made it."*
>
> *"I just got word from Louisa that you have been waiting for me at GoldenEye. I wish I could give you better news."*
>
> *"I thought long and hard about inviting you here. I'm sorry, but I decided I couldn't drag you into this. I can't explain any further, except to say I'm safe and very wealthy."*
>
> *"I don't know what else to say. I can't thank you enough. If it weren't for you, I might not be alive. Michelle told me what you did at the little grocery store. If you hadn't pressed Michael, I'm not sure he would have changed*

his mind about getting us on that plane."

"Goodbye, Becky."

"P.S. I'll send money when I can. You won't be able to reach me this time because we're leaving Bogotá soon. If I can, I'll be in touch. But don't wait for me. We should go our separate ways now."

Ajani waited for Jack to finish. "No good, Mr. Kendall?"

Jack didn't hear the clerk's voice clearly. It sounded distant. He struggled to understand what he had just read. Becky was alive? But she was gone again? He bit his lip.

"No, not good news at all," Jack finally mumbled. "I got my answer."

"Are you all right, Mr. Kendall?" Ajani said.

He slowly took a few steps back from the front desk. He shook his head. His search for Becky was over. Even if he decided to look for her in Bogota, she might not be there.

Suddenly, he longed to be home. He needed to go home. Becky was safe, but she wasn't coming with him. It was time to leave.

"Can you get me a seat on the next flight to Miami?"

"Yes, sir. I have a friend at the airline I can call," Ajani said. "There aren't many flights left tonight, but I'm almost sure my friend can get you a seat. This one leaves at 7 p.m. Hold on."

He picked up the phone and dialed a number. "Hey, Johni, I need another seat on the 7 p.m. flight to Miami. What can you get me?" Ajani said. "Window? 22C. Very good. It's Jack Kendall from Sarasota, Florida. He will be right down."

"Mr. Kendall, go to Air Jamaica and see Johni; he is holding your seat. I'll have a taxi waiting for you. Can you pack and come right down?"

Jack nodded. "Give me 15 minutes." He stuffed the letter into his pocket and quickly climbed the stairs to his room to shower and pack. He had done everything he could.

He wouldn't track Becky from Colombia to wherever else she might be going. Everything he did to find her, to help her, to save her, to protect her, had been for nothing.

Maybe LeCare had been right in the parking lot that afternoon when he said she wasn't worth it. First, it was cocaine. Now, it was drug money. Whatever her reasons, it didn't matter anymore. He wouldn't be fooled next time if she changed her mind and wanted him back or needed his help.

Going Home

Tuesday evening, Aug. 6, 1980

Jack Kendall took his seat on the nearly full Air Jamaica flight. Hurricane Allen was getting closer, and everyone expected it to hit the next night. He was lucky that Ajani had been able to secure him a seat on such short notice.

It was a three-hour trip home, and the approaching hurricane infused the passengers with a strange sense of excitement. Given his somber mood, Jack hoped he wouldn't have to sit next to anyone who wanted to talk. But he knew return flights usually had plenty of people wanting to chat about their vacations.

Becky's letter left him empty, and he was exhausted. Jack felt sad to leave without her, but relieved to know she was safe.

He buckled his seatbelt, pushed the button on the armrest to adjust his seat, leaned back, and looked out the window.

The plush green Jamaican countryside beckoned along the runway. But this was goodbye. He didn't think he'd ever return. He didn't know if he'd ever see Becky again. She'd gotten what she wanted: freedom and wealth. It was hard to compete with that, especially on a reporter's salary.

He almost laughed. That was a good sign. He hadn't laughed in a while.

Before the plane took off, he opened his notebook and scribbled additional thoughts about the past month. He had been writing continuously since the battle on the mountain.

Writing seemed to calm him and help him put everything in perspective. It also distanced him from his experiences. He could hardly believe what had happened. He felt as if he were writing a history of another time and another person.

Funny, he was starting to look forward to work again.

Just then, someone sat in the seat next to him. He pretended not to notice.

"Hello, I think this is my seat," said the blonde young woman as she stowed her bag in the overhead compartment. She wiggled into the adjacent seat.

Jack nodded but didn't raise his head.

"I'm Melanie."

"Jack," he replied flatly, still looking at his notebook.

"Do you mind if I ask what you're writing?" Melanie asked softly.

"A novel."

"About what?"

Jack paused and wondered how to deal with Melanie's enthusiasm. He felt too tired for discussion. He turned his head toward the window and said, "Not much. It's about broken dreams and lost hope."

"Sounds depressing," Melanie said.

"Depends on your point of view."

"That's an interesting perspective. What do you mean?"

"Nothing much."

"Oh, are you a writer?"

"Used to be."

"Used to be? But not now?" Melanie asked. "I thought, you know, once a Marine, always a Marine?"

Jack said nothing. He frowned, shook his head, and looked out the window. "Not the same," he said softly.

He thought about excusing himself and moving to another seat. The jet still hadn't moved. He knew moving would be futile. He turned to Melanie and gazed into her clear blue eyes.

"Yes, I'm still a writer. I'm just tired, I guess," he finally said with a shrug. "Been a long month."

"Well, no matter how difficult the lives of the characters in your novel must be, be sure to give it a happy ending," Melanie said.

Jack grew a little irritated with Melanie's intrusion and her cheery disposition. He replied sarcastically, "I suppose everything always turns out fine for you?"

He looked at her directly for the second time. He was surprised by his reaction because he was usually better with people. But she reminded him of something familiar. He couldn't put his finger on it at the moment.

She didn't flinch and even smiled back.

"Write about Minnesota," Melanie teased.

"Minnesota? That's not much of a state," Jack said, turning away.

"You've never been there."

"It's too cold."

"Yes, but it's a great state. You should go there sometime, during the summer, of course," she said. "You do look a little thin-blooded."

Jack looked at Melanie a third time. She was smiling. His scowl melted at Melanie's clear, bright, energetic face. She was all attention. He relaxed and decided to talk with her a little more.

"Why should I go there?" he asked.

"Because. That's where I was born," Melanie said.

"I see. Just one more question."

"All right."

"Does Minnesota have any mountains?" he asked.

"Uh, not really, but it does have 10,000 lakes," she said with a little laugh.

"Sounds like a good place to live," he said. "I love the water."

"It's just about the safest place in the world," she said.

Jack nodded. Melanie's talk of her home made him think of his own from long ago. He was even more eager to get back now. He smiled at Melanie, closed his eyes, and leaned his head back.

He thought back to a few weeks earlier, when he had lost his memory after Mackey's thugs tried to kill him. He was in the hospital recovering, and the first memories to return were of his youth.

More old memories began to rush forward. He thought of bike riding with his best friends through his old neighborhood, how the wind blew through his hair, and the aroma of dinner wafting through the air.

He thought about sitting in a circle with his friends on the street in front of his house after dinner, having long talks about the meaning of music and books.

He almost heard his mother calling him in for homework and a bath. He longed for that kind of safety.

Then he smiled, for he suddenly remembered the end of the mountain dreams he'd had over the past two months.

He looked over at Melanie, who was reading a magazine. Her angelic face, long blonde hair, and white outfit struck a nerve.

Her face became clearer, more familiar. A warm sensation passed through Jack as he flashed back to the last part of the mountain dream.

Could Melanie be the young woman in his dream, the one dressed in white who had shown him the way down the mountain? He didn't know and couldn't be sure.

But he wondered why he'd had so many dreams about the mountain and what they meant.

Suddenly, it hit him. Coming down from the mountain meant going home. Of course. He had never understood the last part of his dream.

He knew that in the dream, he was the only survivor of the battle atop the mountain and that a blonde girl had led him down. But he never understood where she was taking him. Now he knew.

She was taking him home.

He looked over at Melanie again, smiling. He didn't know whether he had won or lost his battle on the mountain, but he smiled because he knew, after all he'd been through, he was on his way home.

He knew his way this time—by heart.

How to Contact Jay B. Greene

Visit My Website and Sign Up for My Newsletters: www.jaybgreene.com

By subscribing, you'll get:

- Early sneak peeks at upcoming books
- Bonus chapters, deleted scenes and exclusive short stories
- Insider updates on Jack Kendall and Tim and Peggy Smith's worlds
- Special offers and giveaways
- Author insights and personal notes

Sign up now at: **www.jaybgreene.com**

Love My Books? Help Others Discover It!

If you enjoyed one of my Jack Kendall Mystery books or Tim and Peggy Smith Space Adventure books, please consider leaving a review on **Amazon, Barnes & Noble, or wherever you bought your book.** Your reviews help other readers discover the series—and they mean the world to me as an author.

Thanks again for reading, and I hope you'll join Jack Kendall or Tim and Peggy on their next thrilling adventures!

Pursue the Truth, **Jay B. Greene**

Other Jack Kendall Mysteries

Becky—Becky Kendall and Michelle Talley have fled their traumatic past in Jamaica, taking control of $5 million in drug profits. But they are pursued by Gordon Gecht, a ruthless enforcer determined to reclaim the money he believes is rightfully his. When estranged husband Jack Kendall arrives in Bogotá to uncover the truth about Becky, he gets caught in a deadly game of betrayal and survival. As old wounds resurface and trust becomes hard to find, Jack races against time to expose Gecht's crimes. *Becky* is a tense journey through danger, resilience, and the relentless pursuit of justice—set against the gritty backdrop of 1980s Colombia.

Other Jack Kendall Mysteries

Bone Valley—In the third book, Jack exposes the dark underbelly of Florida's phosphate industry, where corruption, environmental ruin, and murder collide. An anonymous tip leads Jack into the heart of Bone Valley's phosphate mines, where toxic spills devastate communities and powerful corporations bury the truth. Partnering with police reporter Bobbie Jackson, Jack investigates murders tied to an industry willing to kill to protect its secrets. As a Category 5 hurricane approaches, Jack faces a vengeful enemy from his past. Can he survive long enough to reveal the truth? *Bone Valley* is an unflinching thriller about justice, greed, and the high stakes of environmental disaster.

Other Jack Kendall
Nokomis Hospital

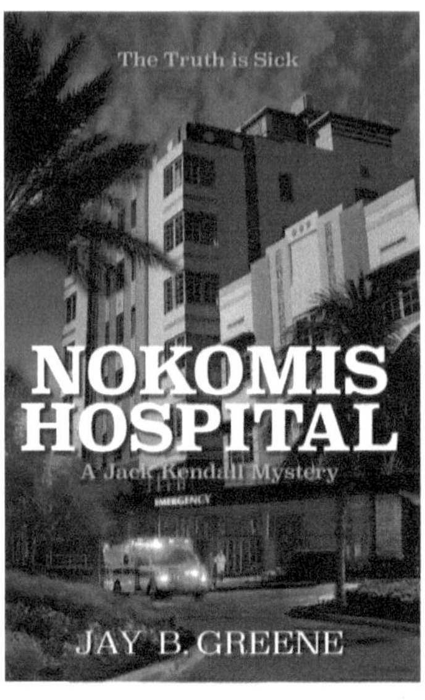

Nokomis Hospital—Jack Kendall suspects financial troubles and healthcare fraud when his wife, Bobbie, is admitted to Nokomis Hospital after she is treated in the ER for pre-eclampsia. While Bobbie has a successful C-section and delivers healthy twins, Jack learns from several employees during her three-day stay that charismatic CEO Mike Lard has conspired with other top executives and board members to embezzle millions of dollars that threaten the non-profit hospital's future. But as the merger with National Healthcare Corp. nears, and a whistleblower and a drug addicted co-conspirator turns up dead, Jack realizes he's not just chasing corruption. He's chasing killers. Join Jack as he discovers the lengths—and crimes—the executives go to cover up their illegal acts.

Jack's Next Adventure
Breakthrough Lies

Breakthrough Lies—When sixteen-year-old Julie France is seized from her home and forced into Breakthrough—a controversial teen drug rehabilitation program—her desperate mother turns to investigative reporter Jack Kendall for help. As Jack digs deeper, he uncovers a tangled web of abuse, corruption, and political protection linking the so-called treatment center to Florida's most powerful political families. Backed by national figures and politicians, Breakthrough hides its cruelty behind a façade of moral righteousness and media praise. To expose the truth, Jack must confront the same forces that built the program—and risk everything to bring its victims' stories to light. *Breakthrough Lies*, the fifth Jack Kendall book, is a gripping, emotional thriller about power, family, and the dark side of institutional control—grounded in the chilling reality of America's most notorious youth rehabilitation programs.

Tim and Peggy Smith
Space Adventures

Danger From Space—Tim Smith gains psychic powers after discovering a mysterious space rock during a summer camp hike. This event propels him into a career as a NASA astrophysicist, where he uncovers an exoplanet called Terra Nova and foresees an alien threat approaching Earth. A massive alien mothership, its AI corrupted by dark matter, emerges from the Kuiper Belt and begins attacking a world devastated by pollution and climate change. Discovering that the Mothership holds technology capable of restoring the planet, Tim and his team race to reset the ship's AI to its peaceful prime directive of "no harm to humans" and "assist in cleansing Earth of pollution." In *Danger From Space*, join Tim and his team as they confront an alien menace and the pressing realities of our world's environmental crisis.

Tim and Peggy Smith
Space Adventures

Flight to the Stars—With Earth's environment cleansed and humanity expanding into space, Tim and Peggy Smith, alongside their psychic children and the faithful *Horizon* crew, are asked to investigate a new wormhole threat. They face hostile and friendly aliens, ancient mysteries, and cosmic trials. But when Earth is threatened again, the crew must race home to defend humanity's fragile future. *Flight to the Stars* is an epic odyssey of discovery, danger, and destiny, the thrilling second installment in the Tim and Peggy Space Adventure series. Join Tim and Peggy on the *Horizon* as they journey beyond the Solar System using alien-developed wormhole technology.

About the Author

Jay B. Greene was born, grew up, and lives in Sarasota. He studied environmental science and journalism in college and graduated from the University of Florida. His love for stories propelled him into a 40-year career covering healthcare, government, crime, and the environment for several newspapers across different states. Greene's lifelong experiences inspired *Mountain Crossing*, the first book in the Jack Kendall Mystery series. He has also published *Becky*, *Bone Valley*, *Nokomis Hospital*, *Danger From Space* and *Flight to the Stars*. In 2026, *Breakthrough Lies* and *Children of the Stars* are scheduled for release.